CW00551250

Memories
of the
Cottage
by the
Sea

BOOKS BY REBECCA ALEXANDER

Secrets of the Cottage by the Sea

Rebecca Alexander

Memories
of the
Cottage
by the
Sea

bookouture

Published by Bookouture in 2023

An imprint of Storyfire Ltd.
Carmelite House
50 Victoria Embankment
London EC4Y 0DZ

www.bookouture.com

ISBN: 978-1-80314-863-2
eBook ISBN: 978-1-80314-862-5

To Wren, my adorable and charming grandson, and his parents Sam and Becky.

PROLOGUE

Isabelle stepped into the beehive-shaped stone hut on the beach, coming straight from work with a bag of shopping. The floor was swept clean as usual, the recycled yacht window was open, and a lazy curl of smoke drifted up from the chimney. The only suggestion that there was something wrong was the way her grandfather was lying down on his bed, fully clothed, as if he needed a nap. The bench was barely wide enough to contain his shoulders; Isabelle's mother had softened it with cushions and blankets. On the table, just big enough for two people to eat at, were his framed photographs. One was of her mother's wedding, the other was of Isabelle as a child, sat on the sand arranging shells. She walked forward to check he was really dead, but everything about him suggested he had gone. His face was pale, his lips grey, his eyes and mouth a little open. And he hadn't leapt out of his wing chair and shouted, 'Welcome, child!' as he had done throughout her life, even when she brought her own daughter Margaret, or her granddaughter, Lottie.

She pushed the rock he used to keep the door open into place, and touched his half-filled mug. It had been a gift from her, years ago, but now the tea was cool. She took his hand, warily, because she hadn't touched a dead person before. His fingers were cold, too, but no more than usual for a man who lived half-wild, all year round, facing the Atlantic winds and storms. She kissed his hand, put it by his side.

'Bye, Poppa,' she whispered, even as she realised that she would have to tell Mam and Dad now, and that she would never see him again.

1

PRESENT DAY, 16 MARCH

Charlotte Kingston leaned against the glass of the ferry window, her dark curls cushioning her forehead.

She remembered this from her childhood. The lift of the ship with each wave, the moment of feeling lighter as it dropped, the clanging and jarring of the deck under her feet. Even the smell of salt and exhaust fumes made her happier, recalling the excitement of travelling from Bath to see Grandma Isabelle on Morwen Island. The stays were usually disappointing, though, as they were out of season, filled with constant wind, mist and rain blown off the sea. Grandma's house was too small, so they usually rented one of a row of damp chalets back from the sea. The bunk beds she shared with her sister were narrow and hard, and she ended up freezing against the outside wall. The room was so small she could step from the top bunk onto the window sill, and out onto the hummocky grass.

But this time would be different. She hadn't been to the island for fifteen years, since her grandma's funeral in the old church off the quay. At the time, she had been standing hand-in-hand with a younger Zach, her impossibly glamorous and clever boyfriend from university. They had been twenty, just kids, convinced they were soulmates and destined to be together forever. She felt a pressure in her chest at the thought of him, and closed her eyes for a moment. *Zach.*

The sea, in grey-green rollers, continued to challenge the boat, with a few passengers already looking uncomfortable. Her phone beeped again – presumably it had caught a moment of signal. She looked out the window, thick with salt crystals, to see the first of the small islands floating as if above the water, hunkered down in the distance. She listened to the voicemail message: 'Call me. Don't leave it like this. It's not over.' There was a choke in Zach's voice, and she could imagine his anguished face as he spoke.

She closed her eyes against this latest heartfelt message. Maybe he'd broken up with Flower or Willow, or whatever her name was. Charlotte knew he had met the tie-dyed, tattooed temptress at a surfing competition at Cocoa Beach in Florida and, while she could try and be cynical, the truth was Zach *wasn't* a heartless womaniser. She knew he still loved her, but he had probably loved the girl, too.

She turned her attention back to the file in her leather messenger bag, a legacy from Grandma Isabelle, softened by decades of use. Her brief from the local education authority was simple: to make all the necessary assessments to see if the school was viable. Otherwise, it would close at the end of the summer term. The timing was perfect, a project that would give her a complete change of location while she adjusted to life without Zach after fifteen years of him by her side. She closed the folder and stared out at the Atlantic. The sky was one shade lighter grey than the water, which matched her mood. A new life, solitude in her own Morwen schoolhouse. Then back to the real world to find a new home and take up her new position as a school inspector.

She looked out at the first glimpse of the big island, St Brannock's, just a low shadow on the horizon. It still gave her a shiver of anticipation. Or maybe she was just cold without Zach's warm hand in hers.

Maybe she would never feel warm again.

2

'Jenofeve! Bring the baby,' Madame Boiteux said, lifting a straw basket onto the seat. 'Marc, sit down, you are in everyone's way.'

Jenofeve, who went by Jenny at home, pushed the perambulator into the corner of the ferry's main passenger cabin and applied the brake. Eight-month-old Adela was sitting up on her pillows and secured with a harness, while seven-year-old Marc was perched on the edge of the wooden slats. Jenny smiled down at him.

She handed a toy to Adela. 'Sit still, now, sweetheart. You shall look out of the windows soon when the ship leaves.' She turned to Madame. 'All the trunks are secured, and Aunt Hélène and Cook may go up on deck because... well, it looks like a breezy crossing, and they aren't the best travellers.' She lowered her voice. 'The Germans have surrounded Paris, Madame. I overheard another passenger.'

'They will be in through Brittany and into Rennes in no time.' Madame sniffed, looked out of the salt-stained window and wiped a tear away with a gloved hand. 'We were in Paris last year,' she said. 'Just before you joined us, Jenofeve. I wonder how many of the galleries and restaurants will survive the invasion.'

'They will surrender, Madame, to preserve the city,' Jenny's Aunt Hélène said, stepping forward to sit beside Madame. She pressed a handkerchief to her lips for a moment. 'However, if Brittany votes to surrender, we will be away from the war on Ushant.'

The island was thirty kilometres from the westernmost point of Brittany. The villa there was a peaceful summer retreat for the Boiteux family. Jenny knew Ushant well; it had been her father's childhood home, and the port from which he sailed as a fisherman. It was where the Boiteux family had engaged her as a governess to teach the children Breton, and to guide their education until they were old enough to go to school. She had been recommended by her aunt, Hélène, the family's house-keeper. Although she had grown up on Morwen, one of the Atlantic Islands off the coast of Cornwall, she was a native Breton speaker and wanted to work in France.

'The Germans won't come this far, I'm sure.' Madame smoothed her dress over her knees. She had been forced to leave many of her silk gowns and furs at Rennes, hoping the house wouldn't be invaded by the German troops. As Maître Boiteux was a principal lawyer in the town, Jenny feared they might commandeer the family home. 'Soon, Maître Boiteux will be able to join us.'

The ship rolled a little as it cruised out of port, the baby bouncing excitedly in her pram. Marc was pale and his eyes were wide. Jenny caught his hand.

'Is it safe?' he asked in a hoarse whisper.

'This is quite gentle weather for the crossing,' she said. 'The ship will go up and down, like a horse, taking us to the island,' she said. 'We will ride him all the way there.'

The nursery maid, Lisette, sat next to the young boy. She offered him a boiled sweet from her pocket. 'This will help,' she

said. 'Until you get used to the motion.' The maid sat back on
the wooden seat, tucking her pale hair into her hat. 'It's just a
few hours,' she said. 'I haven't been on a ferry before. You'll
have to show me things out of the window. Like all the
lighthouses.'

'There are lots of lighthouses on the island,' Marc said.
'Phare du Créac'h is the biggest in the world. Or the brightest, I
forget which.'

'He was so much smaller when we came last time,' Madame
said. 'Of course, we travelled in first class then.' She sounded a
little outraged. 'But all the seats were booked.'

Jenny caught Lisette's eye and smiled a little. Madame
always travelled first class; the servants and children usually
made do with *deuxième classe*.

'Indeed,' Jenny said, putting her arm around the little boy.
She suggested he might like to go on deck with Cook, an idea
which was quickly taken up when he started making odd
retching sounds. Her aunt took him, along with a warm jacket.

'It won't be as comfortable as the Rennes house, with only
half the staff,' Madame said, leaning over to give baby Adela a
rusk.

The rest of the servants had remained in Rennes, including
the maître d'hôtel. Jenny put her gansey – a thick sweater
knitted by her Atlantic Island mother – over her dress, and sat
back to amuse Adela. Mam had made it the same shade as
Jenny's hair, a rich honey colour, and it smelled of the kitchen
stove's smoke, and of home on Morwen Island.

3

PRESENT DAY, 16 MARCH

Charlotte was waiting on St Brannock's quay for the boat that would take her to Morwen. An information map showed all six inhabited islands and hundreds of uninhabited rocks and islets in the archipelago. A colourful sign pointed south, out to sea: 'Twinned with Ushant'.

She was trying to remember where Ushant was when a small boat chugged alongside, piloted by a striking young woman who leapt ashore and tied her boat up.

'Are you waiting for the ferry?' she called, pushing a head of dark curls back with one hand. 'If so, I'm it.' She leaned forward and offered a brown hand. 'Corinne Ellis, ferryman. Ferry-woman, anyway.'

'Charlotte Kingston,' Charlotte said, briefly clasping Corinne's hand. 'But this can't be the ferry, surely?'

'The summer ferry's getting its yearly paint job and over-haul. But don't worry, this is perfectly safe.'

Corinne carried the bags on and steadied Charlotte as she stepped into the well of the boat. 'St Petroc's, St Piran's, West Island or Morwen?' she asked chattily.

'Morwen, please.' Charlotte waved her bank card over a card machine.

'I'm guessing you're the new teacher? Thank God, by the way – we haven't had one for months.'

'I'm not exactly...' Charlotte started to say, but the situation was complicated, not to mention confidential. 'Yes, I'm a teacher. But I'm just helping out.'

Corinne loosened the ropes and started the engine, which phut-phutted away from the quay.

'You'll be staying at the schoolhouse?' she said, putting a cap on her head against the first drops of rain.

'Yes.' Charlotte looked across the water, which was veiled with rain. She wished her coat was warmer.

'It's a ratty little house,' Corinne said, swinging the boat away from the island past a large buoy. 'No one's lived in it for years. Patience Ellis used to be the teacher there, lived in it in the fifties onwards. There were other teachers, but they mostly lived in the town.'

She steered around another buoy and turned the engine up a gear.

'They said it would be ready for me.' Charlotte started to feel even colder as the wind whipped up spray from the sea.

'You could clean it up, but it's not liveable yet. But you could stay at the hotel. Or the pub, now it's reopened? It's lovely, but a bit pricey.'

Charlotte started to worry if her agreed expenses would run to a hotel room when she felt her phone vibrate again in her pocket. It was a text from Zach.

Are you OK? Haven't heard. Worried about you.

No, Zach, I'm not all right. I have a broken heart and I'm going to live in an uninhabitable schoolhouse in the middle of the Atlantic Ocean to get away from you.

But she didn't write that text; she couldn't answer him yet. The sea was darker between the islands, and despite the drizzle, it was beautiful. She took in a deep breath and felt a little of the tension leave her. Whatever was coming had to be better than living in an empty house surrounded by memories of Zach and the ruins of all the plans she had been clinging to. House, wedding, babies...

Corinne tied the small boat up at Morwen Island. The tide was high, but there were two rungs of a ladder to climb. They hauled Charlotte's luggage up, her big case of laptop paraphernalia and paperwork coming last, Corinne heaving it up to her from the boat. The wet cobbles were slippery under Charlotte's feet.

'This is my last stop,' Corinne said. 'Just let me secure her up properly for the night. Then I'll give you a hand.'

Charlotte looked at the cases piled at her feet. 'How far is it to the school?'

'Too far to drag those all the way up the hill,' Corinne said, pointing at the large white building. 'That's the pub, the Island Queen. Well, it's more of a restaurant and hotel now – the food is good and they have rooms above. You might like to stay tonight.'

'I think you're right.' Charlotte stared at the pub, smartly painted, with windows filled with ships' lanterns. 'I'll get a room there, if you don't mind helping me with the bags?'

'Sure,' Corinne said, pushing her cap back and grabbing the biggest one. 'And maybe you could go up to the schoolhouse bright and early tomorrow, get it ready to live in.'

'Can I buy you a drink?' she said, smiling at Corinne. 'Maybe I could ask your opinion of the school situation.'

In answer, Corinne grinned and shouldered the pub door open.

Inside, the inn was a mix of ancient beams, stripped floor-boards and modern walls. The tables and chairs were an eclectic mix of old and new and the bar looked like it had come out of a Napoleonic-era ship.

'Wow,' Charlotte murmured. 'This is lovely.'

A young woman with a name badge saying 'Madi' sat at a reception desk, and looked up as they entered. 'Hi, ladies. Is it raining again?'

'A bit.' Charlotte looked around. 'Could I get a room for a night? My accommodation might not be ready yet.'

'Oh, you must be the new teacher! It's great to meet you,' Madi said warmly. 'I went to Morwen School. I loved it. Hi, Corinne.'

Charlotte smiled back mechanically. 'I'm just here to help. But I'm not sure the schoolhouse is ready for me, and it's getting late...'

'It's fine, we have plenty of space this early in the year. These are our room rates.'

Madi handed over a leaflet. The prices were high but manageable out of season, and the local authority would prob-ably pay for one night. If not, Charlotte was so tired she would pay out of her own depleted pocket. She'd left her previous job after Zach left her, as she just couldn't concentrate, and she was due a change anyway. But nine weeks without wages and having to pay the mortgage while the house was being sold had left her short. Their savings, the money earmarked for their wedding, were all gone. They had agreed that Zach would get most of it in exchange for signing the house over to her.

Charlotte realised she had zoned out, and both women were waiting for her to answer.

'I'm sorry, I was just thinking. Yes, I'd love a room. And could we have a drink now?'

Both Charlotte and Corinne settled for coffee, Charlotte's a frothy latte and Corinne's a large black decaf. Madi also brought them a small plate of cookies and two mini cakes.

'I knew this would be perfect for you,' Madi said to Corinne. 'Our chef is trying these out for our afternoon tea menu. Let me know what you think.' She left two slips of paper and pens, so they could score them.

'This is great,' Corinne said, then demolished a cake in one bite and turned to Charlotte. 'I wanted to talk to you, anyway.'

'Oh?' Charlotte mumbled through a mouthful of delicious mini sponge, filled with a nut and chocolate cream.

'Our previous teacher, Jayne, has just retired from the school. She wants to come and talk to you.'

'That would be very helpful.' Charlotte nodded and reached for the pen. 'I'm giving that cake a ten,' she added, and bit into a shortbread that showered the table with crumbs.

'Jayne had a suspicion that the local authority was trying to close the school down.' Corinne frowned at half a biscuit. 'I'm not sure if that's lemony enough. Anyway, as the parent of a young baby, I want to make sure he has somewhere to go to school.'

Charlotte crunched another biscuit. The chai gingerbread also scored a ten.

'All schools have to justify their place, even big ones,' she mumbled through a mouthful.

'Well, island schools are essential for island communities,' Corinne said, pushing her chair back a little. 'We're just glad they've sent a teacher at all, even a temporary one. We thought the local authority had abandoned us. Jayne retired early because she needed an operation, and they haven't advertised to replace her.'

Charlotte managed a shaky smile. 'I don't know the whole situation yet.'

'Well, Jayne will put you straight. Oh my, this gingerbread! *Mmm...*'

Madi returned. 'We've put your bags upstairs, room five. Best view of the water.'

'Thank you. I'd better go,' she said to Corinne. 'I'm glad to have met you, and perhaps I'll see you around?'

Corinne laughed. 'You'll see *everyone* around.'

4

APRIL 1940

The Villa de Mezareun was a welcoming haven for the tired travellers, surrounded by boxes and bags. The hall, an airy tiled entrance, had chairs placed under pictures and a huge mirror, which Madame refused to look in. She sagged onto one of the chairs and looked at the grandfather clock.

'Three hours late,' she murmured to Jenny. 'I suppose we should be glad we got here at all.'

Jenny was introduced to the village couple who looked after the house while the family were away, and in turn introduced them to baby Adela. Marc was still pale from the journey and drooped against his mother's side, while Cook disappeared to lie down, having also been seasick almost the entire journey.

Jenny explored the house with Adela as soon as she could, finding two large reception rooms in front of the kitchen wing, which had pantries and an old-fashioned wood stove beside Cook's room. Upstairs, two large bedrooms looked over the sea, and behind was a smaller room for the housekeeper, as well as a bathroom. Steps between them led up to the top floor, which had a day nursery overlooking the sea and the many rocks and lighthouses Ushant was famous for. Beside it, the night nursery had a bed and a cot, and two tiny rooms, one for Lisette and one for Jenny, along with a small bathroom and storeroom.

On her first full day on the island, with the children being indulged and petted by the staff at the Villa de Mezareun, Jenny was free to pull a cardigan over her summer dress, slip on some sandals, and go into the town. On the quay, she sat on a bollard and waited for the ships to return from a day's fishing. She could see the tide was already dropping, and brightly coloured trawlers were on the horizon, inside the dangerous shoals. Tad, the Breton name she called her father, had told her many times about growing up on Ushant, the island of her birth. Her uncle's ship, the St *Guillaume*, came in, and Uncle Paol stepped ashore to tie up.

'Jenofeve! Welcome back to the island. Are you here to stay?'

'I am. At least the Germans haven't got here, yet,' she said.

Her Uncle Paol looked up at the sky, shielding his eyes. 'It will rain before dawn. Here,' he said, leaning back to one of the metal fish-wells on deck and hooking out a turbot almost a metre across. 'I'll come up to the house. Madame Boiteux might make an order. This will be a welcome home gift.'

'That's kind,' she said as he wrapped the fish in newspaper for her. 'I'm sure she will order more fish now we're here all year.'

Paol tucked the parcel under his arm. 'All year?'

'Until the Germans have gone, anyway.' She sighed. 'The war won't last too long, will it?'

They walked along the quay road together, past rows of tiny houses, each one white with blue shutters to secure against the storms. The road branched uphill, the stone path filled in with grass and flowers. Walls reared up each side as the path wound back and forth, zigzagging up the slope towards the house. All sounds from the sea died away in the wind.

'I hope not,' he said. 'The Breton nationalists are arguing against the invasion, suggesting we surrender and rule Brittany under the Germans, as an independent state. But I think the Germans will occupy the coast to defend against the British.'

'What can we do?' The rocky path twisted around a corner, lost in deep banks of wild plants, flowers nodding onto the stones.

'I may have to support the Resistance,' her uncle explained. 'We can't give up our homeland without firing a shot. Oh, that reminds me, I have a letter from your father. We crossed paths out in the Channel, under the noses of a patrol.' He paused as the house became visible over the overgrown hedge, pale pink walls punctuated with rows of two windows each side of the door, and attic windows above. 'We have put a rumour about that your father died, a year ago. Which explains you being out of black clothes. He's actually helping the British agents; that should stop people remembering you are half-English.'

'I'll say, if I'm asked, that Tad is gone. Madame will want to thank you for the fish.' She tucked the folded note into her pocket, pointing him to the break in the hedge surrounding the unmown lawn. The grass gave way to steps leading to a broad terrace. The gardens spread in front of the house, giving an uninterrupted view of the sea.

Madame Boiteux was standing by the double doors, shielding her eyes from the sun as she looked out to sea.

'Ah, welcome,' she said, giving just a little look to Jenny, to remind her she was late. 'Get the children ready for their dinner, my dear.'

'This is fresh off the boat, to welcome you back,' Jenny said, peeling the newspaper off the head of the fish.

'How generous, Monsieur. What a wonderful turbot. But I cannot accept such a valuable gift, although the sentiment is much appreciated. Take the fish down to Cook, Jenny. You can see your uncle tomorrow, and take some money down to pay for it.'

'Thank you, Madame,' Paol said, pulling at his mop of curly hair as if it was a cap.

The two women walked back indoors, Jenny hugging the fishy parcel. 'He seems to think the Germans will come even here.'

Madame hesitated. 'Such a poor, rocky little isle. Surely not.'

'Yes, Madame,' she said, smiling to reassure her.

Cook was thrilled with the fresh fish, and Jenny wandered out to a chair outside the kitchen door to read. She took the letter she had slipped into her pocket and slowly opened it.

My dearest Jenofeve,

This may be the last message I can get to you for a while, as we don't know when it will be safe to sail across the Celtic Sea to visit. I have a request for you, don't question it. We're sending my half sister, Augustine, to stay on the island. Please give her what assistance you can, without risking yourself. She won't need much, a few francs, a little food, a room to stay in. She has friends on Ushant, and she is a seamstress, so you might find her work. Your mother sends you her love and hopes for your safety. Destroy this letter, child. I do not want the Germans to know anything about you. Forget your home, forget you are British, and look after your employer and the children.

Love from your father.

Jenny knew well that Tad had two sisters, one a nun in Normandy, the other Aunt Hélène, the housekeeper. But neither were called Augustine. What did it mean? Was this Augustine a secret *agent*?

5

PRESENT DAY, 17 MARCH

Charlotte's accommodation in the pub was comfortable and modern, with the backdrop of the restless sea. The sound reminded her of waking in the old holiday park as a child, the wind rattling the single-glazed metal windows, and the sea becoming the soundtrack of the night that she had always loved. It had soothed her into a deep and dreamless sleep.

The hotel breakfast was delicious, and she ate while reviewing the documents she had been sent about the case for the Morwen School closure.

The problem was obvious. Six inhabited islands had one large primary school group spread across them all, each with a small campus. Morwen, the second smallest of the islands, had recently lost three children from the roll: two to the secondary school on the largest island, St Brannock's, and one to Cornwall. Now, just one five-year-old and one ten-year-old used the school, and had their own full-time teacher, at huge expense.

The ten-year-old posed a difficult question: Rhiannon Pender simply refused to become a weekly boarder at the secondary school on St Brannock's. She couldn't commute daily with any reliability, as ferries could only dock two hours either side of high tide, not to mention the problems of rough weather and the expense. Her parents couldn't persuade Rhiannon to even visit the high school, and Charlotte had read she'd had a diagnosis of autism spectrum disorder. Rhiannon would need additional support and it would be difficult to place her given the limited resources on the island schools.

Charlotte did note that the previous teacher, Jayne Mason, had found the child cooperative and engaged, and that her academic work was excellent. Mrs Mason had a quirky way of annotating reports with little handwritten notes about things Rhiannon could be rewarded with when she got frustrated or anxious. 'Ten minutes cleaning the aquarium' was one, 'collecting dandelions for the rabbit' was another. Charlotte smiled; she was looking forward to meeting Rhiannon and also the retiring teacher, who still lived on the island. That could be helpful if she was to somehow relocate the children to a more appropriate school.

The other child, nearly five-year-old Merryn, also came with challenges for an educator. Taken into care as a baby and adopted by a local couple, she had originally struggled with developmental milestones, but was now catching up. School had been a springboard for the little girl and it was a shame that she would have to adapt to part-time or distance learning. She needed classmates her own age to learn from, share with and socialise with.

The letter from the local authority was tucked in the back of the file. The school apparently came with its own schoolteacher's cottage, which was a Victorian anachronism that she hadn't heard of surviving into the twenty-first century anywhere else. She assumed the single key enclosed would give her access to all the buildings. The school was used for a few local activities, organised by the village committee. That extra use – as well as its responsibility as a polling booth for the voters among the one hundred and forty permanent inhabitants – was another obstacle to closing the school entirely.

'Can I get you anything else?' the waiter asked.

'I was just wondering if I could book another night? I might have to.'

'We're nowhere near full, so I'll leave your room as it is and you can let us know later. That way you won't have to lug all your belongings around all day.'

'That's so kind, thank you. And I was wondering, which is the best way to the school?'

He gave her simple instructions: along the quay, up the lane, by the side of the common. She half remembered the village green from childhood – a steeply sloping field with a few swings and a slide.

Once she'd paid for her meal, she started up the hill between the churchyard and the pub. It had been raining, and the stone cobbles were glossy and uneven. It was as steep as she remembered, and she struggled to keep her footing. A couple of people were out walking their dogs, and they smiled and said good morning. She remembered that as well – everyone spoke to everyone else on Morwen, even when you were just a shy teenager. She heaved her antique bag full of papers onto her shoulder and joined a track that ran along the back of the houses, and turned right, towards the common. A gate had a sign to the school.

She pushed it open and walked along a short path towards two buildings, through hedges filled with honeysuckle, wild roses and hawthorn buds. The buildings couldn't have been more different from each other. One was a flat-roofed tempo-rary building, on a trailer base, overlooking a field full of sheep. A tiny cottage sat to the right of it, with a Gothic arched door in stained wood, and a slab of stone acting as a threshold, worn by the passage of many feet. It almost looked like a tiny chapel. She pushed the door, but it was locked. Walking around to the temporary classroom, she found another door that was also secured but the key she'd been sent fitted the door.

It immediately smelled like a school: paper, pens, paint, detergent, feet. The retired teacher had clearly had a talent for arts and crafts: the walls were decorated with pictures and sewing, 3D cardboard models, some of which were very accomplished. She had managed to get children from the ages of four to eleven to work together. A small nature table was covered with everything from a mini camera and laptop to various skulls and dead insects. Another desk under a wall of windows had more computers, and two tables in the middle had four chairs each. The teacher's desk was crammed into a corner and was littered with piles of books and papers, as well as a sewing machine and a telescope. It was a fantasy version of school. Around the corner from the lobby were two toilet cubicles, a long sink and a small, but well-stocked, kitchen. A packed bookcase included books on the island itself, dictionaries and loads of children's stories, some looking a hundred years old.

Hung on the wall behind the desk were various keys, all marked up. Charlotte lifted the one marked 'Cottage', a heavy, ornate key that felt like it belonged in the church-style door.

Walking outside, she tried the lock to the accommodation. It took a bit of wiggling and pushing, as if it hadn't been used for a while, but the lock clunked around eventually. Charlotte shoved the door open with her shoulder, and it scraped over a flagstone floor.

The single room was piled high with file boxes and plastic-wrapped parcels of supplies for the school. Activity equipment, including camping stuff, was stacked over a kitchen straight out of the seventies, with scratched orange cupboard doors and a fake pine worktop. Everything was covered with dust, and she looked up to see how cracked the ceiling was. It bulged in places, only held up by heavily painted paper. Chunks of fallen plaster littered an old table stacked with books in clear plastic boxes and beyond was a stained two-seater sofa.

In the corner was a small door, which Charlotte pushed open. It led straight upstairs, the steps narrow. She had to squeeze past boxes of books on each stair, onto the tiny landing, and an open door revealed one bedroom. A dirty mattress, somewhere between a single and a double, was pushed up against the wall. A matching bed frame was stacked on the other side. A few old boxes and suitcases covered the floor and everywhere seemed dotted with mouse or rat droppings. She shivered. Mice she could cope with, but rats... The stale, damp smell seemed tinged with the acrid stink of animals.

'I can't stay here.' The words echoed around the dank little room. She snapped a few pictures of the upstairs room, and went back outside with relief. It was oppressive; it was horrible.

A knock on the door made her jump.

'Hi there.' A blonde woman in her fifties leaned in the door-frame, barely holding back a large golden retriever. When the dog jumped at her, the woman couldn't hold it, and the lead slipped. Every night terror that Charlotte had ever had surged forward and she shrank against the stone wall, her hands held high.

'Callie!' The woman apologised and grabbed the dog, but not before she had bounced up, making Charlotte squeak. 'Sorry about that, but she's very friendly. I'm Jayne Mason, I used to be the teacher here.'

'Oh. Hi. Sorry, I'm not very good with dogs.' She breathed a little easier. 'I was just checking the cottage out.'

'It's a mess, I'm sorry. It really needs a complete overhaul as it's only been used for storage for thirty years. Come into the school. Can I bring the dog? She'll settle in her basket.'

Charlotte followed Jayne up the steps into the schoolroom. Under the desk was a bean bag, and the dog reluctantly flumped into it.

'When did the school close?'

'Six weeks ago. I had to have an operation, but we managed to spread the children about a bit to the other islands, and get supply teachers over for the odd day. Now the local authority think we could do that permanently, but I think it would be ridiculous.'

Charlotte looked around. 'Why ridiculous?'

'Even on the highest tides, the students can only go for a maximum of four hours or they won't be able to get home again until the next high tide. That's why the older children are weekly boarders at the high school from the age of eleven. But Rhiannon absolutely wouldn't cope with that.'

'I read that she's had an autism spectrum diagnosis.'

'She does, yes. She's lovely, bright, cooperative, motivated. But even with her older brother boarding, she wouldn't cope socially yet. She's done her homework, and she's decided to home educate herself.'

Charlotte smiled. 'What do her parents think about that?'

'Oh, they know she can do it. But they both work, and she's too young to be left alone all day.' Jayne pointed up at a star-shaped hanging polygon. 'That's one of hers. Each plane is a star chart. The galaxy inside out.'

Charlotte watched the artwork shiver in the draught from the door. She walked to close it, carefully avoiding the dog, who thumped her tail as she passed. 'I'm not sure where I'm going to stay, either.'

'Oh, don't worry about that. A couple of the parents are coming up to clear the cottage out at the weekend. We thought you were coming next week.'

'I wanted to get a head start. I'm planning to reopen the school on Monday.'

'Well, we can get the place organised by then – we have the whole weekend.' Jayne smiled warmly. 'Especially now you have two more students.'

'Oh?'

Jayne dropped her voice even though they were alone. 'Two boys that have just lost their mother. They're staying with Clarrie Tremayne in the town. She's their grandmother, but I don't think she knows them that well. They've been a bit of a handful, apparently.'

'I'll contact the local authority about that,' Charlotte said, mentally adding that to the list that included going back to the hotel and begging them to halve their prices.

'I would. But do it soon – the education office closes at two o'clock today.' Jayne shrugged. 'Tides.'

'How do I let the parents know the school is opening again?' Charlotte looked around the room, wondering if she could camp out in the classroom.

'They'll know.' Jayne lifted a folder with the children's contact details from the desk. 'Sometimes the older kids can't get to St Brannock's, so come here for a storm day as well,' she explained. 'They work from the computers and sometimes join in with what we're doing.'

Charlotte's mind boggled. 'How can you deliver anything like the national curriculum with such a wide range of ages?'

'Oh, we manage. Not on set days, necessarily, but over the term we cover all the major points and assessments.' She pulled out a chair and sat down. 'You should relax, you're going to have a busy few days.'

As she settled down next to Jayne, Charlotte realised it was going to be more complicated than she had thought.

6

JUNE 1940

Of course, the Germans came to the island not long after they occupied mainland Brittany.

It took another few weeks for them to land at the quay, the fishing boats shoved aside to stand out at sea on buoys. The local men muttered about fighting back, but the German boats were packed with soldiers. They had brought their own pilot, a thin man known on the islands as Monsieur Razh, or Rat. He had been exiled three years before, after he attacked another fisherman, and sent to prison on the mainland. Now he was back, strutting around the quayside, ordering honest trawlermen around, telling them they needed licences to go to sea and fish.

By the end of their first day, the German soldiers had taken over the town hall, the harbourmaster's office, and the property of the most prominent landowner – a lawyer and friend of Maître Boiteux. The neighbouring Le Godinec family arrived at Villa Mezareun, clothes rammed into baskets and cases, children crying, dogs barking. Their house had been turned over to the new commandant and his family. Madame Boiteux welcomed and comforted them, but privately she complained to Jenny.

'This is just our holiday place,' she hissed to her. 'We won't have enough rooms, especially when Maître Boiteux gets here.'

'It's only for a few days. I'm sure we will find her alternative accommodation soon,' Jenny suggested. 'It is so kind of you to take them in, especially with the children so frightened.'

So Jenny found herself with eight children to keep an eye on for several days, with just one nursemaid. Madame Le Godinec's governess had succumbed to hysteria. The nursery, never very large, was now a sea of mattresses and beds, the children sharing, clothes everywhere. Just getting them all washed, changed and fed took so long that Jenny missed the evening meal. She scrounged a plate of bread and cheese and excused herself to sit in the garden to catch her breath.

The midges were starting to come out, and the swallows and house martins were just giving way to fluttering, swooping bats. Good news came that the refugee family would be able to stay with Madame Le Godinec's sister, and they would have the nursery back before too long. But the chill in the evening air reminded Jenny that the Germans were a threat, and she was somehow expected to do something about it, with the mysterious Aunt Augustine.

There was talk in the town that a woman called Augustine *had* travelled to the island. Within days, the mysterious woman had walked up to the house and called at the back door asking for Jenofeve.

Jenny found an old woman sitting on the chair outside the back door, smoking a vile-smelling cigarette. Augustine was a short, plump woman in a coat that might have been from the past century, black faded to green. She had grey curls, stained yellow at the front. Her cigarettes made her voice harsh, and her boots had holes. Jenny had never been rich but her family's clothes and shoes were always neat and mended. She wondered if Aunt Hélène would even let Augustine in the house.

'My father said you would come,' Jenny said, staring at the woman. 'He asked me to help you, if I can. But the children...'

'They will be fine for a few minutes, won't they?'

Seven-year-old Marc was awake, working on his arithmetic in the dining room, and the baby was asleep.

'Just a moment, then,' Jenny conceded and nervously sat on a barrel by the gate.

'I am Augustine Berthou,' the woman said in heavily accented Breton, shaking Jenny's hand firmly. 'And you are...?'

'Jenofeve Huon,' she answered. 'But you cannot be my aunt?'

'I am your father's oldest *half*-sister,' Augustine said briskly. 'My mother was widowed before she married your grandfather.' She winked just a little. 'The island is wary of strangers, so it is easier for me if *you* let them know who I am.'

'Is that how I can help?' Jenny asked, awkwardly. Augustine had an enormous straw hamper beside her, buckled with belts.

'You can help first by finding somewhere to put my sewing machine.' She smiled at Jenny. 'Just until I can find a room to lodge in.'

At that moment Aunt Hélène came out with two cups of fragrant coffee. 'Enjoy it while you can, before we have to start roasting chicory roots ourselves. I doubt we will get much imported food now we are under occupation. We can put your case in the pantry.'

'Thank you, Hélène,' Augustine said, laughing with a short bark that made Jenny jump. 'Do you remember acorn coffee from the last war? Oh, my.' Augustine looked at Jenny from under bristly, dark eyebrows. 'Hélène and I got to know each other years ago in Marseille. When I was not such a vagabond.'

'Of course,' Jenny stammered.

'You must have received your father's letter?' Augustine asked.

'He asked me to burn it. I did so, in the nursery grate.'

'Good girl,' Augustine said. 'Please commit my story to memory, then you don't know anything more. That way you can be honest about me if you are questioned.'

'Questioned?' Jenny looked at her aunt in panic. 'By the Germans?'

'It's possible,' Augustine murmured. 'So, the less you know the better. Your father recently *died at sea*, remember that. He had an older half-sister, Augustine, who behaved very badly and was sent away to school at a convent. She left, married and was widowed young, and now travels around mending clothes and doing occasional cleaning work. She is smelly, dirty and swears, so you and Hélène will find a room in the town for her. You are all a bit embarrassed by her but you, Jenofeve Huon, feel a sense of responsibility. That will give you reason to visit me occasionally.'

'If my father died, everyone here would know—'

'News between the islands is impossible since the war started. That's the story we're telling. People will offer their condolences at first, but we will say it happened a year ago, when you were in Rennes. It's now my reason for travelling to Ushant, to be near family. I doubt if the fishermen will talk to the Germans, and many of the older ones only speak Breton. The Germans struggle even with French. Hopefully they will never know you grew up on Morwen.'

At the name of the island, Jenny could almost smell the scents of home, warm linen airing on the stove lid, bread baking in the oven, the sea off the quay adding its salty tang to her tongue.

Augustine put a hand on Jenny's shoulder. 'Go up to the children, now, and learn our story. One day, our lives might depend upon it. Don't engage with the Germans.'

'Tad wants me to help you as much as I am able.'

'Oh, you will be able to help me.' Augustine smiled. 'If you have the courage.'

7

PRESENT DAY, 18 MARCH

After another delightful but luxuriously expensive night in the Island Queen pub, Charlotte prepared for her battle with the one-up, one-down schoolhouse, complete with rats and falling ceilings. Maybe her memory was playing tricks on her – surely it hadn't been *that* bad?

Rocking up at eight thirty was a mistake. It was overcast and the rooms were so dark she could only smell the rats. She tried an old-fashioned light switch, and a flickering light bulb cast shadows in all the corners and behind the stacks of supplies.

Oh. It is really that bad.

'Hi!'

Charlotte jumped at the greeting from a blonde woman, already in rubber gloves.

'We're here to help,' the woman said. She looked a little younger than Charlotte, and had a broad smile.

'Oh, hello,' Charlotte stammered. 'We?'

'I'm Elowen, we live along the lane. Ellie. I'm quite new to the island, so ask me if you need anything.' She peered in, looking completely unfazed. 'This is going to be great.'

'Do you have a child at the school?'

Elowen ran her hand over her tummy and Charlotte could see the beginnings of a bump. 'One day.' She grinned, then nodded towards the door. 'There's Corinne. Now, she and Tink have a baby already. Where's little Kitto, Corinne?'

Corinne strode up to the doorway. 'Nan Sarah has him. Ugh, it's filthy, isn't it?' Both women were taller than Charlotte, and she felt small beside them.

She could feel tears bubbling up and sniffed. 'It's horrible. I was going to carry on staying at the pub, but I can't afford it long term.'

Ellie opened a shopping bag full of stuff. 'The pub's great, isn't it? Not cheap, though. But neither is the hotel, so we'd better clean up here. I've got spray cleaners, cream cleaners, bleach and a load of old cloths.'

'And I brought a mouse trap,' said Corinne. 'Don't be scared, the cottage will scrub up *beautifully*.'

Corinne's optimism was unfounded, but even Charlotte had to admit the house was better after most of the contents had been stacked inside the schoolroom, every surface cleaned and scraped and the floors mopped. The kitchen cupboards were full of black mould but yielded to Charlotte's scrubbing with bleach.

Corinne's partner, Tink, was a whirlwind of action upstairs, every thump and bang releasing a dusting of ceiling plaster (and shouts from Corinne) until he had swept out and cleared the bedroom. Charlotte was amazed. He had put the bed together, turned the mattress over to its less stained side and even laid out a faded rug in front of the tiny fireplace.

'There's a bit of a wardrobe cupboard in the corner,' he said. 'How's downstairs?'

'I think it's liveable,' said Corinne, coming up the stairs behind them. 'But then, I lived in an old lorry for three years.'

Charlotte laughed in disbelief. 'You did?'

'We still use it for lambing. The sheep are ours.'

Charlotte was less confident of sleeping up here. She could hear someone using the vacuum cleaner downstairs and a couple of people were laughing outside, where they had taken mugs of tea. 'The fridge...'

'Cleaned and working. I doubt if the freezer box works, though,' Corinne said. 'Jayne had kept it turned off and the door open, but I cleaned out an inch of dust. You might need a more modern one. I wouldn't use the wood burner until the chimney's swept – I think something's nesting in there.'

Charlotte turned to Tink. 'Thank you both so much. That's amazing.'

'That's Joanna out there – she brought the tea and coffee. She's Rhiannon's mum.'

'That's nice of her.' Charlotte was feeling more uncomfortable now everyone was being so kind, acting as though she was there to save the school.

Tink smiled as he gathered up a bag of rubbish and dust. 'That's what the islands run on, tea and cake. And gossip, of course. We're all hungry for news all the time. That's why *we* came today.'

'We came to find out if our baby boy will have a school on the island he was born on,' Corinne said, looking straight at Charlotte with narrowed eyes.

Ah. Not everyone thinks I rode in on a white pony.

Ellie called up from the bottom stair. 'Lucy sent cakes from the café for everyone. Come and see the bathroom, Charlotte. It scrubbed up OK, although I think the colour choices are very last century.'

Charlotte hadn't been able to get into the downstairs bathroom at first, through a narrow door on the other side of the main room. Boxes blocking the door had been removed and it turned out to be straight out of the seventies, complete with tiled floor, avocado-coloured suite and net curtains that looked iron grey.

'We've taken all the other curtains down for a wash,' Ellie explained. 'But without those you'll be a bit exposed – the glass is clear. I think the bath will work.'

'No shower?' For the first time, hysteria bubbled near the surface.

'Not functional, but there's no hot water anyway,' Ellie said. 'I think the fuse has gone on the immersion heater. You can get that fixed. But we have both hot water and a shower and we're just a few doors along the lane. You're very welcome to pop in. Kittiwake Cottage.'

Charlotte was humbled by all the kindness projected her way. 'Thank you. I may have to take you up on that.'

She walked into the main room and could see the possibilities. It was no worse than a self-catering holiday Zach had once booked in Croatia, no worse really than those chalets from her childhood memories. At least she had a work surface, a cooker and kitchen cupboards, a table with three old chairs and the sofa. She could use her laptop and the phone in the school – she'd been assured there was good Wi-Fi in there.

A tall man about her own age stuck his head in the door. 'One bag of clean bedding,' he said. 'Charlotte, right? I'm Bran, from Kittiwake.'

'Thank you,' she said, rushing forward to take the bag and to shake his hand. The sheets smelled sweet, in fact the whole cottage did. Ellie had said something about lavender in the cleaning sprays that helped cover the sharp smell of the bleach she had used on the floors. 'This is so kind, all of you.'

A red-haired woman was outside, collecting up cups. 'Hi, I'm Joanna.' She shook hands firmly. 'I'm also the teaching assistant. I do three mornings a week.'

'The school has a TA?' It was getting more and more ridiculous; a full-time teacher and an assistant for two children?

When Rhiannon went up to the high school – or home educated herself – there would be two members of staff for one five-year-old.

'My daughter Rhiannon has special needs. Merryn has, too. And both the new boys will need help after losing their mother.'

Charlotte looked around at the small group standing outside the cottage. 'Does anyone know about these two boys?'

There was a small ripple of laughter. Corinne spoke first. 'Of course we all know. There's only a hundred and forty-odd people on the island, two new ones really stand out.'

'Clarissa Tremayne lives just around the corner from my nan and grandpa,' Tink added. 'Everyone knows everyone here.'

'Did you know the children, from before? Did they ever visit?'

This time the group quietened down. 'They never visited before,' Tink said. 'Clarrie had fallen out with her daughter. Chloe was a bit of a wild child, off with different men every few months. Clarrie hardly knew the boys until she was asked to take them.'

'Poor little scraps,' Joanna said. 'The little one, Billy, is just beautiful. But he's no bigger than Merryn and he's nearly two years older.'

This is so unprofessional, getting gossip from the locals.

'Well,' Charlotte said. 'I'll find out more when I get them in the classroom.'

'I just think you'll need me around, at least to start with.' Joanna looked around the group. 'Because Rhiannon doesn't like change.'

'Which reminds me. The previous teacher said there was a rabbit and a fish tank?'

'The boys at the hotel have the tank, Merryn loves the fish,' Joanna said. 'But we have the rabbit. We'll bring him back on Monday. He's very tame.'

Charlotte opened her mouth to refuse but then thought

again. It might help motivate Rhiannon. 'That would be great, thank you.'

'I expect Jayne's dog Callie will be a regular visitor, too,' Tink added, as he packed up a bag to take away. 'She gets bored sometimes, wanders down the hill to join the kids. Bertie pops in sometimes, too, Ellie's cat.'

All thoughts of keeping the classroom allergen-free had already fled when she resigned herself to taking back the rabbit, but the thought of the huge, hairy dog coming in made Charlotte even more certain she would keep the door shut at all times.

Charlotte needed to walk down to the shop to pick up some basics and collect her bags from the pub. Getting into the fresh air and striding down the road lightened her mood. This time, people didn't just say hello, they expected her to stop and be introduced to other people on the quay. In the well-stocked little shop there was more advice on where to get a coffee or a nice meal.

She picked up a handful of tourist information leaflets and a map of the island, along with a book of local history. They also sold her a tide table while she was introduced to several small dogs and one greyhound, which seemed to dislike her on sight. None of the dogs were on leads, but then there weren't any cars. She shut the door with relief when she arrived back at the cottage, before changing the dodgy light bulb to better illuminate the shabby, tired interior.

The fridge was making all the right noises, even if it wasn't very cold. She put some butter, cheese and milk away, then looked through the clean, dry and slightly chlorinated kitchen units. There was an electric kettle in the schoolroom – she could borrow that, and there were a few plates and mugs, freshly washed up. She put soap and toilet rolls in the bathroom, and found a couple of towels folded up with the bedding.

Thank goodness for Ellie and Bran, and all those kind people.

She made herself a cheese and tomato sandwich, almost slicing into her thumb with the blunt knife and mentally adding a new one to her shopping list. Then she sat at the table with a large mug of tea and opened the school files on the new children.

There was little information on the two boys from their previous schools. The elder, at eight years old, was called Beau. A picture showed a boy with dark skin, unsmiling, head tilted back away from the camera. Test scores were poor, reading age undetermined. A little note had been added: 'Very good at faking it'.

She stared at the picture. 'Let's see how much you can fake it with me.' She read through the notes again. It wasn't clear how his mother had died.

His half-brother Billy was also black, but lighter skinned. He had a halo of curly hair and a lovely smile. She held his picture for longer, seeing a little of the baby still in his features.

'Poor little scrap.' She sorted through a couple of standard assessments, and it was clear he had struggled. Barely six, the only subject he enjoyed was art.

The previous three schools had been very short term as the boys had gone into care after the death of their mother. Finally, social services had persuaded their grandmother to take the boys, at least on a trial basis. Charlotte's heart ached for them. Perhaps the grandmother could provide the perfect home.

She brushed a tear aside, not certain if it was the boys' story or missing Zach that had made her sad. She almost reached for her phone to call his number, but a memory made her pull back. Was he with *her*, would she answer his phone as she had before? The memory made her mind skitter away. Instead, she went upstairs, pulled out the book she had bought to read on the ferry, and got ready for bed.

Before she fell asleep, her last thoughts were memories from fifteen years of goodnights at surfing venues, at festivals, or in their own bed. They had shared so much –holidays, struggles, changes – it felt like they were connected by a rope of many strands. Love, that was the big one. Love, laughter, adventure, his extraordinary beauty...

Goodnight, Zach, I love you. She finally let the tears fall.

8

JUNE 1940

The summer had rolled on for Jenny, but not as hot as she remembered from her childhood visits. Few letters came from Maître Boiteux as most non-official post had been cancelled by the German administration.

She received another note from her father, passed between fishing boats to Uncle Paol. Heavily armed German patrol boats were guarding the French coast, and submarines were hunting for British vessels. Even trawlers were targets, as the Germans were hoping to starve the British Isles into submission. Fishing out in the Celtic Sea was more dangerous; her father was having to trawl in shallower waters close to the Cornish mainland.

A single line along the bottom of the note told her to visit Augustine and give her the enclosed tightly folded strip of paper. Aunt Hélène had told her to deliver the sewing machine, so she packed it into the empty perambulator and walked down to the quay to visit the old woman.

The entire fish catch was now the property of the German army, and the prices paid were low. Fish was salted, canned or dried in the old factory, hastily extended. The soldiers were polite to the older locals, but were sometimes rude to the girls. It was a relief to turn into the inn without comments or whistles.

A barmaid explained how to find Augustine. Originally the building at the back had housed a few horses, but now it was converted into half a dozen small rooms for lodgers, mostly elderly. At the back of the stable block was a privy, shared by all the inhabitants, with an outside sink. She knocked on the door marked '4' in blue chalk.

'Aunt Augustine? It's me, Jenofeve. Aunt Hélène asked me to visit you.' She parked the pram outside, and hefted the hamper to the ground.

She heard a little scuffling from inside, then the door opened. 'Come in, come in, bring the machine.' The old woman shut the door behind her and kicked a wedge under it.

'No lock,' she said, smiling at Jenny's raised eyebrows. 'Do you have anything else for me?'

'A note from my father,' she whispered, bringing it out from its hiding place, inside the torn lining in her pocket. 'And Cook sent food from the kitchen. Milk and cheeses are more scarce now, but Aunt Hélène has spared a little. There's a knuckle of ham in there, too.'

Augustine's small room had the traditional blue shutters over the window. It was dark, and after peering out, Augustine opened them.

'Some of the ships can see inside my room when they moor at this end of the dock,' she explained. 'Your cook is a treasure.' She spoke in Breton, but with an odd accent.

'You don't sound like an islander,' Jenny said, sitting on the edge of the tidily made bed.

'I've travelled around a lot. Like you, I have a parent from two different countries. I would say French is my true language, so people look down on me here in Brittany. That means the Germans notice me even less.'

Jenny couldn't imagine what she had to hide. A large table was shoved under the window and Augustine lifted the case onto it. She unpacked the old sewing machine, next to a stack of folded fishermen's work shirts.

'You do mending for a living?'

'Just to get by. People won't be able to get new clothes or even cloth soon. They try to be thrifty, but many families don't sew. These shirts are mostly from widowers or fishermen.' She smiled suddenly, her teeth like little round pearls. It was the one thing that made her worn and faded dresses and ragged-cut hair look out of place. Augustine opened the folded note and spread it out. She showed it to Jenny. '*One bear, 4 cruise, lemons, swallows 56.* Everything's in code,' she explained, sighing.

'I'd better go,' Jenny said hurriedly as the woman went over the note several times, scribbling some words down with a pencil, holding it up to the light from the dusty window.

'No, stay. I have to ask you something.' Augustine crouched down to drag out a leather suitcase from under the bed. 'Do you know what this is?' she said, opening the lid.

Inside was a black wooden box. It wasn't until Augustine unlatched the lid and opened it that Jenny caught her breath. She put her hand to her mouth. 'Is that... a radio?'

'Shush. We don't use the word out loud, ever. This is a *swan.* Remember that? It will have a new codeword next month, when it will be a *stag.*'

'Why are you showing me this?' Jenny whispered. 'It could get you arrested. Both of us.'

'Arrested, interrogated, tortured and shot,' Augustine murmured back without a trace of concern. Her dark eyes were sparkling. 'Which is why we never talk about it. For now.'

'Aren't you scared?'

'I am fifty-three years old,' Augustine said. 'I dress poor, I mutter a bit, I smell bad when I travel. I scratch a lot. That keeps the Germans away. No one notices me; I never get stopped.'

Jenny felt cold inside. 'Why are you telling me this?'

Augustine held out brown, strong hands and after a moment, Jenny put her own fingers in them. There was an energy in Augustine that seemed to warm her.

'I'm an agent,' she said softly, the words barely making it across the air between them. 'My job is to collect and deliver equipment for the operatives already working in France.'

'Are there many?' Jenny asked, her heart beating faster.

'Hundreds. Many of us were here before the invasion. We helped the French Resistance slow the Germans down at Dunkirk and at the Brittany ports.'

Jenny knew thousands of troops had escaped the invading Germans – many of the ships had been visible from Ushant as they scattered towards Britain. 'And now?'

'We are recruiting agents. Don't worry, no one expects you to carry a gun or be a spy. I promise. I have just one tiny job for you, then I will do all the work.'

Jenny pressed a hand to the pulse bounding in her throat, as if it was a drumbeat the Germans could hear. 'What job?'

'I need you to translate some encrypted notes for me. You read both English and Breton fluently.'

'But I don't know about translating anything.'

'Vital messages have been translated into Breton, then encoded. I can decode the letters but then I need someone to translate the Breton back into English for our operatives. The messages will be difficult, and even after translation they may be a bit cryptic. Do you understand the word "cryptic"?'

'Like crossword puzzles?' Jenny's teacher used to bring in old copies of *The Times* newspaper for the students to wrestle with.

'Exactly.' Augustine pulled out a sheet of tiny letters, with no spaces or punctuation. 'Can you work on this? I've decoded it but now it's just lines of text, without spaces, in Breton. Some of the words are misspelled, or they might be phonetic renderings of important words.'

Jenny stared at it, a spark of interest growing inside her. 'I'll try. That's all?'

'You must keep it hidden. Anyone on the island could be spying for the Germans, or the right-wing Bretons, for that matter. I have to go away for a few weeks, taking my "sewing machine" with me. Can you try and decipher it?'

'What happens if someone finds it?'

'Try and destroy it if anyone is searching your house. And leave little traps around your room to make sure you aren't being watched.' She explained how to arrange a hair or a tiny scrap of paper in drawers or closet doors. 'If you have to, eat the paper. Better a stomach ache than an interrogation.'

Jenny wrapped her arms around herself at a sudden shiver. 'What do I say if I am questioned?'

'You don't know anything. You can tell them you were kind to an old lady who said she is a distant relative, although you don't remember her.'

'And if you don't come back?'

'Forget all about me,' Augustine said. 'Forget everything.'

Jenny looked over at the door. 'I'm scared someone will see me leaving now.'

'Here. It's a piece of sewing, just a chemise I darned for your aunt.'

Jenny took it and examined the beautiful stitchwork. 'It's so fine. Did you really do this?'

'I really did.' Augustine rolled her eyes. 'The benefits of a convent education. I used to sew clothes to help the poor.'

'I must go,' Jenny said, folding the worn linen over one arm. She had tucked the paper into her bodice, where it felt crisp against her breast.

'Your father is working with British intelligence. I will be back if you need anything, in about two or three weeks. Work hard with those children, and don't do anything to stand out. Act a little stupid, as I do.' Unexpectedly, she leaned forward and kissed Jenny on both cheeks. 'Go, child. All will be well.'

9

PRESENT DAY, 19 MARCH

Charlotte moved her things into the cottage and set out to walk the length of the island with her history of Morwen book and the map.

She met Tink and Corinne walking with their baby, as well as half a dozen locals. She navigated from the lane, looking for familiar landmarks. She couldn't see where the holiday chalets had been, but thought it might have been where the campsite sat on a windswept and gently sloping field. It had two old buildings that could have once been holiday homes, but were now a utility block and bathrooms. It was opening for the season in a week, and the owner was cutting the grass. She stopped to chat, and he pointed out the commercial washing machine and tumble drier on site, which would prove helpful. A picture in the book showed a dozen windswept chalets from the 1940s, which had been used as an army camp during the war.

Walking north on the path along the back of the island, she could see the whole town curved along the eastern shore: the sheep field beside the school, the village green and churchyard, and behind the path, the cliffs. As she looked west she supposed the next land would be America.

Several offshoots of the path led to flights of rough steps going down to small coves, only one big enough to offer an actual beach. She decided to explore, climbing down the stairs cautiously, avoiding the ones that had collapsed with the winter weather. At the bottom was a gully leading back into the cliffs, bubbling water cutting across the sand. She was contemplating jumping over it when she realised several of the rounded boulders on the beach were actually seals, bunched up in the furthest northern corner, settled on rocks stretching into the water.

The other end of the beach had some kind of structure, and since the wind off the sea was keen, she walked over to find shelter. It looked almost like some sort of Stone-Age hut, a simple circle of stones collapsed at the front, built up at the back into the cliff face. The wall was covered in creepers hanging off the cliff, and a foot of sand had been blown in by the wind. It smelled of seaweed and salt, and apart from a few springs from what might have once been a chair or bed, it was empty. It was eerie, although she couldn't say why. She stepped inside. Every stone in the wall was carefully fitted together, as if someone had taken hours to find and place them with such care that they stayed solid for... how long? It could have been a dozen years or a thousand – there was no modern technology in the making of it. She ran a hand over it, feeling small ferns growing in the tiny cracks, a film of dried salt covering all. The stone threshold must be just a few feet away from the highest tides, in the strongest storms. Dried seaweed formed a broken line only a few metres away. Flicking through the guidebook she identified Seal Cove, and a small article caught her eye.

During the Second World War, a radio operative, Laurence Byers, was recruited into the Special Operations Executive (SOE) as a spy in occupied Brittany. His diaries, written in code, are kept in the museum on St Brannock's. Byers earned a

medal of valour for his actions during the war in Ushant. He
built a small shack from rocks and shipwrecked timbers, living
as a hermit in Seal Cove.

Did Byers live here, in this hut? She had an idea that this
once had a blue door, faded and peeling, a small fire right at the
darkest point at the back. She pulled away dried foliage and
grasses, scooped away the sand and found a hole, barely a foot
high and the same across, venting inside the wall in a sooty
chimney. The whole hut was about twelve feet across. Turning
to the next page in her book, she saw a photograph of a man,
posing with an older woman in a fur coat with a rope of pearls
almost to her waist. Another picture was of the beehive-shaped
hut with its duck-under door.

I've bent under that doorway. I've been here before.

The memory made her shiver.

The smell of burning wood, the odd curl of smoke in the
room if the door was open, candles stuck in tins full of holes, an
old armchair and a tartan blanket... she could have painted the
scene. She ran her hand along the jagged top of the rear wall,
feeling the shaft of the tiny chimney, a little soot clinging to her
fingers even now, the ends of old beams that once held the roof.

Anxiety began to burn in her chest, stifling her breath.
Something happened, some story she was told when she was
little, about dangerous sea crossings, and a dead man in the hut.
She backed out of the doorway, her breath ragged, and staggered across the soft sand to the steps. She ran out of puff
halfway up and stopped to look back at the beach. The seals
had all lifted their heads and were looking at her with curiosity.
Maybe they had picked up on her urgency, her panic.

By the time she reached the clifftop, she was embarrassed
about allowing herself to get so spooked.

But the name Byers resonated with her.

10

JULY 1940

Summer brought changes for Jenny, and plenty of worries. Augustine had been away for several weeks, not just one or two, and Jenny and Hélène wondered if she'd been caught or killed. The passenger ferry had become a troop and supply ship, but at least the Germans hadn't shown any interest in Madame and her household.

Jenny had worked out the meaning of the cryptic, coded note. It had been a surprise. It was a formal invitation for Jenny to work for the Secret Intelligence Service, as an interpreter. The letter was explicit, stating that the risks were high even to young agents. She would know as little as possible so it couldn't be dragged out of her under torture. She had memorised the letter, but she wasn't sure if she wanted to be pulled into her step-aunt's world. Was Augustine dead? Was she being interrogated somewhere, telling the Gestapo about Jenny? But the war looked like it would drag on, even threaten Great Britain, and she decided to do what she could. Knowing her father was working for them gave her a warm glow, a little connection to her old life on another island.

Maître Boiteux was forced to stay in Rennes, and was

working as a civil administrator under the German government. Occasional letters were allowed, but didn't betray any dissatisfaction as they were probably read by his superiors. Instead, he gave news about their house being requisitioned as expected. He was able to report that his wife's wedding coat had been stored away in a friend's house, which gave Madame some relief as it suggested he had hidden her furs and Parisian dresses as well.

Young Marc started his studies at the island school. He had been expected to attend the same school as his father in Brest, but travel in Brittany had become impossible.

Marc's school day left baby Adela with Jenny, Lisette and her bored mother to entertain her. Madame was lonely without similar ladies to talk to or pay calls on. The few families of her own class occasionally invited her to a meagre, rationed dinner. Some well-to-do families also socialised with Germans, although Madame hadn't approved.

'Perhaps we should invite the Kommandant,' Madame said to Jenny one morning. 'I don't want to be suspected of anything unpatriotic.'

'Don't worry, Madame,' Jenny reassured her. 'Without the man of the house, we can just say we are living quietly, just women and the children.'

'You're right. Such an invitation should come from the master.'

Jenny picked up the toys from the drawing room floor and excused herself to the nursery. Lisette was undressing baby Adela and looking out of the window. She had recently become moody, as she had left her sweetheart behind in Rennes, and the embargo on letters had upset her.

'The ferry is coming in,' Lisette said, with a sigh.

'It's two days overdue,' Jenny said, choosing a dress for the baby from a pile of clean linen. 'Now everyone has to apply for travel papers, it's getting harder to go anywhere at all.'

'I just hope they bring some fresh fruit for the island,' Lisette said, fastening the baby's rubber pants over her nappy. 'There you go, little lady.' She lifted Adela up to kiss her nose.

'Are you unhappy here?' Jenny asked gently.

Lisette handed her the baby to finish dressing and gathered up the basket of dirty clothes. 'I miss my parents,' she said. 'I'm sure you do, too.'

'And your boyfriend?'

The girl shrugged. 'I suppose. But it's been months since I saw him. He's found someone else by now, I'm sure.' She glanced up at Jenny. 'Are you missing someone special?'

'No, just my family.' It hurt a little to speak of it, and she smiled at Lisette with sympathy. 'We must stick together. Perhaps we could walk down to the harbour when the children are with Madame?'

'I can't,' the girl said, her face twisted into a discontented scowl. 'I have to iron some laundry. Madame said I left it to get wrinkled.'

'Another day then, perhaps.' It occurred to Jenny that Lisette was her own enemy, cutting corners and avoiding work.

Jenny couldn't wait to put on her jacket and walk down to the harbour, out of the stifling house facing the September sun, and into the breezes along the quay. Fewer people sat around on the dock now, and the Germans would question anyone who had a beer in his hand. *Who are you? Why are you not working? Where are your papers?*

She stopped by the ferry, tied alongside the harbour and rocking in the choppy high tide. Two men were unloading the last of several crates. 'Are you looking for someone?' an older man asked.

'No. Yes. I wondered if there was an old lady on the ferry today?'

He smiled at that. 'There was an ancient who smelled like a

farmyard and had so many bags she had to pay Hervé here to
carry them. She went to the inn.'

Augustine.

Jenny thanked them and slipped along the quay, clutching
her purse as if she was going to buy something. Two German
soldiers stared at her and one said something, but she got past
without being challenged. She made certain no one was
watching when she slid along to the converted stables, to
number four. Augustine answered on the first knock, smiling
broadly, her teeth unexpectedly dirty and with two missing.

'What happened to your teeth?' Jenny was horrified with
the idea of interrogation or torture. 'Were you arrested?'

'A good dentist in Montmartre did it while I was in Paris.
No peasant my age has good teeth.'

'Oh.' Jenny sat down with a bump.

'I used to blacken them but the colour would come off after
a few hours. No, this is better. The Germans are more vigilant
now. People around me were stopped on this last journey, and
they checked my papers several times.'

'I thought you would be back sooner.'

Augustine patted Jenny on the shoulder and sat at the table
with a fresh pile of mending and the enormous sewing machine.
'Don't worry about me. I go where I'm needed. Have you had a
chance to translate the letter?'

'Easily,' she said. 'Well, it took some time – some of the
clues were obscure – but I worked it out.' She hesitated. 'I have
been asked to help with the war effort by the secret service in
London. To do some more coding and pass on information.'

Augustine looked severe. 'And you must say no, if you are
not absolutely certain. Does anyone know you are here?'

She shook her head. 'Not at the house. They know I have
gone for a walk, that's all.' She looked at her watch. 'But I want
to help if I can.'

'Bring me linens to repair,' Augustine said. 'Not tomorrow,

leave it a couple of days. Act casual, don't be nice to me in public, no one is. Just polite. There is a young man behind the bar, he has red hair. Pretend that you came to look at him, if anyone asks. Can you do that?'

'Flirt with a young man? That's easy,' Jenny said, with a laugh.

11

PRESENT DAY, 20 MARCH

For the first day of school, Charlotte had prepared one of her getting-to-know-you exercises, using the island map. She sketched the outline onto big sheets of paper from the well-stocked art supplies, for the children to add their ideas and colour in, focusing on what was important to them.

Morwen Island was different from the other Atlantic Islands. The others had once been connected by sand bars between them, having once been part of a larger island. After the last ice age the water levels had risen and flooded it, creating islands from the high points. But Morwen was a rocky outcrop with steeper geology, higher cliffs, further away into the Atlantic. It was mirrored sixty miles away by the rocky outcrops of Brittany, the islands around Ushant.

The first child to arrive was Rhiannon, with her mother Joanna. She was a nervous-looking ten-year-old and seemed younger than her age.

'I liked Mrs Mason best.' She walked over to one of the tables, then looked around at the stacks of stuff they had removed from the cottage. 'That's where the rabbit lives,' she said, with a frown. 'We're bringing him back. Where is he going to live?' Her voice was starting to rise.

'It's just temporary.' Charlotte showed her a bag of drawing paper. 'We just need to find homes for all this extra art stuff.'

'Oh. I like art,' the child confided. 'Can we do drawing today?'

'I'd like to make some maps.' When Rhiannon looked blank, she added, 'So we'll need to draw things on the outline of the island. Like roads and houses and special places. Like your house and the school.'

Joanna put an animal carrier down. 'We'll get Percival's cage sorted out. Come on, Rhiannon, you know where it goes.'

An older woman, maybe in her sixties with greying hair pulled back into a bun and wearing jeans and jumper, walked into the classroom and stared at Charlotte over thick glasses.

'I expect you got the notes about my grandsons starting at the school? And their school records?'

'Yes, thank you, I did.'

A small boy, recognisable from his photo as Billy, peered around his grandmother. He scampered over to the animal carrier where Rhiannon was talking reassuringly to the rabbit.

'I'm Clarissa Tremayne,' the woman said, holding out a hand. 'My grandsons are Beau and Billy. They arrived after Jayne retired, unfortunately. They hardly seem to have had any education,' she added.

'I'm Charlotte Kingston,' she replied, shaking her hand. 'I'll have a better idea where they have got to after this week.'

'Good,' the woman answered, allowing a small smile. 'I'm just sorry to give you so much more work.'

'Not at all.' A second boy, tall and slim with a scowl on his face, slipped around his grandmother. 'You must be Beau, is that right?'

He shrugged one shoulder, but seemed more interested in Joanna, who was setting up the indoor cage. She was filling it with sawdust for Billy and Rhiannon to spread around and adding a feeder and water bottle.

'I suppose I ought to meet this rabbit.' Charlotte knelt down beside the carrier and Beau shuffled over to watch her open the door. Joanna was right, the animal was large, grey, tame and very inquisitive, hopping towards her knees and standing up against one. 'Oh, he's very cute,' she said, as Beau crouched down beside her and petted the animal. 'And so soft.'

Rhiannon walked over and picked him up. 'He likes me best,' she said, possessively.

'Percival is everyone's rabbit,' Joanna reminded her. 'Put him in the cage so everyone can stroke him.'

Rhiannon did, explaining to Billy where he liked his fur touched and how he liked to be brushed.

'Can I leave them here, then?' Mrs Tremayne had already moved towards the door.

Charlotte could see apprehension building on Billy's face, and Beau seemed withdrawn. 'They'll be fine. Can you leave your number so I can call if necessary?'

Joanna got the grandmother to write it on Beau's file.

She hesitated by the door and turned to the boys. 'Be good for Miss Kingston, boys, and I'll see you this afternoon.'

Billy launched himself at her middle, wailing as he went, and she shot out an arm to stop him.

'Now then, don't be silly.' His grandmother bent down to his level, still holding his arm. 'Be a good boy and we'll watch television together this evening.'

Charlotte put a hand on his shoulder. 'Come on, Billy. Perhaps we'll pick some grass for Percival Rabbit. Or maybe he likes carrots?'

Billy was easily distracted into a conversation with Rhiannon about the extensive list of vegetables the rabbit would eat. As they were talking, a slim, dark-haired man brought a little girl in. She was dressed in ballet shoes and a princess costume, complete with plastic tiara.

'I'm Robert, Merryn's dad,' he said. 'I assume you're the new teacher?'

'Charlotte Kingston.' She looked down at Merryn, who went over to the rabbit, crooning at him. 'She probably knows her way around the classroom better than I do.'

'We all do. I came to this school as a kid. There were nine children then. My husband and I run the hotel on the north corner of the island, along the beach. Feel free to come up for a coffee and a chat, or a meal. It's going to be lonely in that old cottage.' He smiled. 'It's nice to see two more kids, too. At least there's still hope for the school.'

She opened her mouth to argue, but thanked him instead. He kissed Merryn goodbye and waved at the rest of them. Finally, the door was shut and she and the children looked at each other.

'OK,' Charlotte said, looking around the room at them. 'Let's sit down, and you can teach me all about your lovely island.'

The children worked together better than she expected. Little Merryn was bright and enthusiastic, even if her language was unsophisticated, and she matched Billy's level of understanding well. Rhiannon was enthusiastic about drawing, colouring and illustrating the pictures she created for the map. Beau was able to draw a reasonable plan of the island as he knew it, and while he didn't speak much, he did engage with Billy and, through him, with Merryn.

As Charlotte read through the scant records from Billy's previous school, she became aware of his bladder problems, and silently showed the relevant information to Joanna, who suggested more breaks than usual and escorted Billy back and forth when needed. At the lunch break, the children wrapped up warm and walked around the sheep field.

'These sheep are about to have babies, did you know?' Joanna said.

For the first time, Beau looked interested.

'Where do they have their lambs?' Charlotte asked.

'Tink will move them into the special field with the shelters,' Joanna explained.

Charlotte looked at Beau. 'Maybe we could ask him to move them in school hours, so we could watch.'

'And help,' said Beau, with a little spark of interest.

'Oh, yuk!' Merryn said, scraping sheep poo off one of her ballet shoes. The other children laughed, and Merryn didn't mind being carried back in. Her shoes, scrubbed clean, were put to dry on the radiator, leaving her to dance around in her sparkly tights.

Later that afternoon, Charlotte traced the little cove on the west side of the island on the map with her finger, still puzzled by the emotional reaction she had experienced in the hut.

'We should learn about the history of these places on the island, too. Maybe there was an older farm in the fields at one time.'

Beau drew some sheep on his map. Charlotte's history book had a Victorian plan of the fields and farms on the island; each one had been tiny. Bee Farm, School Field, Noah's Farm, Lighthouse Acre.

'The sheep keep moving,' he said, frowning, looking out of the window and rubbing out a faint outline.

'That's OK.' She had an idea. 'How about you draw some on card, and we'll cut them out? That way you can move them around, and move them to the right field when they have their babies.'

She got some card from a stash in a stationery cupboard. He started drawing, tiny sheep-like figures, with individual faces and markings.

'People kill lambs,' he said, his face still expressionless. 'And then they eat them.'

'When they grow up, they do. Not all of them, though. Some of them get chosen to be the mums and dads, the ewes and rams. Do you want me to cut them out?'

'I can do it.' He reached for the scissors and started cutting around them roughly. 'My dad showed me how.'

'I didn't know about your dad,' she said, looking at the map, not challenging him with eye contact. She knew the boys had different fathers, although neither were in contact. At least, neither had stepped forward to take their child when their mother had died.

'My dad is Daddy Ash,' he said, leaning forward to cut carefully around a tail and some legs. 'He's our stepdad, really.'

'What's he like?' Charlotte was aware that Billy was listening, watching his brother.

'He's dark, like me, not lighter like Billy. He's a diver in the North Sea. That's a very long way away. He doesn't live with us any more.'

'Oh. I'm sorry.'

'Mum made him leave. She had a new boyfriend.' He shrugged one shoulder. 'I didn't like the new one.'

Billy leaned forward, over his own map, planting one elbow in wet paint. 'He was cross with us all the time.'

'That's sad,' Charlotte said, trying to keep her voice neutral.

'Then he left, and Mum died.' Beau's words were plain, matter-of-fact, but Billy shrank back like he was hurt. 'She was dead on the sofa,' he added, and now Billy's eyes were filled with tears, one spilling down his cheek.

'Her heart was broken,' he said.

'I am very sorry,' Charlotte said, reaching over to touch Billy's hand. 'That must have been very sad.'

'It was a heart valve, it went wrong,' Beau added, very softly. 'No one knew about it until too late.'

Charlotte couldn't find the right words. The boy seemed wrapped in a blanket of desolation, his face blank and lost. She couldn't touch him; his whole body was stiffly pulling away from her. Billy walked over and hugged his unresponsive brother.

'You need more sheep,' he added, and Beau went back to cutting them out.

12

PRESENT DAY, 21 MARCH

Jayne had offered to walk over on the second day of school to help out, thankfully without the dog. She arrived after lunch and sat in the corner with each child in turn, reading with them. Charlotte noticed that Rhiannon's reading was fluent and she was ready academically to go to the high school. Behaviourally she wasn't; she needed a lot of supervision and returned again and again to touch the rabbit cage.

The atmosphere in the classroom was quiet, three adults and four children all working together. Joanna went off an hour early and Rhiannon coped well with her absence. Charlotte worked on maps and planning walking routes with the younger three children. It had been many years since she had taught a small group of primary-aged children – it was a pleasure even as it stretched her imagination. By the time Merryn was finishing colouring a unicorn for what she called the top field, her other dad Justin was waiting, and Mrs Tremayne was waiting for the boys.

'Did Joanna tell you I was walking Rhiannon home as well?' Justin asked. He was fairer than his husband, with a big smile and a close, ginger beard.

'She did.' Charlotte showed him the map his daughter had been working on, and he exclaimed over it, then moved on to praise Beau's accurate sheep pictures and Billy's strong colours.

'There are going to be baby lambs!' Billy told him.

Justin smiled at him. 'I hope so, or those sheep will pop.'

Clarrie Tremayne arrived and asked what the boys had done at school, listening intently to the answers.

'And Billy hasn't wet himself or had a tantrum?' she said quietly.

'He's been great. They both have. Beau is going to be our resident sheep expert by the end of the week.' She turned to Beau who stared back, unsmiling. 'See you tomorrow.'

The room seemed very quiet once the children had left. Jayne put her coat on. 'Do you want me to come in later in the week? It's nice to give the girls a little continuity as they cope with the changes.'

'If you have time, that would be great, thank you.'

Jayne pushed the open book on the desk around to look at it. 'Are you interested in Laurie Byers?'

'I think my grandmother Isabelle knew him. The name's familiar.'

Jayne turned the page and showed Charlotte a photograph. 'I love the symbols he used to code his diaries. The older children had a go at translating a few pages a couple of years ago.'

'Maybe there's something about my grandma in there.' She gathered up the papers she had been using. 'I'd really like your advice, informally, if that's all right? I haven't taught for seven years.'

Jayne looked at her thoughtfully. 'Come for a walk with me and Callie, tomorrow evening. I'll answer your questions and then you can start making your report.'

Charlotte caught her breath for a moment. 'Look, I know the parents want to save the school at any cost, but the local authority might not be able to pay for it.'

'Oh, I know why you're here,' Jayne said, picking up her bag and putting it over her shoulder. 'They asked *me* to make the report, get Rhiannon to school on the big island any way I could, and close the school. I couldn't do it, and neither should you.'

Charlotte made two mistakes as she celebrated her first day teaching in seven years. The first was that she bought a bottle of wine.

The second was that she called Zach.

He didn't answer right away. After three rings she almost hung up, and after four she took a big glug of wine. Her finger was hovering over the cancel button as he answered.

'Char? Is that really you?'

He had a lovely voice. He was a great singer, too; he'd sung to her regularly, especially around her birthday. He'd sung when he asked her to marry him. When she lifted her glass for another gulp, a tear plopped into the wine.

'Charlotte, are you there?'

The memory of the last time she rang his phone filled her mind. That soft voice, the puzzled enquiry. 'Are you...?' Her voice came out squeakier and more childlike than she had hoped. She cleared her throat and tried again. 'Are you on your own?'

'I am. Except for my new flatmate, but he's gaming in his room.'

Charlotte sat back, spilled a drop of wine on her T-shirt. 'You've got a flat?'

'Just sharing, in Newquay. I've got a teaching gig at the surf academy for the summer. How are you?'

There were so many answers crowding forward she couldn't voice any of them. She topped up the glass, realising she was probably a bit drunk.

'I'm in Cornwall too. Well, sort of. Atlantic Islands. Middle of nowhere.'

He sighed, and a little curl of warmth spread up from her belly. It was the sound he made when he was content – falling asleep on the sofa or walking home late at night after a great meal or gig.

'Are you inspecting a school there?'

'No. Just looking after it until...' She didn't want to say it. She didn't want to be the cold-hearted bureaucrat he had accused her of being in their last row. 'How was Portugal?' The words came out clipped and snippy.

'Good. First in the surfing *veterans'* longboard class. Came over fiftieth in the main competition. I missed you.'

'You found a replacement quickly enough.' There it was, the spiteful, jealous tone in her voice that she hated. 'I'm sorry. It was already over.'

'If you had come to Portugal...' She could hear the old frustration in his voice. 'Let's not rehash things. We wanted different things, Char.'

'We did. We do.'

But now Zach was doing what Charlotte had always hoped he would. He was settling down, had stopped chasing 'one last championship'. He was teaching the sport he loved every day, instead of shouting about how he qualified for Maui or Portugal or some contest in Australia, chasing the elusive win.

'So, you're nearby.' His voice had dropped into a soft rumble. 'We could meet up, if you like? Just as friends...'

'But we're not friends, are we?' The tears trickling down her face had made her words husky. 'We hurt each other.'

'We were friends first and last.'

'But you were *unfaithful*.' The words jumped out easily after a second glass of wine. She winced, and wished she could take it back.

'I didn't have sex with her. Honestly. I drank too much and

got into some deep discussions with Fleur. We didn't sleep together until afterwards. When you left me.'

He made it sound as if she forced him into it. 'But you *kissed* her.' Her voice was thick with tears now, tickling her cheeks. 'You wanted to have sex with her.'

'Listen,' he said, his voice calm, objective. 'I'd won the longboard veteran pro competition and I wanted you there to celebrate. I hadn't seen you for nearly three months. But you refused to fly out.'

'Maybe it was over already.' Rehashing the old argument was agony. 'I hate you. You hurt me, I can't sleep, I'm miserable and lonely and cold.'

He gave a little cough of laughter. 'I don't think I can be held responsible for you being... *cold*.'

She drained the last of the wine. 'But you are,' she cried. 'You should be here, I'm always cold now...'

'Char.' He sounded closer to the phone now, as if he'd tucked it under his chin.

Don't call me that. Words were difficult to form, and the tears were coming too fast.

'Char. I love you. We could still be together.'

Now you've lost your stupid dream to be the world champion longboard surfer.

'Please let me see you,' he said. 'Just meet up somewhere nice, neutral. Go for lunch, talk about old times. We can see if the spark is still there.'

He sounded so reasonable. She managed to press the red button on the second try.

She hadn't been able to cry before. Now she let go, and the alcohol smoothed the way.

I love you. You know I still do.

13

JULY 1940

Along with Augustine, the ferry had brought post from the mainland. Madame received three letters, all from Maître Boiteux, increasingly worried that he hadn't heard from his wife. She spent the evening in tears and went to bed early, leaving Lisette to reread an old romance novel from the study, and Jenny to walk out into the gardens.

'*Dimezell!*' someone hissed from the shrubbery. It was the Breton word for mademoiselle, clumsily said.

'Who is there? Show yourself,' she commanded, backing towards the house.

A pale face emerged from the leaves, followed by half a thin body. 'I am unclothed, I am sorry. I have just come from the sea.' His French was better than his attempt at Breton. At least he had long trousers on, and she averted her eyes from the bare chest.

'Why?' she hissed.

'I-I fell overboard. I am looking for someone, do you know her? An old lady, a seamstress.'

She marched across the terrace and flapped her hands to get

him back into the shrubs. 'Be quiet! Do you want to get me into trouble?'

In the softest voice, so she could barely hear, he whispered, 'Our ship was shot up.' In English.

She shook her head. 'No, you must speak in French or Breton,' she hissed. 'French is well understood here but never, *ever* speak in English.'

'My code name is Fox,' he said quietly.

Oh. An agent.

'I am Jenofeve Huon.'

He smiled then, and the low light gleamed in his teeth and eyes. 'I was supposed to land at Kerzoncou. But our vessel couldn't get close enough once it was shot at, so they dropped me in a dinghy offshore. I must have rowed too slowly so the current brought me here. This is Ushant, isn't it?'

'The west of the island, yes.' He was carrying a bundle of wet clothes and a leather bag. 'Why are you here?'

'My cover story, if I get caught, is that I came here to beg money from my grandmother, Madame Berthou. You have met her?'

'Augustine? Yes. You must be cold – should I get a towel or something?'

His teeth were chattering, but he said, 'I'll be fine. Walking will warm me up.' He hesitated. 'I had a letter for you, as well as one for Augustine. The fishing boat that brought me was the *Westerly Murrelet*. Do you know it?'

'I do!' She could hardly keep herself from shouting at the mention of an island boat. 'It belongs to my uncle, from St Brannock's. Is the letter from my family?'

'From our masters in London, but there is a note from your family as well. I hope the ink is waterproof. The dinghy broke up on the rocks offshore. I had to swim for a long time.' He reached into the bundle and brought out the leather bag, about the size of a large book, with black straps. 'I also have things for Augustine.'

'You should get them to her, then,' she said, smiling at him. 'I am glad to have met you. Call me Jenny.'

He grasped her hand with his fish-cold fingers. 'Byers,' he said, shaking it firmly. 'Laurie Byers.'

14

The following day, Charlotte had an unexplained headache that she refused to think of as a hangover.

Tink walked up to the school, banged on the door and warned them he was about to move the sheep. Getting the kids into coats and boots was fine. Beau was the first out, taking instructions from Tink and listening so carefully that he was allowed to handle the long-handled crook. Corinne had come up to guide the sheep towards their lambing quarters. It was hard to believe the sheep could get any bigger – some of them looked like they were carrying panniers on their sides, like overloaded donkeys.

'They're mostly carrying twins,' Tink pointed out. 'So, Beau, which ones do you think will have their lambs first?'

'That one,' Beau pointed. 'She's the fattest.'

'You might be right,' Tink said, grinning at Charlotte. It was nice to see Beau out of his shell a little. 'Run, head those two off.'

Beau shot off, then slowed to gather the ewes into a loose bunch. Billy and Merryn held hands, periodically jumping and giggling. It took Charlotte a few moments to realise they were jumping in heaps of sheep poo, splashing their trousers and coats. By the time she had got them to stop, the sheep were already by the gate, jostling to get out.

'Up, sheep,' Tink said, with some theatrics. Beau echoed him, laughing when one barged past Tink, knocking him aside.

Rhiannon walked by Charlotte's side, matching her footsteps, making sure they kept an arm's length apart.

'My mum says you're here to shut the school. But you can't, can you?'

She was blunt, the words hard for Charlotte to bat away. 'I need to see if the school is big enough to work. If the boys stay on the island...'

'I heard someone say they might move away. Maybe their dad will come.'

'I promise we'll work together to do the right thing,' Charlotte said, as diplomatically as she could. Rhiannon turned to stare at Charlotte directly.

'Don't shut the school.'

That evening, after a ready meal from the shop heated up slowly in the rickety oven, Charlotte put on her coat and wellies to walk the dog with Jayne. Callie looked even bigger close up, with a pink tongue over long teeth.

'So, she's friendly? I mean, even to nervous people?'

'She wouldn't hurt a fly.' Jayne let the dog off the lead. 'I thought we could go along the cliff path.' Callie shot off, sniffing all over the field where the sheep had been. 'I just hope she doesn't roll in anything.'

Jayne set a fast pace up the lane, around the corner with its viewpoint, above the fields and eventually, the campsite.

'I remember being here as a child,' Charlotte said, a little out of breath as Jayne powered ahead of her up the hill. 'At the old holiday camp.'

'It's the campsite now,' Jayne said, stopping for Charlotte to catch up. 'It was originally a barracks in the Second World War.'

'I thought it was all about fishing rather than the forces.'

'This was a base for the secret service. There's a whole archive over at the museum,' Jayne said. 'The kids might like it. The islanders talk about a real character who lived here who was a war hero. Or not. It depends who you talk to.'

Charlotte started up the stone track alongside the cliffs. The drop-off was getting higher. 'Do you need to put the dog on the lead?'

'I shouldn't have to but if there are rabbits...' Jayne secured the dog. 'I thought you would know more than me. Didn't your grandmother know him?'

Charlotte could only remember Isabelle – a hardworking, fisherman's wife – with a sense of humour and a lightning temper. 'I thought I remembered something in his hut. Like I'd been there before.'

'She used to take shopping down to him, at the end. She was the one who found him when he died and arranged his funeral.' She called to the dog again as Callie tugged her lead at the top of the steps to Seal Cove.

Charlotte didn't know what to say. Maybe Grandma Isabelle had taken her to see him in his little house, before he passed away. 'When did he die?'

'I think in the late nineties. There are several coded diaries in the museum, found in his house. No one's ever bothered to decipher them. Well, not yet, anyway.' Jayne slowed down as they reached a white stone platform. 'But enough of that. You wanted to talk about the school.'

'You know the local authority wants to close the school.'

'I do.' She gazed out to sea, the dog leaning against her. 'But they can't. The islands are at a turning point, changing post-fishing. New people are coming in, like Ellie and Corinne, both likely to want to bring up their children here. If there isn't a school, those families would be forced to move away.'

Charlotte couldn't see the problem beyond individual children. 'If people with kids want to move elsewhere...'

'No, you don't understand. The average age of a resident on the island is over fifty, whereas the UK average is about forty. We have a lot of people like me, newly retired, looking after a lot of much older people. We need young people, but they struggle to find houses and jobs. Taking the school away would be the last straw.'

Charlotte ran her hand over the huge block that must have supported a building, maybe a lighthouse. Fragments of the walls lay around, covered in climbers. 'I don't see how I can help.'

'Emphasise the needs of the children you have now. Explain how the school will meet the requirements of the new children that will come.'

'But if Billy and Beau move away, that will leave just Merryn. That's a miserable school experience for one child.'

'If that happens, engage more with the island communities, the way home-educating parents do. Create new opportunities.' She let the dog off the lead. 'Don't just give up.'

15

JULY 1940

Jenny had given Laurie Byers strict instructions on how to get to Augustine's accommodation and, over his complaints, lent him a towel that needed mending to stop him shivering. 'I can pick it up another day,' she had said, telling him where the night patrols usually walked.

When he had gone, she was on edge knowing he was walking past the German guards, and locals who would know he was a stranger. She couldn't sleep, wondering if he was hiding at Augustine's, whether they were both safe.

Her everyday work seemed mundane the next morning as she dressed the children. She got Marc ready for school even though he already hated going, and sat them down for breakfast.

Madame Boiteux was downstairs unusually early. 'Did you hear the commotion last night?' she said placidly. 'An arrest in the town. I heard gunshots. Pass the coffee pot.'

Jenny's stomach flipped, she felt sick. 'No. I didn't hear anything.'

'Lisette told Cook when she brought up the milk,' Madame said. 'Timbers from a boat washed up on the other side of the

island. They thought it could be a British airman, trying to get
back to England. Sacré bleu.'

Jenny squeezed her hands together under the tablecloth to
stop them shaking. 'I thought I could take Adela into the town
for some air. It looks like a lovely day.'

'Wrap her up warm.' Madame buttered a sliver of toast.
'And Lisette can help Cook with the laundry if you can take the
baby.'

Armed with a shopping list and some money, she left the
house with both children – the baby in her chariot and Marc
walking behind them to school. She prayed she would get some
news on the Englishman, sending a silent prayer that he wasn't
already captured. She took a few minutes at the school gate to
reassure Marc, who was getting paler and more scared as the
term went on, then walked through the little town and slid a
note under Augustine's door. She walked on to a square with a
garden, the grass clipped short enough to let Adela crawl
around on a rug and wave at white butterflies. Augustine found
her there.

'There you are,' she said, wincing as she sat down. 'Oh,
those wooden seats in second class! They are bad enough on the
trains but the one on the ferry was cruel.'

'What's happening?' Jenny hissed. 'People are talking about
gunshots.'

'Nothing serious. One of the fishermen brought his skiff in
while he was drunk. They had to fire over his head to get him to
identify himself.' She looked around before dropping her voice.
'Byers is hidden in my room. He'll be gone on the next tide,
hiding on the *Colombe de Sainte Marie*. It's the old cargo ship.'

'Won't the Germans search it?' Jenny sat the baby up when
she fell over, and gave her a rusk.

'They won't find him,' Augustine said.

'What was he even doing here?'

Augustine waggled her fingers at the baby. Heavy footsteps

clunked behind the hedge of the garden. An officer in a grey uniform walked onto the grass with two soldiers.

'Is this old crone bothering you?' The man was tall and dark, with thin lips, and had riding boots so shiny they reflected the sunlight. His French was precise.

'No, sir,' Jenny said, surprised. It was the first time a German had addressed her directly and her heart began beating faster. She kept her voice calm. 'This lady is repairing some linens for the family I work for. We must make do and mend now clothing is rationed.' Clothing wasn't just rationed, it was scarce, more and more being sent to the German markets.

Augustine mumbled something, hunched over now like she was a generation older, shrinking back from the men.

'She is harmless,' Jenny said. 'Just old.'

Adela started to cry. The officer bent down and smiled at the baby, and she stopped crying to stare up at him. 'You have nothing to fear from us,' he said in clipped French. 'Have you seen anyone new in the town, that you don't recognise?'

Jenny shrugged. 'Not since the ferries don't run so much. People aren't coming here on holiday any more.'

'All will go back to normal shortly, when the war is won,' the man said, courteously. But his eyes seemed to bore into her, as if looking for secrets. 'There will soon be a weekly ferry service for people with the correct travel papers.'

'I'm glad,' she said.

He stared at her again, probably at her accented French. She just hoped it sounded like a peasant Breton rather than a hint of English.

After the German officer left, she headed back up the hill to the house. The baby was happy to crawl around her bedroom while Jenny sat in a chair and searched through her hiding place – beneath her dirty laundry – for the packet of papers. Despite

her composure in the moment, meeting the enemy had made
her feel quite hot and faint. It made it real – these would be the
people who arrested or interrogated her if she was caught
helping the Secret Intelligence Service.

The paper Byers had given her had once been folded into a
cube. It had been soaked in seawater, too – she could smell the
salt on it. There were hundreds of characters on the paper this
time, three or four times more words than the previous one.
How did they know she had agreed to work for them? Then she
remembered Augustine had access to radios. She memorised
the first line, sat on the window seat and tucked the paper into
her liberty bodice before buttoning up her blouse.

She carried Adela into the nursery, sat on the floor with her
and concentrated on the remembered letters. It was hard to
disentangle the long trail of characters into separate words, and
even then the meaning wasn't always clear.

This time, she got the gist quickly while baby Adela played
with her bracelet. Laurie Byers was 'Law cattle sheds', the only
English words, so 'cattle sheds' became Byres/Byers and times
and dates were spelled out. November eleventh was clear,
'under-ship' in Breton must be U-boat, and some coordinates
followed. She lifted the baby into her arms to consult the map of
the island on the wall. The coordinates suggested a location
north, some fifty or sixty miles away, beyond the map. Her heart
lurched in her chest. Her father, her uncles, her friends all had
crew on fishing boats from Morwen, St Brannock's or West
Island.

She was still feeling faint when Lisette's voice floated up
the stairs. 'I'll bring the baby's food up, shall I? Marc is staying
with a schoolfriend until eight.'

'Yes, yes,' she stammered. 'Thank you. I'll just get a bib for
the baby.'

By the time Lisette had come up the stairs, Adela was in her
highchair. 'I saw you looking a bit flushed when you came in,'

Lisette said, sitting down and stirring the fruit puree Cook had made for the baby. 'And now you look very pale.'

'I bumped into a German officer today,' Jenny said, cutting some bread into soldiers. 'Here you go, little one.' Adela rewarded her with a toothy grin as she took a bite.

'That must have been scary.'

'I was just in the town garden, with Adela.'

'I saw you, when I went to the shop to wait for bread,' Lisette said, calmly spooning more food into the baby, who banged her fists on the tray. 'With that old lady, the seamstress.'

'I thought she might do some sewing for us. There's hardly a sheet in the house that doesn't have a hole in it,' Jenny said quickly, glancing back to see Lisette staring at her.

'It might look a bit suspicious,' she said. 'I mean, she seems to travel about a lot.'

Jenny was finding it hard to breathe, and her hands were shaking. She passed the baby a sliver of her favourite cheese. 'She was visiting a sick relative,' she improvised. 'I think I heard that somewhere.'

'Maybe,' Lisette said. 'Since that boat washed up, the Germans are suspicious of anyone new. Even of me, because I'm not from here.'

'Has anyone questioned you?' Jenny's fingers were trembling, and she had to concentrate on the cheese so she didn't cut herself.

'One did, just a little.' Lisette had a little smile on her lips. 'He's really nice, he just asked me to watch out for new people.'

'Did you say anything about Augustine?'

Lisette stalled for a second. 'I didn't, but I could have done. I mean, she is new, isn't she? The Germans pay for information.'

'That's collaboration with the enemy. That's how the villagers will see it,' Jenny said, sounding calmer than she felt. 'You know you can't trust the Germans.'

Lisette's mouth was sulky. 'They're not all the same. Some just want to sit out the war, like us.'

'Aunt Hélène says "We are all islands in a stormy sea."' Jenny smiled at the baby, who was starting to nod off. 'We don't need to make it stormier. Adela's had a good day in the sunshine,' she said, changing the subject quickly and wiping the baby's face with the bib. 'You'd better get her in the bath before she falls asleep. Then she'll go down better.'

'She's always good,' Lisette said, lifting the baby and trying to get her attention.

Adela put her fat cheek on the maid's shoulder and her eyes closed.

'It's bath time, button!' Jenny moved into the children's bathroom to put the taps on.

As she passed the window, she caught sight of a trawler coming in from the sea. It was running before the tide, with the turquoise and white colours of Uncle Paol's boat.

'That looks like *St Guillaume*,' she said, standing on tiptoes to see.

'If you want me to bath the baby, you could go down and meet them,' Lisette said. 'Ask Madame. Maybe they will have more fish for us. I'm sick of vegetables.'

Jenny walked to the door then paused. 'Don't be cross with me for saying something, but please be careful.'

'*You* be careful,' Lisette said suddenly serious. 'You know about Yves, your uncle Paol's son?'

'I thought he was working on the trawlers with his father.'

Lisette shook her head. 'He's got caught up in his work with the Strollad Broadel Breizh,' she answered. 'He's in Brest at the moment. It's the talk of the port.'

'Nationalists?' Jenny said. 'Right wing?'

'Yes, but not Nazis,' Lisette said, feeling the water and lifting the baby into the bath. 'There you go, kitten.'

'Not anti-German, though.' Jenny thought about the nationalists' passion for Brittany. 'They will ally themselves with whoever offers them a separatist agenda. Be careful. Don't talk to the Germans about... well, anything.'

'I know.' Lisette leaned her head on the side of the bath and rolled it to look at Jenny. 'I just want to talk about something other than this dreadful war, being stuck on the island and food shortages.'

'I know,' Jenny said, changing her shoes. 'But not to the enemy, promise me? Get the baby into her nightdress and Cook will bring her bottle up.' She picked up the dirty clothes. 'I would give anything to travel home whenever I liked. I miss my island of Morwen more than anything,' she admitted, as much to herself as Lisette. 'The fishing boats along the quay remind me of home, and the smell of the sea.'

'We all want the war to be over,' Lisette said. 'Is Morwen like Ushant?'

Jenny shook out a creamy, soft towel. It smelled like baby powder and milk. 'It's rocky, so it's similar, but it's a kind place. Everyone knows and trusts everyone.'

'The Germans don't want to be away from home any more than we want them here,' Lisette said, as Jenny lifted the baby out.

'Maybe not,' she said. 'But while they are our enemies, we shouldn't help them.'

16

PRESENT DAY, 24 MARCH

After a couple of uneventful days – unless she counted the moment when Percival the rabbit escaped and ran behind the stacks of stored boxes – Charlotte was surprised when Clarrie Tremayne was late to pick up the boys.

Charlotte got the feeling looking after the two boys was quite a challenge. There didn't seem to be anyone else. Charlotte had asked about 'Daddy Ash', but Clarrie told her he had worked away for long periods and the relationship broke up less than a year before Chloe died.

Charlotte did up the boys' coats, slipped on her outside boots and walked down to the huddle of cottages in the town. The door to number seven, Noah's Drang was ajar when they got there. Many of the older residents in the tiny street left outer doors open in the day. She knocked, then opened the inner door.

'Hello? I just walked the boys back—'

She saw Clarrie's collapsed body in the tiny hallway at the same time as Billy. He let out a scream that deafened her in one ear.

'No, no, no,' Beau moaned. He put his hands over his ears and screwed his eyes up.

'Wait outside, Billy. Your grandma isn't very well. Beau, out, now!' Charlotte wasn't sure the boys had even heard – her focus was on the woman slumped in a heap against a doorway. 'Clarrie, it's Charlotte...'

She pressed two fingers to the woman's throat. At the contact, the boys' grandmother opened her eyes and mumbled something. Charlotte could immediately see that her mouth was drooping, her face lopsided.

Oh God. They've just lost their mother.

'It's OK, I'll get help right away.'

She glanced through the two doorways, one to a kitchen with a tiny table and the other to an even smaller living room. A crocheted throw on the back of the sofa would have to do, and she grabbed a cushion too. She grabbed the phone and dialled 999 on instinct. She could hear a strange keening, like an animal, outside the window. She put the phone under one ear as she tried to straighten Clarrie, drop the throw over her and slide the pillow beside her head.

'Ambulance, please. Yes, she's breathing. I think she's had a fall and she's struggling to talk. No, I'm on Morwen Island, one of the Atlantic Islands? Hang on.'

She put the phone down and lifted Clarrie's head a little to push the cushion under. She'd gone quiet, and for an agonising moment Charlotte wondered if she was dead.

She grabbed the phone again and walked to the front door. Beau was huddled on the tiny square of front garden and Billy was wailing.

'Billy! It's going to be OK.'

She put the phone back up to her ear. 'Please, she seems to have had some sort of stroke. I need help right now.' She listened to the calm questions and tried to answer them, but she couldn't. She'd met the boys' carer exactly eight, nine times, when she dropped them off and picked them up from the tiny school. 'I don't know, about sixty-five? She never mentioned anything about her health. I hardly know her. Hang on a minute.'

She pulled the phone away and screamed, as loudly as she could, through the open door. 'Help!'

At least it stopped Billy screaming, and she could hear the scrape of another door. A man with thick white hair leaned out. 'What's the matter, maid?'

'It's Clarrie. She's collapsed,' she managed to stammer.

'I'll get help.' He disappeared, shouting to someone.

Charlotte put the phone back to her ear. They wanted to know if she needed the coastguard. Well, they weren't going to drive across from the big island, were they? She supposed a ship would be involved. Or a helicopter. She turned back to look at the silent, unconscious woman.

'Just send help, as quick as you can.'

Billy, whose lips were grey in his brown face, was still standing in the doorway.

'We're getting help, Billy,' she found herself saying, before she registered that her face was running with tears. She put her arms around him, but he was stiff. 'The paramedics will know what to do. They are coming in a boat as soon as possible.'

Beau spoke from his huddle on the grass. 'She's dead.'

'No, no! She's not. I have to go and check how she is. Oh, thank God.' The old man and a little woman in her seventies bustled out of their doorway.

'It's all right,' the woman said. 'Iona's on her way, and the fire brigade are coming.'

Charlotte could feel hysteria rising like vomit. 'She's not on fire!'

'No, lovey. They are all trained in first aid. Iona's a nurse and Ed and Tink will be here very quickly. Let me look after the boys.'

Charlotte realised her fingers were cramped around the phone handset, almost crushing it. She put it to her ear again.

'Yes, I'm still here.' She walked back into the cottage and followed instructions, kneeling beside the stricken woman, who opened her eyes again. 'Oh, she's awake,' she mumbled. 'I'm so sorry, Clarrie. But the boys are all right, and help is coming.' She followed the calm instructions, aware that the woman at the other end of the line was having to repeat herself. Clarrie didn't seem able to do much, just lift her head a little and wave one limp hand in her direction. It was a relief when a woman in her fifties spoke with a warm, authoritative voice.

'You're the new teacher, aren't you? I'm Iona, I'm a nurse. Let me help Clarrie, and you go and be with the boys.'

Charlotte passed the phone to Iona, and walked to the front door, shaking with adrenaline. Tink and an older man barged past. The tiny doorway was packed with loud, encouraging voices and people who seemed to know what they were doing. Charlotte walked over to Billy, and after a moment he put his arms around her waist.

'Is she going to die?' he mumbled into her jumper. He was short for six and his curls were long.

'Help is here,' she finally said, then looked at Beau. He was frozen, looking out to sea, shaking. She dragged Billy over to him. 'It's all right, they're going to get her to hospital.' Her voice was high with panic. She managed to swallow hard and try a more teacher-like voice. 'Beau, it's going to be all right. Look at me.'

The boy, whip thin and shaking so hard he looked like he was going to faint, turned towards her. His eyes were wide and he didn't seem able to focus on her.

'Look, Beau. Billy's upset. Can you hug him for me?'

Transferring the clinging child was difficult, but eventually

Beau put his arms around Billy, tears dripping onto his sweat-shirt. Charlotte rummaged in her pockets and found a tissue. Billy hardly registered her as she mopped his face. She put her arms around both of them. She was cold and both were shivering so she hugged them closer.

The older man walked out to the quad bike parked just along the lane and rummaged in a trailer for a bag of supplies.

'She's awake and a bit better already,' he said cheerfully, looking at the two boys. 'My name's Ed, by the way. I'm the chief fire officer.'

Beau swung his head around. 'She's not dead?'

'She certainly isn't,' Ed said. 'But she fell over and had quite a bump. I bet you've fallen over before, haven't you?'

Charlotte could feel Billy nodding. 'But she's a bit better?' she asked.

'On the mend, hopefully. We'll get her to hospital and give her the right medicine.'

'We have to go too,' Beau said, his voice cracked and strained.

'No room on the boat,' Ed said, dropping down to one knee. 'Look now, Miss here will look after you until we sort it all out.'

'No,' Beau shouted, waving both hands. 'We're not going back into care. We can look after ourselves at Grandma's house.' He stared around, looking panicked. 'I can look after Billy until she comes home.' His voice broke up on the word.

Ed put a hand on his shoulder, squeezed it. 'I'm sure you would do a great job. But right now you've had a bad shock and you're too young to care for yourself. Let your teacher look after you.'

One hundred reasons why that was a stupid idea crowded into Charlotte's brain. 'I don't have anywhere...' she started to say. 'I mean, I'm living in the schoolhouse.'

'Exactly. The best place for them, away from the cottage. Social services will work out how to help them. Iona will pack a few clothes for them and then you can take them away. It's better if they don't see the coastguard carry her out.'

The argument Charlotte was mentally forming evaporated when she caught Billy's trusting gaze.

'OK. I'll do it.'

17

AUGUST 1940

Jenny put her coat on and ran down to the quay. The ground was damp from a rain shower and the cobbles were slick. Her uncle was just putting the last boxes on the quay to be picked up by the cannery.

'Uncle Paol,' she said, out of breath. 'I saw the boat. Madame wondered if there was any fish?'

'Maybe, for you. A few mackerel the Germans don't know about, still flapping.' He wrapped up a dozen fish and she tucked the parcel under her arm.

'How much do we owe you?'

He shook his head. 'Those fish threw themselves into the boat, just to meet you,' he said, laughing. Then his smile faded. 'You heard from your tad?'

'A little. They're all well, staying out of the way of the enemy.' She couldn't mention her fears of U-boats and raids on the British fishing grounds.

'Good for them. We can only get a licence to fish twice a week. We can't get fuel or parts for repairs. We'll be back to sailing boats and handlines in no time. Take care, girl.'

Jenny shouted goodbye as she ran along the dock, skirting

piles of lobster pots, disturbing clouds of gulls and flies as she passed, the stink of decayed fish following her. She slowed when she got to the door of the inn, propped open with an old keg, and walked around the back.

Number four was locked shut, no one was home. She slid a note under the door, hoping Augustine could get news to her of Byers. She left the pub and stumbled into a run up the main road. She took a shortcut onto the high-sided lane towards the clifftop house. As the lane zigzagged up the hill, she turned a corner, almost running into a man walking a big dog. It barked and jumped up, and she screamed as the man pulled its leash.

'*Runter, böser,* Bruno!' he shouted, almost pulled off his feet as the dog's huge teeth gleamed from drawn-back lips.

She half fell against the bank, her nerves already raw, recognising the officer from the morning in the garden.

'Stay still and be quiet,' he snapped in French. 'He's just doing his job.' He started talking to the dog, and let it sniff at her skirt, then her hands.

'Is he... dangerous?' She had heard stories about German attack dogs.

'Only if you are a spy.' He smiled, chuckled a little. 'But he likes nice girls. Stroke him, he'll be polite.'

She cautiously held out a hand and stroked the dog's long head. He was a German shepherd and was beautiful, his amber eyes watching her neutrally. He must have decided she was harmless and curled his tongue around her wrist for a lick, making her laugh nervously.

'Your name is...?' The man lifted a finger and the dog sat, leaning against her leg, looking far less dangerous.

'Jenofeve Huon,' she answered, piling on the Breton accent. 'I work for Madame Boiteux at Villa de Mezareun.'

'The house of women,' he said. 'Are you the maid?'

'Governess, sir,' she said.

'From Rennes?' Of course, he knew everything already.

'Yes, Monsieur. This is their holiday home.'

She ran her hand over the dog's head. Now his tail was wagging, Bruno looked a lot less dangerous. He slid to the ground and she couldn't resist patting his exposed chest.

'Do you see? Not much of a guard dog. Do you know many of the residents of the island?'

'No, not many, Monsieur.' She felt suddenly nervous and kept stroking the dog to hide her change of expression in the twilight. She had no doubt he knew the answer already. 'I was born here, but I grew up away.'

'You visit Madame Berthou,' he said amiably enough, although his eyes were sharp, staring at her. 'Who also grew up away from Ushant.'

'Everyone knows her,' she said, standing back up. 'Augustine is the cheapest seamstress on the island, and cloth is scarce. I will be late, Monsieur. Good evening.'

'Good evening,' he said, pulling the dog back on his leash. He clicked his heels together and bowed a little as she quickly started back up the hill to the gate into the grounds, her heart pounding against her chest.

The man had looked at her as if he could see through her, to the secrets she was carrying.

18

PRESENT DAY, 24 MARCH

Once the helicopter had been called to take Clarrie to hospital, Charlotte walked the boys back to the classroom and flicked on the lights.

'We can't live at school,' Beau said, looking around. Billy had already run over to the rabbit and crouched down. He started crooning to the animal.

'I know,' Charlotte said softly. 'I have to call social services on the school phone, and they will tell us what to do. Do you know anyone else on the island that you could stay with?'

Beau shrugged and walked over to the bag of clothes one of the rescuers had packed for him. They hadn't given Charlotte or either of the boys a key to Clarrie's house; she just hoped they had everything they needed. There was spare underwear for Billy, who had already wet himself on the walk back to the school.

'Why don't we clean you up, Billy?' She held out the packet of wipes. 'Could you help him, Beau?'

Why they were occupied, she called the duty social worker, who was on the mainland.

'The social worker on St Brannock's will be in contact as soon as she can,' a man reassured her.

'When will that be?' She stood on tiptoes to look towards the quay. 'The tide's going out.'

'It won't be today, but she will be in touch tomorrow. Her name is Traci Penrose. I'll make sure she calls. There's a foster family on St Brannock's. She'll see if they have room.'

Charlotte dropped her voice. 'But what about tonight?'

'You are a safe and qualified person to look after children. You have had an enhanced police check as a teacher. They couldn't be in better hands.'

'But I hardly know them!' She lowered her tone as she heard the boys returning. 'Look, I have a tiny cottage. They need proper care. Can't you send a helicopter or something?'

He laughed. 'Two small boys for less than twenty-four hours? I think they'll be OK.'

Yes, but what about me?

Charlotte turned to the boys, faking a smile. 'It looks like we'll all be sharing the schoolhouse tonight, and then help is coming tomorrow. Who knows, your grandmother might be a lot better by then.'

'Where will we sleep?' Beau's voice was flat, and Billy froze.

'Do you have bedrooms?' Billy asked.

'Well,' she said, putting the phone back. 'I have one bed but it's quite big. Just enough for you two.' She thought through the options. 'I suppose I could sleep on the sofa.' A small two-seater that smelled like mould and dog.

'No!' Billy shouted. 'I want to stay in the classroom with the rabbit.'

'I think you'd keep him awake,' she said, gathering up the bags. 'One bed and the tiny sofa it is.'

. . .

It took hours to calm the boys down. Charlotte did manage to feed Billy a few crisps, although Beau refused anything but full-sugar cola. Once they were wearing pyjamas and ready for bed, she was able to go downstairs and call the hospital.

The news wasn't good. Mrs Tremayne had suffered a major stroke, and was only responding slowly to treatment. They couldn't guarantee that she wouldn't have another stroke, but she was being closely monitored and carefully treated. As Charlotte listened, she looked up to see both boys huddled at the top of the stairs.

Although the boys couldn't hear the words, she was worried they could read her face, no matter how neutral she tried to keep it.

19

AUGUST 1940

Jenny had agreed a place to leave messages with Augustine. Behind the summer house was a space just under the floor, and she checked it regularly, picking up letters decoded into Breton, and replacing them with simple translations.

The messages made little sense to her, all names and places and numbers. The Breton they had been translated into was odd in places, and she recognised a few variations which felt more like Cornish. Her mother's mother grew up speaking fluent Cornish and had often teased Jenny into bantering back and forth in the two related languages. Translating information into Cornish or Breton and then into code must be especially hard for the Germans to decipher.

She realised the British were landing agents on the coast of Brittany to deploy all over the occupied zone. She was sure Laurie Byers must be one of them by now, away on the mainland. She was so sure, that she was astonished to find him waiting in the shrubbery cave backing onto the summer house. He was dressed in blue overalls, like he worked on the dock, and had a short beard. She didn't recognise him for a moment.

'Mr Byers?'

'Jenofeve.' He smiled then, and she was sure it was him.

'Do you have papers for me?' she whispered to him, bending under the evergreen branches to join him.

'Not this time,' he said, his teeth white against the black beard. His hair was long too, falling onto his dirty collar. 'I'm just on my way home, to England. I wondered if you would like me to take a letter for your parents?'

It was like being hit in the heart. No letters were allowed to travel outside the occupied zone, let alone to England. 'That would be wonderful! But how can you get back?'

'I sail with a local boat, fishing far out in the Channel, then hopefully rendezvous with a British ship.'

She closed her eyes. 'Shall I write in English or Brezhoneg?'

'Breton. Definitely not English, and don't mention specifics, first names only. And don't write about what you are doing.' He hesitated. 'Your father already knows. He dropped me halfway across the Channel a few months ago. A remarkable man. I wish we didn't have to involve you, but we needed someone who can decipher our mixed-language notes.'

She sat back against the planks at the back of the summer house. 'I'm scared all the time. I met a German officer.'

'If you mean the man with the grey uniform, he's the Kriminalrat liaison for the German garrison. Gestapo.' He hesitated again. 'He's a very dangerous man. Stay away from him, Jenny, and don't draw attention to yourself.'

'He seems interested in Augustine...'

'She'll be away for a month or so. Maybe he'll be reassigned before she gets back.'

'What does she do?' *I shouldn't ask.*

He looked at her thoughtfully before answering. 'Augustine is an electrical engineer. She replaces components and repairs our radios. People think she fixes sewing machines and travels around as a seamstress.'

'How can she operate in France?' She was overtaken by a sudden fear for Augustine.

'She soaks her underclothes in urine when she travels,' he said, very softly so she had to lean closer. 'She makes her hair greasy with lard, she wears her oldest clothes. She travels in third class, no one even looks at her. She told me, no one notices an ugly, smelly old woman travelling alone. The Germans even help her off the train with her heavy bags, just to get rid of her.'

Jenny put her hand over her mouth to stifle her laughter. 'That's so clever.'

'She is,' he murmured, close to her ear, then froze.

Jenny caught her breath as she heard something nearby, a footstep on the grass perhaps.

'Quick.' Laurie leaned over, opened his arms. 'Kiss me,' he said, urgently.

Before she had time to answer or protest, he had pulled her into his arms and put his lips on hers.

She'd been kissed before, but this was different. She became acutely aware of the scent of his warm skin, the softness of his beard, his lips clinging to hers.

'*Jenofeve!*' The voice sounded outraged, then Jenny recognised Lisette and the shocked laughter in her voice. 'Don't let Madame or your aunt catch you with your sweetheart,' she said, staring at them both.

Laurie said something incomprehensible about getting back to his ship in French, then he scurried away from Jenny.

'Lisette, don't you dare tell Madame!' Jenny cried, who was sure she was scarlet-faced. 'We were just talking.'

'I saw you *just talking*,' Lisette said, making it sound cruder than just a kiss.

'Well, I don't want to tell Madame what you get up to on your days off, either.' Jenny stood, sweeping dried grass off her skirt, and guided Lisette away from the summer house. She could hear Laurie rustling through the dense shrubs behind the path, making his escape.

'You don't know what I do!' Lisette said, in a scandalised voice.

'Then I'll make something up,' Jenny said. 'I just met him on the way up from the village and we started talking. I didn't want to kiss him, he grabbed me.'

'He looks like a tramp,' Lisette said, as they headed through the back porch and into the kitchen.

'Who looks like a tramp?' Cook asked. 'And the baby will be waking up soon.'

'I'll go,' Jenny said, shooting a look at Lisette, who stuck her tongue out.

Jenny ran up the stairs, her lips still tingling.

20

Charlotte had finally persuaded the children to go to bed. She'd brought down a pillow and blanket for herself. Beau had turned away from her, burrowed into the duvet, and fallen silent. Billy had wriggled and kept calling down but, eventually, both had fallen asleep.

As she was trying to sleep, curled on the settee like a pretzel, she heard something upstairs. It was a soft, repetitive sound, like a dove cooing. She checked her phone: eleven thirty. She crept up the first few stairs and pushed the bedroom door ajar. Billy was sitting on the rug, his face in his hands, softly crying.

'Billy?' she whispered, and he looked up, his face flooded with tears. His pyjama bottoms were darker around the crotch.

'I didn't wet the bed, Miss,' he managed to say. 'I got out.'

'It doesn't matter,' she said softly, craning her neck to see if Beau was awake. 'Come downstairs, we'll sort you out.'

He froze. 'I don't have any more pyjamas.'

She held out her hand to him until he crept to his feet and put his fingers into hers. 'Let's run a bath,' she said. Her chest ached with sadness for this lost little boy.

'With bubbles?' he asked, letting her lead him downstairs.

She did a mental inventory of the toiletries she had brought with her. Shower gel would just have to work. The water tank was already hot, so she walked through to the bathroom and started running the bath.

He wrapped his thin arms around himself, stepping from foot to foot on the cold floor. She grabbed a couple of clean tea towels from the stack by the cooker and made up a bath mat. She found an old-fashioned metal heater on the wall, which glowed red thirty seconds after she turned it on. With the hot water running and the door shut, the room warmed up quickly.

'I need the loo,' he said, looking at it.

'OK. You go, and I'll get you a towel,' she said, swiping the water with one hand and adjusting the cold tap. 'Don't get in the bath yet, it's still too hot.' She glugged an inch of shower gel into the warm water and left him to it, pulling the door mostly shut.

'Miss! Miss!' she heard him cry out, and came back to find he had shed the wet pyjama bottoms, but the bubbles were satisfyingly rich and high, the water warm but not hot. She turned off the taps. 'Can you get in by yourself?'

She looked at the high enamel side as he slipped off his top and held out a hand to her. 'Grandma says I have to hold hands,' he said confidingly, and climbed into the water. Then he beamed, the first real smile she had seen since they found his grandmother. He was beautiful when he smiled. He had huge hazel eyes and a tiny gap between his front teeth. He was small for his age; she had seen reception children the same size.

'You get warm and clean in there,' Charlotte said. 'I'm going to get you something to wear to bed.' Closing the door halfway to reduce draughts, she rummaged through her bag for sanitary towels. 'Have you wet yourself before, Billy?'

'Every night,' he said, and when she poked her head around

the door he was piling double handfuls of bubbles over his head into a white wig. A memory from decades ago, when she shared a bath with her sister, floated to the surface of Charlotte's mind.

'Oh, very good,' she said, grinning back at him. 'What does Grandma do for bedtime?'

'My mum used to get me pull-ups.' He stopped smiling. 'But Grandma says I'm too big for nappies.'

'Can you do this?' she said, kneeling down on the makeshift bathmat. She scooped up huge handfuls of foam and clapped. The bubbles exploded all around the room, all over Charlotte and Billy, and this time he really chuckled, a proper belly laugh. He couldn't wait to do it back, and the floor was soon wet and the room covered with soapy froth.

'I have an idea,' she said, wiping the suds off his face. 'I'll go and get you some clothes to sleep in, OK?'

His face fell. 'I don't want to wet the bed. Beau will be angry with me.'

'He won't,' she said. 'If I help you out, can you dry yourself off?'

He nodded, and took her hand to clamber out. She enveloped him in the bath towel and guided him to the sofa.

Upstairs she found the superhero pants she had grabbed earlier, and an old T-shirt of hers from Glastonbury 2012. When she came down he was curled up in his nest of towels. She fitted two night-time sanitary towels inside his pants.

'Look, these will catch the wee.' She bent down to his level and helped him put them on.

He was almost asleep. His eyes were closing, and when she pulled the T-shirt over his head, he dropped his head against her. The shirt was down to his bare feet, so she lifted him and carried him up to the bedroom. Beau had insisted she leave the bedside lamp on, so it was easy to lie Billy beside him and tuck him in. Beau frowned even in his sleep. By the time she had rolled the rug to take it downstairs, Billy's thumb was already in his mouth.

She had a strong urge to kiss him on the forehead, but something stopped her.

I'm just his teacher.

21

SEPTEMBER 1940

The autumn dragged on, and the winds picked up over Ushant.
The weather raced across the sea all the way from America,
lifting the waves until they were the height of a house. Fishing
was restricted to days when vessels could safely get out of port.
After two weeks of the ferry not being able to run, the ship
finally made its way into the harbour.

On it was Maître Boiteux. The letter he had written to
warn Madame had not arrived, so no one was sent to meet him
on the dock. A weary master and two stewards carrying his
luggage arrived at the front of the house. Lisette opened the
door, and her surprised shriek brought Jenny downstairs and
Madame running from the drawing room. The couple were not
usually publicly affectionate, but his return to the island gained
him a hearty embrace from his wife and a kiss on each cheek.

'My dear!' she stammered. 'You are here!'

'Let me sit down,' he said wearily. 'The ship took twice as
long because the weather was so bad.'

Madame guided him to the seat referred to as the master's
chair in the drawing room and sat on the sofa beside him,
reaching for his hand. Tears sparkled on her eyelashes.

'I am so surprised,' she said. 'I thought we might not see you until the end of the war.'

'Which looks like going on a long time.' Her husband leaned back and closed his eyes. 'The room is still moving,' he said, managing a little smile. He had always been a short, stout man, but he had grown thinner over the last five months. He also had grey hair; perhaps he had stopped having his hair dyed at the barber.

'Jenny, tell Cook to make up a tray for the master,' Madame said, then turned to Lisette. 'And take his luggage upstairs and unpack it.'

'Better take my cases into the kitchen first,' he said. 'I mostly brought food.'

The women exclaimed at the contents of the largest trunk, which was surprisingly heavy. Inside was a whole Timanoix cheese, straight from the abbey dairy. There was a wrapped ham as well, and some quinces from the town gardens at Rennes. There was a bag of flour, soft and white and spilling out, so much nicer than the gritty flour in the larder. Underneath it all were a dozen bottles of wine and a large one of cognac. Once the provisions had been put in the larder, Jenny went upstairs to bring the children down to see their father.

Maître Boiteux had two cups of weak tea without milk and the last slice of apple cake as he greeted his children, before going upstairs to rest before dinner. Jenny took the children into the garden, while Lisette and Cook tried to create a meal fit for the master out of some beef bones, some young leeks from the garden and the ham and cheese. Madame sent the gardener down to the neighbouring farm to purchase some eggs, off the rations, an indulgent treat for his breakfast. At least they had fresh fish, and two boxes of mackerel that Cook and Aunt Hélène had smoked over several aromatic days. By the evening, the master was enjoying a fine beef broth, a *lotte à l'armoricaine* monkfish stew, and a sliver of cheese to finish.

'I have dreamed of this,' Maître Boiteux said as Jenny cleared the plates. 'Sit, Jenofeve, tell me how are you coping, so far away from your parents?'

Jenny knew she couldn't tell him about the letters she had received. 'I miss Morwen,' she said, sliding onto the edge of a spare chair, 'but I am happy here, thank you, sir.'

'You have done a wonderful job with the children, all of you,' he said, smiling at Madame. 'The island air suits them. Marc has grown inches, and Adela, she is running already.'

'His studies are advancing very well,' Jenny said.

'Soon the war will be over,' Madame added, 'and he will be able to attend your old school. Jenofeve has been a great support to me. Especially with Cook moaning about the rations, and that flibbertigibbet Lisette sneaking off to see men at every opportunity.'

'She is young,' Monsieur said, lifting his glass to his lips and draining it. 'I see young people acting incautiously in Rennes,' he added. 'We are dealing with many young girls who have fallen into sin.'

Jenny could understand why the girls were behaving recklessly. Life felt fragile for all of them, like shifting soil under their feet. She had spent hours remembering a kiss from a young man with a soft beard and greasy overalls...

'I must check on the baby,' she said, leaving the couple together.

The brittle veneer of joy had cracked. They looked old and frightened, alone in their shiny dining room.

22

PRESENT DAY, 25 MARCH

Sleeping on the small sofa was uncomfortable and Charlotte woke frequently. By seven the next morning she was already dressed and waiting for the boys to come down. Billy was first, rocketing to the bathroom shouting 'Gangway!' and triumphantly returning to show Charlotte his dry pads.

'I wasn't even worried,' he said, bouncing onto the sofa.

'I'll still get you some pull-ups for night-time,' she said, throwing the pads away and sending him upstairs for the rest of his clothes. He came down dressed and smiling, with Beau treading cautiously behind him. 'We've run out of clothes, now,' he said.

'We'll make do with what you're wearing,' she said. 'I'll see if I can get some more from your grandma's house. We have cornflakes for breakfast.' She wondered if there would be enough milk for all of them.

'I don't like cornflakes.' Within seconds, Billy had echoed him.

'How about toast?'

Beau shrugged one shoulder. Billy smiled, though. She had a pack of butter in the fridge but it was rock hard, so she put it in the microwave to soften up. Puzzling over the controls, she selected ten seconds, only to realise it was probably set to ten minutes. It took valuable seconds to work out how to turn it off, by which time melted butter was dribbling out of one corner of the paper.

The bread was easier: she already knew the toaster burned everything, so popped it up every twenty seconds until two pieces were brown. Billy watched her solemnly pour the yellow butter on, which made him laugh.

'Do you have any jam?' He looked over at Beau. 'He likes jam.'

Beau's arms were so tightly folded his knuckles were pale. 'I don't want toast,' he said, lips pressed together.

'What jam do you like, Billy?' Charlotte spread a bit of the soft butter on the other piece and held out a piece to Beau. He shook his head, and she took it back, took a bite. Billy allowed her to add strawberry jam.

'Beau, you need to eat something. We've got a lot to do today.'

Beau looked down, his long eyelashes fanning over thin cheeks. He looked many years older than Billy, careworn and hopeless. Charlotte licked the last bit of butter off her fingers and grinned at Billy when he did the same.

'We could get some food from the shop if you just tell me what you like.'

Beau stood up, looking at his feet. He mumbled something.

'I'm sorry, you need to speak a bit louder.'

'Go to Grandma's,' he mumbled.

'I don't have a key,' she said. 'But I suppose one of the neighbours might have one.'

He was staring at her, and she was drawn in by his dark, greenish eyes.

'I mean, I could look after me and Billy until Grandma gets back.'

'I'm sorry,' Charlotte said. 'But an eight-year-old isn't allowed to look after a six-year-old.'

'I can cook, I can do housework.' There was a determination in Beau's stance, his arms straight by his side, hands clenched. 'I've done it before, when Mum was out.'

'It's too much responsibility for you,' she said softly. 'I know staying here is not what you want, but we can make the best of it until the social worker calls.'

His chin was up now. 'We'll go to foster care. They will split us up.'

'Why would they?' She looked at Billy, now running one finger over his plate and licking it.

'That's what social workers do. They decide where we go, they don't listen to what we want.' His eyes were suspiciously bright now. 'Last time I ended up staying with two girls who were mean to me, and Billy was a hundred miles away.'

'Well, I'll definitely ask them to keep you together. It's only until your grandmother comes home from hospital.'

Beau shook his head. 'I want to play video games,' he announced.

'I don't have any of that stuff,' she said, remembering Zach's collection of consoles and games. But she didn't even have a television yet. 'Look, if we go down to the village, we can get you something to eat there.'

'Not hungry.'

Billy handed Charlotte the polished plate. 'I was,' he said, with another big smile.

'You must eat *something*,' she said to Beau, with her best teacher voice. 'I bet they have fruit, or bacon and eggs.'

'Or ice cream,' Billy said helpfully. 'Or cake.'

At a flicker of Beau's eyelids, Charlotte pounced. 'I suppose we could all have cake if we go now,' she said, feigning giving in. 'Just this once.'

After a round of trips to the bathroom and putting on shoes

and coats, the three of them left the house. Charlotte couldn't find the key and Beau almost smiled.

'Nothing worth nicking,' he pointed out as Charlotte gave up.

He led the way towards the quay where Charlotte had noticed a café. The pastel houses looked like they were leaning back from the sea, into the wind running down the hill. Charlotte had to grab Billy as he scampered towards the edge of the quay, drawn to a blue and white boat pulling up alongside the wall.

A tall man in his fifties stepped from the side of the boat onto a ladder and up. 'You waiting for the ferry?'

'No, we're going for cake!' Billy said excitedly, looking up at the pilot of the rickety craft.

'I had a feeling you weren't off to do ballet,' the man said, winking at Beau. 'Ah, there she is. Merryn, sweetheart.'

Merryn stepped aboard with a hand from the pilot.

'Hello, Miss,' Merryn said, waving. She was wearing dance clothes, a thick jumper, pink wellingtons and an open waterproof over the top.

Justin leaned forward. 'We heard about Clarrie. Is she all right?'

'She's in hospital and they've given me the boys. I have literally no clue what to do,' she confided, out of earshot of Beau and Billy.

His smile was sympathetic, but Merryn was already calling him to get on the ferry. 'Call social services. See what they have to offer.'

'Already on it,' she said, as he stepped onto the boat.

'We can lend you stuff if you need it. Spare beds, that sort of thing,' he shouted, as the engine started.

She waved. 'Thank you, I might take you up on that!'

Charlotte watched them pull away, feeling cold and scared again. She checked her mobile phone. Two bars of signal but no message from the social worker. She sighed. It was still early, but waiting was agony for the boys.

'Come on, let's see if the café is open.'

Billy slipped his hand into hers as they walked along the quay, a little sheltered from the westerly wind which still had quite a bite. The Quay Kitchen was just opening, a tall young woman arranging a menu board outside.

'First customers of the day,' she said, taking in the trio. 'This is a wild guess, but I think you might be the new teacher? I'm Kate.'

'Charlotte. We thought we might have cake for breakfast.'

'Our speciality,' Kate said, smiling down at the boys. She was blonde and about Charlotte's age. 'I heard what happened,' she said to them all. 'I hope Mrs Tremayne is back soon.'

'I've been told to call the hospital about midday,' Charlotte said quietly, Beau swivelling his head to hear.

The café was dark inside, the building old, with exposed brick between ancient timber uprights, and boards as wide and solid as a church floor. Kate showed them to a table in the window.

'We have apple and sultana cake, lemon drizzle and Victoria sponge this morning. Chocolate brownies and scones as standard.' She gave the menu to Beau. 'I'll be back in a minute to take your order.' She pointed to a line on the menu. 'There are milkshakes if either of you want them, or we can do hot chocolates to warm you up. With whippy cream and marsh-mallows.'

Charlotte noticed how Beau studied the menu, his eyes looking up and down as much as along. *He can't read.*

'Let me read it for Billy,' she said, reaching for it. 'Although he should be full of toast.' He handed it over and went back to staring out at the quay. She read the items out to Billy, who narrowed it down to a strawberry milkshake. Beau shrugged when she asked him, so she ordered the same for him, with a slice of cake.

He did eat, when the food came, and Charlotte nibbled on a brownie while drinking her coffee. This was all more complicated than she had expected.

'Where was Merryn going?' Billy suddenly asked, looking up with a milkshake moustache. She lifted her phone, took a picture and showed it to him. He laughed and licked off most of the foam. Kate had given him a little bowl of marshmallows as well.

'He said ballet, I think.'

'The boat driver's name is Bird,' Billy said, loudly slurping through his straw.

'It's Birdie.' It was the first thing Beau had said since they left the schoolhouse. 'He brought us over here to live with Grandma.'

'I'd like to do ballet,' Billy said.

Beau pushed his drink away. 'Boys don't do ballet.'

Charlotte wiped some of the cream off Billy's jumper with her napkin. 'Actually, boys and men *can* do ballet. Some of the best ballet dancers in the world are men.'

'I'd like to,' Billy said. 'Is it on the mainland?'

'I imagine it's on one of the other islands.' Charlotte caught Kate's eye. 'Where is the nearest dance class?'

'There's ballet on the big island, and I think there's Irish dancing and tap on West Island. There's modern dance here for all ages, Tuesday night. We used to have a couple of kids as well as the adults. One of the staff here, Emily, runs it fortnightly at the school, six to seven thirty.'

'Oh. That's great.' Charlotte looked at Billy, now squashing marshmallows between his fingers and eating them. 'Do you want to try out a dance class, Billy?'

'No.' He closed down as quickly as he'd cheered up. 'Can we call Grandma now?'

'You get the best signal out on the quay, if you're on a mobile.' Kate picked up the empty plates. 'If you change your mind, you can always watch the dancing. Merryn will be there, she's about your age.'

'She's a baby. She's only four.'

'She's very nearly five.' Charlotte smiled. 'Now, let's try social services again, they might have good news for us.'

23

SEPTEMBER 1940

Not wanting to appear to snub the Germans now that he had arrived, Maître Boiteux had to pen a hospitable invitation to the Kommandant, Herr Richter, to dine on Saturday evening. They also invited a few of their more well-to-do neighbours. Maître Boiteux was surprised to see how many accepted his offer, while Madame bemoaned the difficulty of getting food for a party. Large numbers of francs changed hands secretly for a pig to be slaughtered for the occasion, and the family managed to source some root vegetables from a farmer's winter storage. The centre-piece would, as always, be a whole fish. Everyone at the villa prayed for a large turbot to be caught before the party.

Herr Richter was bringing his wife and two of his junior officers, but he wrote a pleasant note asking if he could introduce an officer of the Geheime Staatspolizei, Kriminaldirektor Wolfgang Albrecht. The Nazi police commander, from the Gestapo.

Whenever Lisette or Jenny could be spared from nursery duties they helped with the preparations. They extended the table and polished the stale dullness off the extra leaves. Lisette ironed the only tablecloth long enough to cover the whole thing, while Jenny cleaned silver not used since before the war. Madame had found two old maids' uniforms in matching grey that could be mended and adapted to Lisette's plumper and Jenny's taller frames. The dresses were more than thirty years old, and Jenny loved the feel of the almost floor-length hems sliding over the beaten and brushed carpet.

Madame Boiteux had a selection of her summer jewels polished in the town by the only watchmaker and jeweller, a tiny shop run by one old man. Both of his sons had died in the first war, and Jenny had to plead with him to clean the diamond and sapphire tiara. As Madame's personal maid had left at the outbreak of war, Jenny also had to dress Madame's luxuriant hair, blending in the bemoaned streaks of grey as best she could.

'You look wonderful,' she said, as she set the tiara in Madame's coiffure. 'Like you did before the war.'

'It's the only Paris gown I keep here,' she replied, meeting Jenny's eyes in the mirror. 'I feel like I'm going into battle.'

'To keep the Germans happy and quiet,' Jenny said, tucking a few hairs into the side of the tiara. 'And to keep the island peaceful.'

Madame's hands were shaking as she clasped them in her lap. 'We tiptoe about trying to appease them,' she said. 'We're eating roots grown for cattle, our children are eating bread from barley meant for beer.'

Jenny patted Madame's shoulders once, not disrespectfully but in support. 'We will do everything we can to make this a success,' she said. 'And we will always have the sea to sustain us.'

'Are they roasting the turbot?'

Jenny started to tidy up the brushes and combs. 'Cook had to beg our neighbours for butter, but yes, the fish is magnificent.'

'I worry about Lisette,' Madame said, just resting her fingers on Jenny's for a moment. 'If she is talking to the Germans...'

'Lisette would never do anything to harm any of us,' Jenny

said in surprise. 'She is just flirting, and I've told her to be careful.'

'There is talk about resistance in the countryside around Rennes, in Finistère.'

Jenny smiled as reassuringly as she could. 'How could that spread to the islands? We would know straight away. We know everyone.'

'But they have stationed a secret police officer here,' Madame said. 'Gestapo. He is spying on us all.'

'Just one officer. What could he possibly find?'

Maître Boiteux walked in through the half-open door. 'Marthe, you look wonderful! As if the war had never started.'

Madame laughed shakily. 'I wish it *had* never started. Thank you, Jenny. Go and get yourself ready – you'll be serving with Hélène and Lisette. Let's hope there's enough wine to keep them all happy.'

Jenofeve found herself playing tag with Lisette to take coats and hats in the hall as Madame and Maître Boiteux greeted their guests. Their Breton neighbours were on edge, in their best clothes. Close friends of the family greeted Jenofeve by name, but in French. The Boiteux family had asked that the conversation be entirely in French, to help the Germans, who didn't seem to speak any Breton. Many local people had recently fallen back into speaking the language of their childhood, and had very rustic accents.

The Germans came in last. Kommandant Richter was a man in his fifties, with a range of medals on his chest from the first war. He looked like a gentleman with his uniform and formal manners, a handlebar moustache spreading from under his nose almost to his ears. He bowed to Madame and shook Maître Boiteux's hand genially. Frau Richter was a rounded woman, in pale blue satin with a lace shawl. Two officers, young enough to be their sons, wore suits. At the very back of the group was the man Jenny recognised from the town garden and the clifftop, in a sombre grey uniform.

He didn't wait to be introduced. 'Kriminaldirektor Wolfgang Albrecht,' he said, putting a hand out to Jenny as everyone in the hall fell silent.

She reluctantly allowed her fingers to be clasped briefly before Maître Boiteux stepped forward.

'Herr Albrecht, welcome.' He shook his hand and waved him towards Madame. 'May I introduce you to Madame Boiteux?'

'You must forgive me for being forward with your servant,' Albrecht said, shooting a smiling glance back at Jenny. 'I have met her on my walks with my dog.' He shook hands with Madame as Jenny shrank back to hang up hats and coats.

Lisette served trays of drinks to the guests as Jenny tried to calm down in the kitchen. Gestapo. Did he suspect anything? Did he *know*?

She had regained her composure by the time they served dinner, a crystal-clear bouillon with delicate milk rolls, flavoured with a hint of fresh herbs from the garden. Jenny kept her face averted from the Gestapo officer, who looked very official among all the other gentlemen. He kept his conversation light, talking politely to Madame. Jenny slipped upstairs to check on the children. The baby was asleep in her cot, but Marc was sat hunched in his bed like a frightened deer, turning huge eyes to the door every time she walked in.

'They say they kill children,' he whispered to her, the first time.

'Marc, it's fine. They are just being polite and having dinner. They aren't monsters, they are just people: fathers and husbands and brothers.'

He shrank away from her. 'They might arrest us and we will be taken away.'

'You are a good boy,' she said, and kissed his forehead. 'Why would anyone arrest you?'

As she stepped back onto the landing, fear clenched her heart again, making it beat unevenly. *Calm, calm*, she told herself. *They don't know anything. Madame invited them here.*

She needed Aunt Hélène to carry the other end of the silver platter holding the giant fish. It had been roasted on the bone, skinned and carved then delicately reassembled. Lisette brought the vegetables, which were small potatoes from the garden glistening in butter, heavily augmented with oil and herbs. Cook had seasoned the turbot with the best caramelised salt she could find in her stores, as Brittany was famous for its butter. A round of applause greeted the fish.

The last of the sliced beans made a green mound in the serving dish. Madame had daringly offered her guests a choice of island cider, still scented with local citrussy apple, as well as wines. The Germans approved of the choice and everyone went back for more fish.

Jenny started to calm down as the meal progressed, concentrating on serving the food. She tried to stay blank-faced while she carried plates and dishes. The compliments went around until a flushed Cook was called up to receive the guests' praises.

The guests sat around afterwards, chatting and eating tiny sweetmeats that had used up a month's worth of sugar. Jenny finally escaped to help Cook with the piles of soiled plates and cutlery, Lisette staying in the dining room in case anyone needed anything. Madame's friends had finally relaxed with more wine, and Jenny could hear Madame Carrère's horsey laugh from the kitchen.

She couldn't get her mind off the Gestapo officer in his uniform, his shiny hat sat on the floor. She had been too frightened to take it, and he had left it under his chair. He smiled all the time, the skin around his dark eyes crinkling, and he looked amused by everything. His hair was very dark, with just a hint of grey at the temples, but she got the impression he wasn't old, maybe thirty. He was also very handsome, in a lean-faced way. She was, as Madame would put it, a little a-flutter at him.

Because he's the enemy. Because he's Gestapo.

Marc was asleep when she crept past the drawing room door and up to the nursery. He'd fallen asleep, vigilant, at the end of his bed. In his hand was his penknife, folded neatly in his slack fingers, ready to hold off the whole war.

24

As they walked back up to the schoolhouse from the café, Charlotte's phone rang. Traci Penrose, the boys' new social worker, explained the best thing to do would be to bring the boys over in a few days to see her. Maybe to visit Clarrie in the hospital as well, if their grandmother was recovered enough for visitors.

'At least she's talking again. She's been worried about the children,' the woman said. 'She was so reassured when she was told you were going to take them.'

'But I'm not,' Charlotte said. 'I mean, I have them now but I'm not a foster parent. I'm not a parent at all.'

Her words rocketed her back to the many conversations she'd had with Zach, now forever unresolved. *Not likely to ever be a parent, either*. The idea hurt, the loss of something she had taken for granted.

'We're working on it. If you could just look after them until Monday, we can work out a plan.'

'I literally live in a one-up, one-down house. They have the clothes they are standing up in and the ones they wore to school yesterday.'

'I can authorise buying more clothes and we'll get you assessed as a suitable guardian as fast as we can. At least the boys are safe, fed, dressed and have a place to sleep. You know, Clarrie Tremayne was never very keen on taking them,' Traci said, the voice tinny in her ear. Charlotte turned away so the boys wouldn't hear her.

'Why not?'

'Honestly, she hardly knows them. Her daughter was estranged from her. She didn't want to be a mother again, she wanted to be a grandmother.'

Charlotte stared over at the heaving, grey water. 'What does she suggest?'

'She had a few ideas. There was a stepfather that the boys talked about – we've left messages for him. He's inaccessible for a few days but his employer has passed on the message. We also contacted both biological fathers. Beau's dad has a sister who might take them.'

'Do the boys know this aunt?'

'Not since Beau was a baby. I'll make contact.'

Charlotte turned back to the boys, who were listening intently. 'They have spoken about Daddy Ash. They seem to be very fond of him.'

'There is a complaint against him on file. Chloe claimed he was overly strict with the boys, even smacked one of them.' She sighed. 'There's a fine line between discipline and abuse.'

Charlotte stared at the boys. 'They mentioned another step-father being very strict, but they seem very fond of this Daddy Ash. Are you sure there isn't a better place for the boys than a teacher with no room and no experience?'

'We don't have anywhere else. Our foster carers in the county are all full. The best we could do is try and place the youngest here and send the older one out of county.'

Charlotte could see Beau had heard that. He seemed to

close in on himself, looking down, his hand gripping Billy's so hard the little one was pulling away.

'We'll manage, thank you.' *Somehow*. 'Let me know how you get on with the family.' She rang off.

Beau looked at her, narrowed his eyes. 'You're going to keep us? In that horrible little house?'

'Well, yes,' she said, as Billy jumped up and down. 'It may be horrible, and too small, and I can't sleep on that sofa, but I think it's better than the alternative.' She flicked her eyes over to Billy, and Beau nodded. 'I think I will take up Merryn's dad's offer. Maybe we could borrow a folding bed or something for me, and they might have a spare TV. We could all go out to dinner at the hotel, this evening, as a bit of a treat.'

'And then we can phone up Daddy Ash, so he can come and get us?' Beau suggested.

'I don't think that's possible just yet,' she said, her imagination seeing a big man with his hand raised over Billy. 'They don't know if he's the right person to take care of you.' She rubbed an unfamiliar pain in her chest, like heartburn.

Later that afternoon, Charlotte and the boys walked along the foreshore to the northernmost point below the lighthouse cliff. The hotel was a stone Victorian building, set almost on the beach. It had a wide terrace bounded by a thick wall to keep the storms back, covered with drifts of pink flowers growing between the pavers. The hotel only took guests nine months a year, but the restaurant was open at the weekends.

Robert had given them a table in the bay window, and asked if Merryn could sit with them for her dinner, too. The children ate burgers and chips quite happily; Charlotte was just pleased to see Beau eat a whole meal.

Justin and Rob served her a seafood dish at the bar, and made themselves available to answer her long list of questions.

Their experience of adopting an older child was helpful. Beau and Billy weren't doing anything that Merryn hadn't done, or they hadn't met in their extensive training. They lent Charlotte a waterproof undersheet for Billy and a box of toys they had for visiting children. They also offered her a folding bed that would be a lot more comfortable than the tiny sofa, especially with a memory foam topper.

Justin offered to help carry it down, along with a portable television. 'Mind you,' he said, leaning on the bar, 'I'm not sure you'll get much signal down there.'

She couldn't help getting teary as she accepted all their help. 'I'm sorry,' she said, pushing her empty plate away. 'I look at Beau and he's so unhappy, it breaks my heart.'

Justin put his head on one side. 'These kids carry this hurt, underneath. They must have been to hell and back, or they would still be with their family.'

'Their mother died,' she said, sniffling. 'I don't know how I'd cope if I lost *my* mum, and I'm an adult.'

'Just listen. Be available, and try not to lose your temper because these kids can really push your buttons.'

'Why would they try?' she asked, as he put a coffee in front of her.

'They don't believe you care about them,' he said. 'They are desperate for love, but they don't trust it. At least the boys had a healthy attachment to their mum, before she died. The ultimate abandonment.'

She glanced over at the children, still eating. Billy was blowing bubbles in his drink, making a mess and making Merryn laugh.

'What about Merryn? She looks so settled.'

Justin managed a hollow laugh. 'It's early days, even after eighteen months. She's attached to us, sure, but she's not rock solid.'

Charlotte looked at the little girl, who had her hands over

her mouth to stop herself laughing too much. Beau was trying to mop up his brother. 'She's so beautiful. They all are.' The thought of the agony they carried was answered by her own grief at losing Zach. They seemed more able to deal with loss than her.

Rob gathered up some paper napkins and walked over to the children. 'Mucky pups,' he said. He indiscriminately wiped down the younger two and handed Beau one for his own use.

'You've been so helpful,' Charlotte said, sniffing back tears again. 'Honestly, I'm a wreck after two days and I have to work again on Monday.'

Rob came forward with a piece of paper. 'Here you go. The number for the doctor, in case they do anything odd. Our mobile numbers if you want to talk, and Ellie and Bran are just along the lane and would help at any time.'

Charlotte tucked it into her jeans pocket and wiped her eyes. 'You've set me off again.'

Justin smiled. 'You aren't on your own. This island is like one huge family, with all the advice, interference and support that entails.' He rolled his eyes. 'Just don't expect to keep anything secret.'

25

NOVEMBER 19

Jenny regularly checked for messages under the summer house, in an old rat hole. Lisette might be curious about her hidey-hole, but she wouldn't risk touching one of the vermin, and the island seemed to have more rats than usual.

'Overrun with rodents and Germans,' Cook had grumbled.

Perhaps the animals were more visible because there was less food thrown away, and people guarded their vegetables and chickens more carefully. The occupying garrison had grown to ten men. Albrecht now had a fellow Gestapo officer; wandering around, smiling, their eyes missed nothing. They would oversee the soldiers on the docks weighing every catch that must be preserved and sent to the army. Jenofeve wondered how much food was getting to the people of Brittany.

Official news came very slowly. The ferry now ran infrequently, only able to visit when it had enough fuel for the return journey as coal and wood were scarce, and all the oil was requisitioned by the Germans. But Maître Boiteux would be able to return to Rennes, and Madame was upset and listless once he'd planned his departure. The ship was also bringing essential supplies, and some kind merchants wrapped bottles in local newspapers, so at least a little information came in. The news was bad. Much of the best food was being sent to Germany. France, once proudly self-sufficient in wonderful produce, was struggling to feed its people.

A batch of buckwheat flour arrived on the docks in great sacks. Maybe the Germans didn't like it, but the locals would make their galettes – crisp pancakes – even if they had little to go in them. A rind of ham or cheese, a spoonful of potato with garlic and herbs, a Breton could always do something. And always, the ubiquitous fish. Their heads were used to make stock, and most housewives had a fish soup on the fire several times a week, perhaps with some foraged leaves from the hedgerows.

Every few days, a new message would come in for Jenny to translate from Breton. She would then leave it in the rat hole and find it replaced by another a short time later. She knew the messages were coordinates, references to moving ships, or perhaps code names of people travelling, but it made little sense to her. Twice, tiny notes in crabbed Breton were folded up tight inside, with loving messages from her family.

Storms blew in and over the island, the keepers struggling to keep the lighthouses blazing out. Of the nine, only three were kept running, to confound potential invaders from the north. But without the lights, the ferry crossing became far less safe, especially in dark conditions at the end of November. The islanders hunkered down for an isolated winter.

The Germans brought in their heavily armed patrol boats, but often holed them on rocks or crashed them into the harbour wall. By the end of November, most were sitting at anchor and they instead sent launches in to bring supplies and information to the garrison, rather than risk the rocks. The rest of the time they were hunting for British ships, including the Atlantic Islands' trawlers.

Jenny was relieved to see Augustine back on the island,

though thin and looking tired. She met her outside the shop, where Jenny had been sent to queue for milk. It was only delivered to the island once a week and she was entitled to claim a little extra and a few tins of evaporated for the baby.

'I didn't know you were back,' Jenny said quietly, nodding to Augustine, not wanting to act too friendly in the line of a dozen people.

'I came back early, because this might be the last ferry for a few weeks,' Augustine said. 'I hope you have some *mending* for me?'

Jenny nodded slightly. 'We may have to make winter clothes for the children, though. We didn't bring enough warm things.'

'And your master, is he still on the island?'

'He is going back today,' Jenny said, looking over at the superstructure of the sturdy ship, just above the quay at low tide.

'I pray he gets home safe,' Augustine said, crossing herself. Jenny noticed a couple of other women did likewise.

'It's a long journey,' Jenny said, shivering inside her coat. 'And the winds are harsh.'

Augustine turned away, and no one else spoke to her. Jenny turned her attention to the maid of one of the other ladies on the island. They chatted about the rationing for a few moments before the woman dropped her voice to pass on a titbit of gossip. Jenny couldn't help noticing heads leaning in, conversations stopping.

'Your maid, Lisette, is she well?'

'Yes, thank you,' Jenny answered. She looked around, seeing the tight lips and averted gazes of the older women. 'Why?'

'She has been seen out with a young man,' the woman said. 'Perhaps you should keep a closer eye on her. Give her more work.'

'She is young,' Jenny said, trying to understand the

tension in the people behind her. A woman left the shop, the bell ringing, and another woman walked in. They all shuffled forward another few inches. 'Her sweetheart is back in Rennes.'

'She was seen late one evening last week, with a man. A soldier. One of *them*.'

Jenny straightened her headscarf against the wind and tucked her empty shopping bag under her arm. Lisette was only allowed out until eight, even on her day off, but Jenny suspected her of sneaking off after she had brushed the coats and cleaned all the shoes.

'Thank you,' she said, through tight lips. 'I will have a strong word with her. She is very young.'

The crowd seemed to bunch up behind her as another person left, and Augustine went in the shop. When she left with two items, Jenny could have almost cried for her. One small tin of something and a bag of roots. The rations might restrict how much you bought, but they didn't guarantee anything. Madame Boiteux always received her household's full rations, but many of the poorer people went without. Jenny would have loved to share more of her mistress's shopping with Augustine, but she dared not.

When she was called in, she handed over the list without comment. The price had gone up again. Madame had added extra money but Jenny had to hand over every cent and still leave eleven francs on account. She filled her bag with the fresh things, and the shopkeeper promised to send a boy up with the rest.

'Trugarez-vras,' she murmured gratefully. 'Merci, Madame,' she added when she remembered the shopkeeper's wife was from Gascony.

'Perhaps we will see you in church,' the woman said. 'It is at these times that we need the comfort of faith.'

Jenny didn't attend church, except on special occasions

when the whole community was there. Being brought up on Morwen, in the English Atlantic Islands, she was Protestant.

'You're right, I should,' she conceded, thinking again of how she should try to fit in better.

She started back along the quay, knowing that Lisette would have her hands full as Adela was teething and was red-cheeked and grumpy. The glass milk bottle had been refilled, the cans were cushioned between paper packages of the limited meat. Pigs' trotters from the farm over on the east of the island, a few rashers of fatty bacon, more bones. The shopkeeper had also spared an egg for each person at Villa de Mezareun, individually wrapped in newspaper. There was no sugar, no bread flour and no dripping. Cook was having to be more inventive every week.

On her way up the hill she heard a footfall behind her, catching up with her, but she dared not hurry and jostle the shopping.

'Mademoiselle Huon,' came an amused voice. Albrecht, the Gestapo officer. 'Or may I call you Jenofeve?'

'I can't stop you,' Jenny said, looking around and leaning away from the dog, uncertain of its mood.

'He won't hurt you,' Herr Albrecht said, a fur coat over his uniform.

'I don't want him to break the eggs,' she said, frowning at him, and starting back up the hill. 'Or the children's milk.'

He fell in step with her, breathing the sharp air with satisfaction. 'I see why consumptives used to stay here,' he said, his tone friendly. 'The sea air. I never thought you could smell the ocean, but you really can.'

'I know little else,' she said, watching the road ahead so she didn't stumble. 'I grew up by the sea.'

'But not this sea,' he said, his voice cool and calm. 'An English sea.'

'Don't let my family hear you say that,' she said, rounding

the last bend before home. 'They don't even like being called Cornish.'

'But you *are* a British girl.' Her knees almost gave way as she fought to keep her balance.

She stopped, turning to face him and trying to freeze her expression into polite interest. 'I don't know who you've been talking to,' she said, taking another deep breath, the salt scent in her nostrils giving her courage. 'I'm Breizhadez. Breton. My father was born here, my grandparents came from here. He married a Cornish woman and he travelled from one end of the Celtic Sea to the other, my whole childhood, fishing.'

'But you must have some English... sentiments. Is that the right word?'

She turned to face him. 'Would I be here if I had *English sentiments*? I came to be a governess, to speak Breton, to be part of my home island.'

He put his head on one side, dropped his hand to his dog's sleek head. 'The local people don't think of you as one of theirs.'

She shrugged. 'My family are seafarers, not bound to any place. Now I am a governess to a prominent Breton family.'

He followed her around the house to the porch. 'I think my dog smells something delicious in your bag.'

'Well, it is to make broth for the children, sir. I'm sure the shop will be able to provide you with bones for Bruno.'

'I'm sure it will.' He tipped his cap to her, bowed a little, then grinned. 'You remembered his name.'

She looked down at the dog. 'It's not his fault he is German, Herr Albrecht.'

'Nor yours that you are, ah, Cornish.' He turned away as she pushed open the front door.

26

PRESENT DAY, 26 MARCH

After a Sunday of walking, games and another meal out, Charlotte had just made up the fold-out bed late in in the evening when she heard a tap on the front door. At first she thought it was just the wind, but when someone rapped louder she went over and leaned against it.

'Who is it?' she hissed.

'You don't know me, but I'm here to see Beau and Billy. My name is Ash Stewart, I am their stepfather...'

She glanced over at the clock and frowned; it was after ten o'clock. 'This is no time to bang on the door, Mr Stewart.'

How did he even get here? The ferries all stopped hours ago.

She rolled the key in the lock, the thud reverberating around the cottage, and peered out.

He was slim, middle height, younger than her. His close-cropped hair was dark, his face much the same skin tone as Beau's, so the only thing that stood out was a reflective strip on his coat. 'Can I come in? I'm frozen.'

'No, you can't just walk in,' she hissed back. 'And keep your voice down, I've only just got the boys to sleep.' She thought fast, as he hunched his shoulders and shivered. 'I'll meet you at the school. We can talk there.'

He looked over at the brooding cube of the classroom.

'OK. But I do want to see them.' His voice was low.

She grabbed her coat and the school key from the porch hooks and crept outside, gently clunking the door closed behind her. She had to walk past him to open up and turn on the lights. There was little residual heat in the poorly insulated building so she switched on a heater.

'Thank you.' He pulled a child-sized chair close to it and sat down.

'How did you get here?' She was still suspicious, folding her arms over her chest.

'I came on a trawler, with a fisherman called Ellis.' He looked up at her and managed a small smile as he shivered. 'I can't remember ever being so cold, and I work in the North Sea.'

'How did you find the boys?'

'I went to the address a social worker gave me,' he said, holding out a scrap of paper with Clarrie Tremayne's address on it. 'Only there's no one there. The neighbours told me to try here.'

'OK.' She sat down as well, crossing her feet in the guinea pig slippers her mother had given her last Christmas. Billy loved them. 'Their grandmother had a stroke. She was taken to hospital, so I took the boys in. I'm their teacher, Charlotte Kingston.'

'Well, I'm here now. I can take them back with me.' He held his hands out to the heater.

'I can't just hand them over like strays,' she said, anger flaring at the thought. 'And social services have received a complaint against you.'

'I was their stepfather for more than two years. Chloe adored them but she was volatile. She made the complaint against me after we split up; it's completely unfounded – she didn't want me to apply for custody. Ask the boys.' He rubbed his hands over his face. 'And now she's dead...' He sighed. 'They must be devastated.'

Charlotte looked at his bowed head. 'They are, and the proper care for them has to be established.'

He looked up, making eye contact. 'Well, it can't be with you, you hardly know them.'

Charlotte flushed. She couldn't identify the rising emotion inside her, but it was a big one.

'I'm a qualified and police-checked education professional,' she said. 'I'm the best person for them *right now.*'

'Chloe's mum never wanted them,' he said. 'And their biological fathers have never shown any interest. Or paid much maintenance, either. *I've* been sending money to help Chloe look after them, even after we broke up. I only found out she was dead when the payments were returned.' His eyes were brimming with tears. 'I loved her. But no one can cope with a partner who impulsively sleeps with other guys, and moves in with one without warning.'

Charlotte looked down at her hands, tightly clenched together in her lap.

'I'm not blaming you—' she started.

'You have no right to,' he snapped back.

'No. But they are homeless right now, and social services placed them in my care.'

He looked back at the heater. 'It's frosty out there, it's freezing. Can't I kip on your sofa or something?'

'Certainly not,' she said, the words tripping out primly. 'Actually,' she said, losing the attitude, 'the room barely holds a tiny sofa and my camp bed.' That reminded her. 'How about I get you a sleeping bag from our camping supplies, then you can sleep in here? You'll have to get up by seven thirty, though. I'll need to get the classroom ready for school. You can see the boys then, under supervision.'

'I'll bang on the door at seven thirty, then. Will you tell them?'

She thought about Billy's tendency to get overexcited. 'You can surprise them after I've got them up and dressed.' She walked through to the store cupboard and extracted a couple of camping mats and a sleeping bag. 'Bathroom's out the back, kettle is in the kitchen.'

'Thank you. I'm very grateful, Charlotte.'

She paused at the door. 'You should know, the social worker was talking about a sister of Beau's father who might take the boys.'

'Chloe talked about Beau's aunt. Beverley Goodwin is a very driven and successful woman, that's all I remember. She has several older kids.'

'I just thought you should know.' As she walked through the door she looked back. 'They are lovely children. They talk about you with such affection.' The tears were back. Since Zach went, she realised she'd become an emotional watering can.

He smiled then, and she noticed how very good-looking he was: long face, big eyes, strong chin. 'I came as soon as I could.'

'I can see that.'

'Goodnight, Charlotte,' he said, walking up and closing the door gently behind her.

27

DECEMBER 1940

The winter rolled in, with sea mists so thick they coated the windows, winds that rattled the slates like castanets, and hail that broke one of the windows at the little school.

Marc was now eight; he was growing more afraid as the months went on, sharing lurid stories with other pupils about the Germans in France. One of the children, Pierre Keller, had a Jewish grandmother and was classified as a *Mischling* – second class. His parents had had a large red 'J' stamped in their identification papers, and the children would have them when they reached ten years old. The priest, Abbé Jean-Marie Le Houerou, was old and too tired to get involved with politics. Nevertheless, he had gone to the trouble of visiting the Keller family, with their distant Jewish connection, to reassure them of his support and a place of refuge if needed. The Germans had bolstered their small garrison with some Polish workers, who were clearing ground on farmland on the north of the island, a rocky field of no use to anything but sheep.

'They are building a gun emplacement, mark my words,' said Madame Boiteux darkly, when Jenny was helping her brush her hair. 'On the site of the old fort.'

'Maître Boiteux thought they were creating a jetty, for patrol boats.' Jenny met Madame's eyes in the mirror.

Madame caught Jenny's wrist in one plump hand. 'I want to tell you something, but please don't tell Cook or Lisette or anyone else. I have only told Hélène.'

Jenny nodded. 'Of course.' The work she had been doing raced to the front of her thoughts, and her face grew hot. 'Madame?'

'I am to bear another child,' she said, dropping Jenny's hand.

'Oh, that's wonderful news,' Jenny exclaimed.

'Yes. My husband will be pleased. Of course, at my age, there may be complications. I will need to give birth in a large hospital with modern facilities, on the mainland.'

Jenny went back to teasing tangles out of Madame's thick russet hair. 'Of course.'

When little Adela was born, Madame had been rushed from the house in Rennes to a hospital. She had needed a blood transfusion, a modern invention only available in the best infirmaries. Madame covered her face with her hands.

'Oh, Jenofeve, I am so afraid,' she sobbed. All Jenny could do was pat her broad shoulders.

'The war may be over by next year,' she offered.

'If I could just go back to my life in Rennes,' Madame said. 'But our house is gone, most of our money. Even my husband's business is failing because no one can pay a lawyer nowadays.' She pointed to her ormolu jewel case. 'I asked Monsieur Boiteux to sell most of my grandmother's jewels, for food for the children. But he has few people to sell them to except the Germans, and no safe way to send me money.' She stared at Jenny, reflected in the dim mirror. 'Cook tells me that sometimes fishermen from Ushant meet other trawlers, British ships, in the fishing grounds.'

Jenny chose her words with care. 'I suppose that's possible,' she said, smoothing the hair at the back with a comb. 'There, Madame.'

'You could go out with your uncle Paol – perhaps they would meet a British boat. What is it called, your island?'

'Morwen, Madame.' Jenny's hands shook. 'I do miss it. But the Germans have armed patrols, and planes searching the Channel all day long. It must be very dangerous.'

'We hear about British agents and our own resistance all the time. How else do they get here?'

Jenny shrugged and tried to hide her shaking hands. 'I suppose I thought they would parachute in at night. Or land on an unguarded part of the coast.'

The idea of going home, away from all this fear and bleakness, was intoxicating. Every folded note to translate took her deeper into fear, leaving her nights racked with nightmares of the smiling Herr Albrecht. There were other dreams too, of the face of Laurie Byers, his quick grin, his soft beard and lips.

'I don't think it would be safe to go, and how would you explain my absence?'

'I only wonder if we will all perish here if we don't get back to Rennes...'

Jenny put a hand on each of the woman's shoulders for a moment, meeting her gaze in the mirror.

'We will survive because we have to. We will fight for the family, all of us.' She turned away to hang up the day dress – it could do for one more day. 'We're all healthy. You have had two children before, and you are an educated lady. I'm sure we will find the best care when the time comes.'

'I have had three babies,' Madame said, her voice bleak. 'Just a year after our wedding, we had a baby girl, Marguerite. She was small and weak, and she didn't feed properly despite my best efforts. In the end she was too sick. She died at two months.'

'I'm so sorry.' Jenny didn't know what to say, her throat thick with sadness. 'How awful for you. Was that in Rennes?'

'No. that was in Rochefort-en-Terre, where my father had his business.' She waved a hand at the room. 'This was *my* family's summer home, I inherited it from my parents.' She looked like she was going to cry again. 'This is where I shall die.'

Jenny shut the wardrobe with a snap. 'No, Madame, you will not die, because we will all look after you. I couldn't think of leaving, none of us could. Tomorrow, if you permit, we will ask the doctor to visit, and we will contact a midwife. That will put your mind at rest.'

'Thank you, my dear.' Madame turned to look at her. 'You remind me to be strong and brave. But if an opportunity arises, I expect you to put your own safety first. I don't like anyone knowing your mother is English. Suppose the Germans find out?'

The thought of Herr Albrecht made Jenny's heart lurch in her chest, but there was no prospect of leaving the island now.

28

PRESENT DAY, 27 MARCH

Charlotte didn't sleep well, although the bed was more comfortable than the sofa. At least she didn't lie awake thinking of Zach, and instead she thought about the quiet man sleeping in the schoolroom. She also wondered what she was going to tell the boys.

She was already up and dressed by the time Beau padded downstairs.

'Why are you awake?' he asked, glancing at the clock. He squinted at it and she wondered, not for the first time, if he needed glasses. Or if he could even read the time.

'It's nice and sunny,' she said. 'Is Billy still asleep?'

'Yes.' He stared at her, a little frown between his brows. She turned around to put the kettle on, filling it again for Ash. When Beau returned from the bathroom, she asked him to get Billy up and get dressed because they had an early start.

'Why? Are we going to see Grandma?' His distrust was palpable. 'Is someone taking Billy away?'

'No! It's a school day. For goodness' sake, Beau, I have a *nice* surprise organised. Just wake Billy up.'

He must have believed her because he stamped upstairs shouting for Billy. Within ten minutes both children were down, watching her suspiciously from the table.

'Apple juice for Billy,' she said, sticking the straw into a mini box of juice. 'And chocolate milk for Beau. Right, I want to tell you about the nice thing that happened after you went to bed.' Neither boy moved, and she filled the cafetière to the top. 'We had a visitor. He's coming for breakfast.'

Beau looked at Billy, then at her. 'Who?' She could see he was shaking with adrenaline.

'Oh, I'm sorry, Beau, don't worry,' she said, patting his shoulder gently. 'It was Ash. He wanted to see if you were all right.'

Billy leapt out of his seat, knocking over the juice. 'Where is he? I want to see him.' His face was a picture of joy. Beau's reaction was slower but different, his face creasing as if in pain. He dived for the stairs and vanished into the bedroom, banging the door shut.

Charlotte picked up the drink. 'You can let him in when he knocks. I'm just going to see what's upsetting Beau.'

On her way upstairs, she heard Ash knock and Billy wrenching the door open, shouting for him in high-pitched excitement. Beau had shut the bedroom and the door wouldn't open. She didn't want to force it.

'Beau. Please tell me what's wrong.'

The long silence was broken by Ash's deep voice, calming Billy down.

Something of Beau's silence connected with the emptiness in Charlotte. 'Why are you so upset with Ash?'

'He left.' Then the sobbing, great tearing cries through the door. 'He left, and then Mum died.'

'Oh, sweetheart.' It scratched at her heart, hearing his distress. At the age of eight the worst thing that had happened to her was losing a pet. 'Please let me in.'

'Can I help?' Ash was on the bottom step, Billy had a death grip on his waist and was trying to drag him away.

'No, it's OK. Beau isn't ready quite yet. He's still very emotional about his mum.' She tried to smile but the crying was hurting her. 'There's coffee in the pot. I'll have one too, Billy knows where the mugs are, and there's milk in the fridge.'

She sat on the top step and waited. At some point, Ash came halfway up the steps and brought her a coffee, then vanished downstairs. The outside door banged.

'Has he gone?' Beau's voice sounded just like Billy's. The door creaked as he moved his weight away, and Charlotte stood up and pushed it open.

Beau was curled up in the middle of the floor, wrapped completely in the quilt.

'I think they are going to feed the rabbit.'

'I said I hated him.'

Charlotte had heard that before, from her own lips.

I hate you, Zach, I never want to see you again.

'Sometimes we say we hate the people we love the best,' she said, sitting on the edge of the bed. 'They disappoint us the most.' She was wondering if he could understand that when he emerged from a fold of duvet.

'He left us.'

'He probably had a good reason.'

Beau shrugged, then pulled the quilt off, moving closer to Charlotte, leaning against her leg. 'She was mean to him,' he whispered. 'But he could have taken us with him.'

She pressed her hand to the ache in her chest, right over her heart. 'Oh, sweetheart, he wouldn't have been allowed,' she whispered back. 'But he came all this way, didn't he? Because he heard you needed him. He even caught a fishing boat to get here in the middle of the night.'

She could hear Billy's voice as they came back in. Beau shut his eyes so tight the tears squeezed out of the corners of his eyes. 'Can we go for a walk?' he said.

'We have plenty of time before school.' She looked over at the clock. 'Half an hour, anyway. Why don't we see if any of the lambs have been born yet? You can explain the sheep to Ash.' Tink had promised them lambs any day now.

I can't just hand the boys over to a stranger.

Downstairs, Beau managed to sidle around the room to get his coat, keeping the table between Ash and himself. Billy bounced out after him, down to the lane.

'Did you find out what's wrong?' Ash asked Charlotte as she followed them.

'I think so,' she said, although she couldn't break Beau's confidence. 'Wait for him to talk to you. He wants to go for a walk, see the sheep. Give him time.'

I should take my own advice, dealing with Zach.

She walked down the frosted lane, watching Ash listen to an excited Billy, who clung to his hand. After a minute or so, Beau caught a fold of her sleeve in his hand and hung on. Charlotte was afraid to say anything or even look at him; it was like having a wild bird take food from her hand.

Tink was already at the sheep field, filling a manger with hay, sheep butting at each other to get the first bites. They were so pregnant they looked like they might explode.

'Hi, Charlotte,' he said, his gaze sliding over to Ash. 'I'm Tink Ellis. And you are...?'

'Ash Stewart. The boys' stepfather. I came over last night with a fisherman called Ellis.'

'I heard. Uncle Mike.' Tink smiled at Beau. 'Brilliant timing.'

'Why?' Charlotte asked.

'Come and see what happened overnight.'

The boys looked at each other and Billy screamed 'Lambs!' so loudly several of the ewes scampered away.

Corinne was in the shed looking into a pen. Baby Kitto was strapped to her chest, just a few months old. 'Shush, boys, don't scare them,' she said, holding a finger to her lips. 'They're new babies.'

Charlotte's eyes brimmed with tears at the sight of the two staggery lambs wandering around their mother. She was also a little uncomfortable with Ash's proximity, but Billy was hugging one of his legs. She wondered how he could be that secure with someone who had hurt him.

Tink introduced Ash to Corinne, and Beau came to life, asking him rapid questions. When were they born? Did someone have to help? Were any of the other sheep in labour? Was the mother a Cheviot cross?

'Yep. The Exmoor crosses will lamb a few days later,' Tink said. 'This young man has been learning all about sheep,' he told Ash. 'He's getting pretty knowledgeable.'

'I want to do farming,' Beau said, giving a cautious side glance to Ash. 'And help with the lambing.'

'That's a great idea.' Ash turned to Charlotte. 'Look, I have a few weeks off work. I thought I would stay on the island until the custody situation becomes clearer.'

'OK,' Charlotte said slowly. She noticed Billy was jiggling up and down. 'Billy, do you need to pee?'

Corinne took his hand and led him off to the hedge beside the gate. Beau moved over to Charlotte and leaned his head against her arm. He sighed as if all his energy had gone.

'Is that OK with you, Beau?' She crouched down and looked into his downcast face. 'Tell me if you mind Ash being around. If you don't want him to visit, just say.'

'I don't mind if he stays on the island,' he whispered. 'I just don't want to see him right now.'

'Right.' Charlotte looked up at Ash. He glanced at Beau then away, his mouth downturned. 'Sorry.'

Corinne came back, the baby starting to fuss. 'I was just

wondering whether Ash needed somewhere to stay, if he wanted to be near the boys. The campsite will be opening soon,' she said. 'And there is the pub, and the hotel opens next week.'

He winced. 'A bit rich for my blood at the moment. I haven't been paid for my last job yet, and my saving are locked in bonds.'

Tink and Corinne exchanged glances. 'This might sound a bit strange,' Corinne said, 'but our lorry conversion is vacant at the moment, if you don't mind being interrupted occasionally by two shepherds. Or if you could do a few rounds some nights, save us coming out every couple of hours?'

'Really? That would be great. But you would have to do the actual... lambing.'

'That's fine.' The baby was really starting to wail now. Corinne looked at the boys. 'Come on, let's show Ash the lorry. Then I can feed Mr Fusspot.'

After an excited exploration of the lorry conversion, which was lovely but cold, Charlotte dragged Billy and Beau away from the sheep and back to the schoolhouse to get some breakfast. She left Ash behind and told him he couldn't come back until after school.

They arrived at the school at the same time as Rhiannon and Joanna.

'I'm so sorry, we're late and we haven't had breakfast yet,' Charlotte said, letting them into the building, and scooping up the neatly folded sleeping bag. 'We had a surprise visit from the boys' stepfather last night.'

'That's OK,' Joanna said, tidying the tables and chairs back to their normal position and switching on the lights and heating. 'You get some food, we'll get ready.'

Charlotte realised she hadn't prepared anything educational. The weather was bright and cool, the children restless and excitable, so she decided to clear some space in the classroom and play some games to burn off a bit of excess energy. She was taking her turn to be a pirate captain, running around the rope outline of a ship, calling her hearties to order, when she realised someone was looking in through the picture window.

She shrieked in surprise and slapped her hands over her mouth. The children ran over to the window to look at the stranger, as she took in what she was seeing. Zach, in warm clothes, his shoulder-length hair flying around his face in the wind. Her heart did a slow somersault, leaving her somewhere between excited to see him, and nauseous at the emotional baggage he threw up in the air just by *being*.

She wrenched open the door. 'What do you want?' She moderated her voice. 'I mean, why didn't you tell me you were coming?'

'I tried to. You keep ignoring my messages or hanging up on me. Not fair, Char. Don't you think fifteen years together gets me more time to explain myself than leaving messages on your answerphone?'

'Well, I'm working,' she hissed back.

'Looks like fun. Can I wait in your house?' he said, his gaze scrolling across the children.

'Certainly not. There's accommodation at the pub on the quay. They take people out of season. I'll meet you after work.'

'Hi, kids.' He waved at them and they all waved back, except for Beau, who stepped nearer her, like he was guarding her. 'I'd better let you get back to work.' He waved again then gave Charlotte a lingering glance that still had the power to make her flush and her heart bound.

'I hate him,' she whispered to herself, even as she waved a piece of paper to fan her face. Maybe it was early menopause. *Really* early.

Joanna stared at her. 'Wow. He's a looker.'

'Ex,' was all Charlotte could offer as explanation.

'He doesn't look like he wants to stay an ex,' Joanna said, her smile sympathetic.

'He has to *stay* ex,' Charlotte said. 'I can't cope with crushing disappointment any more.'

29

FEBRUARY 1941

Soon everyone on the island knew Madame Boiteux was with child.

Away from their commanding officers the soldiers leered and shouted after girls until Jenny was only allowed to walk with the company of Cook or Lisette, which Lisette took very badly. Jenny spent more time walking around the large grounds and terrace with the children, or helping in the vegetable garden and small orchard, and checking the back of the summer house for notes. There had been none for weeks, since a small and sad Christmas.

One morning, Jenny was joined by Aunt Hélène in the garden.

'Let's go down to the quay for a walk,' she said, tucking her arm into Jenny's. 'Lisette can mind the children for an hour.'

'You tell her that, she won't listen to me,' Jenny said, surprised. 'Is Madame all right?'

'She's laid down for an hour. It will do her good. She's frightened at the moment, and quite overwhelmed. Oh, and fetch those two worn towels from the laundry. Maybe Augustine can do something with them.'

Jenny hadn't spoken to Augustine for months; it was dangerous to visit and draw attention to herself. There were rumours that she was hardly seen in the town and might have gone a little senile.

The wind was fierce off the sea and it was a relief to slip into a warm hat and gloves. It blew relentlessly from the west, and it carried rain as well as mist. Walking with Hélène meant she could step out and walk faster than with Lisette and the children. She filled her lungs with the salty air, stopping at one of the bends to look over the steep hillside down to the quay. Three fishing ships and a couple of inshore lobster boats were rolling in the falling waves, starting to settle on the sand at low tide. The turquoise and white St Guillaume was there, but rust streaked the sides.

'Do you still hear from your cousin Yves?' Hélène caught her arm. She had brought a stout stick, not so much to lean on but for their protection.

'No. Uncle Paol says he's very involved with the nationalist movement now. My uncle is always worried about him.'

'French Nazis,' Hélène said. 'No better than the German ones.' She pushed a dangling bramble out of their path with her stick. 'How are you feeling? I think it's sad that a young girl of twenty-one has the worries of the world on her shoulders instead of thinking of young men.'

'Oh, I still think about them,' Jenny said, feeling her smile twist with sadness. Unbidden, the memory of warm lips on her own intruded, and she shook it off. 'There will be time for that after the war.' Her coat was beaded with water and the mist was deepening.

Hélène led her not into the town but to the north, further along the coastal path onto farmland. In the distance, a working party moved in and out of the fog with heavy tools and wheelbarrows. She stopped behind a stand of elder bushes. 'You haven't had any notes recently?'

'Notes?'

'Augustine told me you were helping transcribe some notes.'

'I... I wouldn't be allowed to talk about it. If it was true.'

'Quite right. But I have found out that Laurence Byers has been arrested,' Hélène said quietly. Jenny staggered, as if the news had dealt a blow to her midriff. A picture of him in chains, dragged through the streets of some town towards a Gestapo interrogation, filled her mind.

'W-why? When?' she managed to ask.

'Before Christmas. That's why he hasn't been bringing letters. He was taken to London.'

Jenny stared at her aunt. '*London?* I imagined him being arrested here.' She shuddered. 'Interrogated or shot.'

'He may still be,' Hélène said, looking away. 'Treason is a hanging offence. No lawyers, no jury, just three judges and a noose.'

'*Treason?*' Jenny leaned against a wall. 'No. He's a British spy, he's helping Augustine, and leaving messages for me to translate.'

'He passed some information that was false.'

Jenny felt sick. 'Was that a mistake I made?'

'No. He altered the message he gave you. Another agent has had to go into hiding; a rescue mission has been cancelled.'

It felt like the world she thought she knew was being thrown upside down. 'But, I...' She couldn't finish.

'I know. We all trusted him. But we must protect Augustine. If he has told anyone about her, she could be arrested. Even killed.'

Jenny tried to think what the messages were even about. 'What happened?'

'A Royal Navy ship was protecting a convoy of ships from America. The message was to confuse the Germans, to misdirect them to another location.'

'But... How would they know about the times and places?'

'They find out about them all, in time. Which is why we hide messages inside messages, things that only a Breton speaker would know.' Hélène took her arm and shook it. 'What you do, what you *all* do, is life and death for France, for the whole war. Both sides have spies and double agents. The Resistance isn't one movement, it's different groups with differing agendas. Take your nationalist cousin. Some factions are working for the Resistance, some are working for the Nazis, all to get independence.'

Jenny pressed her mittened hands to her eyes for a moment. 'Will he – Laurie – be hanged?'

'Maybe. Maybe he'll be found innocent. Everyone is paranoid at the moment.' She turned to Jenny. 'Which is why I want you to take the first opportunity to go home.'

'I can't,' Jenny said, eyes filling up with tears. 'Madame and the children, they all need me. Especially now.'

'They have me and Lisette and everyone else on the island. There's a chance we can get you to the mainland with Madame, to Rennes to have the baby. We might be able to smuggle you to the coast from there, and an agent could get you to Britain.'

'I couldn't leave Madame. Not yet. Don't ask me to go.'

'Those are your orders,' her aunt said, staring deep into her eyes. 'If we can get Marthe onto the mainland.'

Back home. It seemed a million miles away and a hundred years ago now. Jenny hugged herself, more because she was frightened and uncertain than cold.

Laurie.

30

PRESENT DAY, 27 MARCH

Zach was still sending affectionate texts, and Charlotte was still working out how to answer them, when she got a call from Traci the social worker. Investigations into the children's situation were ongoing and, in the meantime, Ash could only see the boys under appropriate supervision.

'Am I appropriate supervision?' she asked Traci.

'Certainly. But please limit contact. Mrs Beverley Goodwin wants to come to the island to meet the boys. She has asked to be considered a suitable kinship carer for Beau. We hope she will be willing to take Billy as well.' Charlotte could hear the relief in the social worker's voice. 'This could all resolve itself quite well, if she decides to help. And Ashley Stewart can ask for visits as well, if he likes, once the investigation into physical abuse is resolved.'

'What do you mean by physical abuse?'

Traci's voice gentled. 'Occasionally, separating couples make claims about each other's parenting. On this occasion, Chloe was responding to a claim by Mr Stewart that he'd found the boys left alone in the house overnight, and that she neglected them on other occasions. She retaliated by saying he physically punished them. We had to take both seriously.'

'Of course.' Her head was spinning. 'But you're not going to take them straight away?'

'You did say the accommodation was very limited.'

What about me? Could the boys be taken away so soon, forever? Billy's smile jumped into her mind.

'We've adjusted,' was all she could come up with. 'And the boys are just starting to settle down. We just hope their grandmother will be able to come back home and look after them.'

'I'm going to see her again today, but I don't think that's on the cards. Or in their best interests.'

Charlotte ended the call and looked around the schoolroom. Billy seemed oblivious but Beau was watching from a chair in the corner, his body tensed. She walked over to him.

'Shall we get the rabbit out? I think he needs a cuddle.'

'No, he doesn't,' Beau said, his eyes wide and, Charlotte thought, accusing.

Charlotte sat on the floor next to the cage, opening the top and stroking the impossibly silky animal. 'Well, I do,' she said.

'Are they going to take us away again?' Beau kept his voice low and glanced over at Billy.

'No. I'm what you've got.'

'And you're trying to get rid of us.' He lifted one shoulder and turned away so she could only see his profile.

'Actually, I'm not.' She lifted the fat rabbit onto her lap, where it looked puzzled then went back to chewing some hay. 'I didn't know how it would work, but now I just want you to be happy. Being with you makes me happy too.'

'Could we go and live with Daddy Ash?' It was the first time he'd seemed interested in Ash.

'Is that what you want? I thought you were upset with him.'

Beau dropped his head, his face screwing up as if he was going to cry. 'He went away. He left us.'

'He didn't want to,' she said. 'I think he only left because your mum met someone else and told him to go. He had to, you know?'

'We didn't like Harry,' Beau said, hunched down on the chair. She handed him the rabbit and he made room on his lap for the animal, who settled into the hug. 'He was mean. He hit Billy when he was naughty.'

'I'm so sorry. Did he hurt you as well?'

Beau shrugged and glanced at her. His expression of acceptance was worse than his anger or sadness. 'I don't care, I can take it. But Billy was only little.'

'Did you tell your mum?'

He nodded and buried his face in Percival's long fur. 'But Harry told Mum that Daddy Ash did it when he took us out for burgers. He lied.'

Charlotte closed her eyes and realised she was hugging herself. She wanted to reach out for Beau. 'Well, you need to explain it all to the social worker when you meet her,' she said, faking a smile. 'Let's clear the tables and get some maths out.' Despite Beau's reading difficulties, his ability with numbers was good. She glanced at her phone to see Zach had left a message.

Booked hotel for a meal. 7.30. Is this OK?

She reached for Percival and placed him back in the cage. It was only then that she saw the rabbit's head was wet with Beau's tears.

31

APRIL 1941

The stormy winter gave way to the first signs of spring. Surrounded by water, the island rarely had hard frosts, and the family had all started working in the vegetable garden early. Except Madame Boiteux, who was too tired and frightened to do much beyond sitting in a chair and writing increasingly desperate applications for a travel pass that would allow her to visit her sister in St Malo and then return to her husband's side in Rennes.

'But where will we live? Monsieur has just two rooms,' she bemoaned, lying on her bed, 'and he has to share a bathroom with two other families. There is no room for a baby, and I cannot imagine being there on my own all day.'

Jenny folded more baby clothes, which had been used to line trunks to bring china and glassware from the mainland a year ago. She had washed them in rose-scented soap and they smelled lovely. Adela was now running about, and some of her wardrobe could be adapted for the new baby.

'The midwife is calling later,' she said, critically holding up a knitted cardigan with a small milk stain. It would have to stay.

The local sheep's wool was harsh, and wouldn't suit baby clothes, although a local family were spinning it for the locals to make coats. 'She says the old doctor has come out of retirement, since our own was taken away.'

'The midwife,' Madame said, looking out to sea, her voice dull. 'What midwife can help me? I'm too old to have a baby on this savage island. I need to go to hospital.'

Jenny sat beside her for a moment, taking one of her cold hands. Madame's rings were loose on her hands now – she had lost weight as the quality of the food deteriorated. 'I think you will be safe, even if we have to stay,' she said, trying to summon up some confidence. 'The midwife has helped bring many babies into the world, and we have a doctor just in the town.'

'But I'm forty-one,' Madame said, pulling her hand away. 'My mother died at forty-four.'

'Not in childbirth,' Jenny said, holding up the last of the tiny dresses. 'Look, was this one of Adela's nightgowns?'

Madame took it, and for a moment her face softened. 'It was Marc's before her,' she said. 'Look at that exquisite stitching. That was embroidered by my mother for her youngest son, my brother Pierrick. He lives on Corsica. I wish I could get a letter to him but...' She handed it back. 'I just hope someone wears them again,' she said.

'Well, Cook has made a soup from the spring vegetables and the last ferry brought us two sacks of flour. We'll have proper bread for lunch.' The smell of the baking dough was already filling the house.

Madame looked over at her. 'You seem sad,' she said, abruptly. 'Are you worried about someone, too?' She swung her legs over the side of the bed and eased herself to standing, rubbing her back. She was almost seven months gone, but she already looked huge.

'Just a friend,' Jenny said, closing the drawer, scented with last year's lavender which had bloomed in abundance in defiance of the Germans stomping all over the verges. Her dreams were full of prison cells and Laurie, taken to a secret court.

'Perhaps you are homesick,' Madame said, walking to the window with a sigh. 'I know I am.'

The family house in Rennes, with three storeys and five bedrooms, had an enclosed walled garden which had been a trap for the morning sun and was where the gardener grew flowers for vases, and fruit and vegetables. For a moment, Jenny salivated at the memory of warm raspberries, figs ripe from the tree, apples growing up cordon hedges in their hundreds. Fruit trees were stunted and twisted in the salt-laden winds on Ushant.

'Perhaps I am homesick. For Rennes, for Morwen. I miss my mother.' Her voice broke on the word. 'But I have my second family here. I love looking after the children, and the island is truly beautiful. It reminds me of Morwen every day.'

Madame held out her arms and for a moment they clung together. 'Well, we love you like one of our own, and you're right, we are a family. We will face what comes with the courage of Breton women.' Still, she shuddered as she let go. 'I will speak to the midwife, see if I can be as healthy as possible.'

'With fresh bread,' Jenny said. 'What heals faster than real, French bread?'

Her heart, if not broken, was bruised. Laurie Byers, the romantic secret agent hero of her daydreams, had turned out to be a traitor. The only other man on the island who showed interest in her – even as she was repelled – was the smart Gestapo officer. He walked past the house often, and sometimes called in to offer his compliments to Madame. If one of the island ships was in port he sometimes delivered a letter from Maître Boiteux. He treated Madame with respect, but as Jenny was often the one to open the door, she had no doubt it was her he wanted to see. His dog Bruno had also become very friendly, at least to Jenny, although he barked at Lisette and made her jump.

One day in April he came to see Madame and asked that her household be present.

'As I'm sure you already know, we are building a lookout on the bluff overlooking the tallest lighthouse,' he started, as soon as he and Madame were seated in the drawing room, the servants standing behind their mistress, Adela in Jenny's arms. The dog sat at his feet, vigilant. He had not asked permission to bring Bruno in.

'So we understand,' Madame said, folding her long skirts over her embroidered slippers. Her back was as straight as if she were in front of a firing squad.

'It is necessary to increase the workforce on the island,' he said, and Jenny's heart sank at the further strains on the island's food supplies. 'Many households will be asked to accommodate one or two Polish or French workers. Hosting families will receive an extra ration for them, and preferential treatment.'

'Herr Albrecht—' Madame started to say before Jenny jumped in.

'That is not possible here,' she said hotly, her sharp voice making the baby jump and the dog utter a sharp bark. 'Madame is presently unwell and is expecting to be confined in the coming months,' she continued, in a more moderate tone. Hélène frowned at her but she carried on. 'And what about the other children?'

'I can assure you,' Albrecht said, 'many of our workers have children and wives of their own. They will behave in a polite and respectful fashion, *as per my orders.*'

The last words were said with cold certainty; even the dog looked questioningly at his master. He stood up and slapped his walking stick against his heel.

'Excellent. I am glad we are in agreement. Your boarders will arrive in the next two weeks, on the cargo ship. Please make accommodation available.'

He clicked his heels together and bowed as Madame put her handkerchief to her mouth in shock.

32

PRESENT DAY, 27 MARCH

Having organised Ellie from the neighbouring cottage to babysit the boys, Charlotte took a couple of hours for herself. Or, more accurately, for Zach, who was waiting for her at the hotel.

When she got there, Robert explained that they weren't opening the whole dining room, just the bar, but they wouldn't be the only couple. For some reason, that made her feel safer. Maybe they could keep it civil.

'Thanks, Rob. Can I have something light, maybe a white wine spritzer?'

Zach was already drinking, she noted, her heart sinking. He tended to be relentlessly 'honest', or as she thought of it, 'confrontational' after a few drinks.

Robert leaned forward. 'Did you know we're looking for seasonal staff? A man came up here this afternoon looking for work for the summer, Ashley Stewart. What do you know about him?'

'He was the boys' stepfather,' she replied, looking back at an impatient Zach. 'I don't know him otherwise, but he seems nice.'

'Would it be OK if we gave him a trial?' Rob asked. 'He says he's found accommodation with Tink and Corinne.'

'They offered their truck. He's just trying to stay close to the boys.'

'I can't fault him for that,' he answered.

Charlotte grabbed her glass and bag and walked over to Zach, who smiled broadly. He was dressed in a soft tartan shirt she'd always loved, and jeans.

'Hi,' she said. 'I have to be back by ten. Babysitter.'

'That's something I didn't expect us to be worrying about just yet,' he said.

'No.' The whole fantasy that Charlotte had been nurturing for fifteen years replayed in her mind. 'No. I always thought we'd have a family house by now, and be having a baby of our own.'

'I thought you wanted the wedding first,' he said. He laughed softly. He loved to tease her about her wedding plans. She'd been to bridal shows with friends, seen both her best friends through their wedding dress consultations and fittings, and visited venues with her aunt when she remarried.

'I thought you shared my dreams,' she said, and took a bigger sip of the wine.

'I did! I still do,' he answered quickly. 'Only I would have been happy with a beach wedding in Hawaii. And there's plenty of time to settle down and have a baby. When we are too old to have any more adventures.'

There it was: the problem. While Charlotte had been indulging Zach in his dreams, she'd been ignoring her own.

'I think having a baby would be a huge adventure,' she said.

'Sure. And it's not like you can't take kids with you when you travel. Remember that couple in New Zealand with the two toddlers in the van? They were all having a ball.'

Charlotte took the menu and studied it. She remembered the dark circles under the mother's eyes, the time the youngest one almost roamed into the sea unattended, and when the children were kept awake by the partying in the surf camp. That wasn't what she wanted for her baby.

'Can I have the lamb, please?' She almost ordered Zach's ribeye steak for him – he'd always been predictable. But he surprised her, ordering a butternut squash curry and more beer.

'I don't think we should go over the same ground again, do you?' she said calmly. 'I have loved you, so much, for fifteen years. But we've grown in different directions.'

Your direction was straight to a twenty-year-old. The idea still made her angry, jealousy cramping her chest. Was Zach becoming the cliché, endlessly trying to revisit his youthful successes?

'But I still love you.' He reached over, put the tips of his fingers over hers. She slowly withdrew her hand from the familiar touch. 'I miss you more than ever.'

'I loved you less with each month apart,' she said, deciding to be brutally honest. 'The first few years I missed you terribly when you went away. I would grieve for you, and get excited when you were due back. But then I made a home, I made my own life.'

'Surfing wasn't just my hobby,' he said, staring at her. 'It was my living, my passion. Thousands of pounds of sponsorship, big competitions, travel. It became my career. I never demanded you gave up teaching, or being a school inspector.'

'You're right.' She smiled at him without warmth. 'Because my career was just a job, and yours a God-given talent.'

'Are you still angry about Fleur?' He put his head on one side. 'I can explain that.'

'No,' she dropped her voice. 'No, Fleur was a *symptom*. You weren't really happy with me, in our long-distance relationship.'

'I was lonely without you. I *am* lonely.'

The food came and when Charlotte leaned forward over her plate, tears rolled down her cheeks. She hadn't known she was that upset. She dabbed at her face with a napkin and picked up her knife and fork. The lamb was garlicky and flavoursome, and she got through two bites before Zach started talking again.

'We can't throw all that time away.'

It was the banality of it that cut through her sadness.

'We are different people now,' she said, looking up at him.

He had a fabulous tan; he'd spent the winter in tropical seas, gradually placing lower down in all the elite events, only qualifying for the veterans' competitions with their minimal funding. He wouldn't choose to retire – it was going to be forced on him once his knees and back went.

'After I stepped down, life with you *was* going to be my new adventure,' he said, smiling with beautifully white, straight teeth. Californian teeth, she'd always thought, for all the publicity.

'I'm trying to find my own life,' she said, cutting into the seared kale.

'So, you're living on an island with a dying school, trying to close it down, and you're stuck with two kids that aren't even yours?' He was starting to sound angry.

She recognised the signs that he wasn't getting his own way, was trying hard to persuade her. She wondered whether their whole relationship had been like that. *I've been an idiot.* No, not an idiot, an optimist. And a lot of their lives together had been lovely, exciting, freeing.

'Those two kids need something from me that no one's ever asked for before,' she answered, simply. 'They want the real me, warts and grumpiness and strict teacher and sentimental foster parent and all.'

'I want the real you,' he said softly.

'No, you don't,' she explained. 'You wanted me to become someone new, give in to my wild side. Find my free spirit, my inner mermaid.'

'And you did.'

'I did, *for you.*' It had been uphill sometimes, skinny dipping with strangers, feeling awkward, drinking and singing with people she didn't know just to keep him company.

'I can't believe you're giving up fifteen years of a great, loving relationship, just like that.' He snapped his fingers.

'But it wasn't *just like that,*' she said, drinking in the beloved features, the sharp cheekbones, the curved lips. 'I gave up seven years ago when I took on the school inspector job and stopped travelling to most of your competitions. You strung me along with promises of a wedding and a baby.'

'I meant every one of them.' A frown crinkled the sun-browned skin on his forehead. 'So there's really no way back?'

She thought back to the afternoon, the boy holding the rabbit. 'I want to pursue my own life. Maybe it will be a disaster. Maybe I'll end up an old spinster and have lots of cats. But I want to chase *my* dreams now.'

She could hear the words shatter in the air. She stared at him, seeing the first white hairs curling among the sun-bleached blonde, the lines across his forehead, the thinner hair at the front. Yes, he was still beautiful in her eyes but there was something else she hadn't noticed before. Sadness. Maybe he'd changed, too.

He sighed. 'You're different.'

'I know.' She did feel more alive, some sort of energy thrumming through her veins. Anxiety for the boys, maybe, for the task she'd been given. 'I'm doing something important.'

'You seem older.'

She laughed out loud at that. 'I've always felt older than you.' It felt like a familiar argument. 'You've been living your best young life, and I've been at home being a grown-up.'

'Well, I'm grown-up now. Teaching surfing doesn't pay the bills. I'm barely managing to share the rent on an apartment.'

'Cornwall's expensive,' she said gently. He'd never really

had to pay for anything, he'd always found sponsorship. 'But there are cheaper places to surf.'

'Nowhere worth surfing, though.' He reached out a long, tanned hand. 'Char, I'm serious now. I'm ready for babies, puppies, whatever you want. I saw you with those kids today, you looked so happy, so confident.'

She looked at his hand, thought for a moment what to say, then squeezed his warm fingers.

'No. It's over,' she said firmly. 'You will always be my wild, adventurous, young love.' She pulled her hands back and watched as Robert came to clear their plates. 'Is there pudding? I feel like a big plate of sugar.'

She selected a meringue, cream and chocolate concoction and Zach went with coffee.

'I'm watching my weight,' he said. 'I've got to be careful now I'm not training.'

'You will always be athletically slim to me,' she said. 'Handsome and young and out of my league. This is our goodbye, so let's enjoy it.'

His eyes were red; she couldn't remember the last time she'd seen him emotional. 'OK. But we can keep in touch, can't we?'

She had a mental snapshot of what he could look like, be like, in twenty years. Over-tanned, balding, rangy rather than athletic, still trying to impress young women.

'Of course,' she said, as her enormous pudding was placed in front of her. 'Do you want an extra spoon, Zach? There's enough for two. Call it a goodbye dessert.'

33

Before their uninvited Polish workers arrived, Jenny saw a note sticking out from the rat hole under the summer house. It looked like it had been there several days and was damp. It wasn't written in any kind of cipher this time – it was in French.

'I need to see you,' it said, in flowing cursive, very different from the printed capitals of the codework. 'Please meet me here at one a.m.' The note didn't give a day, and Jenny had a horrible feeling someone had been here every night for a week, staring at the house like a ghost.

She twisted up the note and dropped it in the kitchen stove. She walked upstairs to the nursery just in time for Marc to come home from school. His shirt was torn, his face muddy, and there was a blue bruise under his chin.

'What happened?' she said, rushing towards him. 'Here, in the bathroom, let's clean you up before your mother sees you.'

His lip was wobbling, but his face was tense. 'Guillaume said Lisette was a spy for the Germans,' he said.

Jenny ran some water into the sink and started dabbing at his face with a cloth.

'Why would they say something like that?' she asked.

'They said she has a soldier boyfriend.'

Jenny had wondered for a while if Marc had a boyish crush on the pretty, flirty girl.

'You mustn't mind if she has friends outside the house,' she said, trying to be gentle around the bruise.

He winced anyway. 'But they say it's one of the soldiers,' he blurted out, tears tracking through the dirt on his cheeks. 'One of the *enemy*.'

'Oh, Marc,' she said, putting the cloth down and cupping his face between her hands. 'I don't think it's as easy as enemy or ally any more.'

Her mind was buzzing, though. She dropped a kiss on his forehead and went back to cleaning him up.

'You'll need to change your shirt. I'll try and mend it tonight.'

'And we're going to have more of *them* in the house.'

She ran her hand over his soft, honey-coloured hair. 'We will. But they will be working most of the time, and they aren't German. I'm sure they will be no trouble, and you can always spend more time up here with me, Lisette and Adela.'

Lisette was moving into Jenny's room next to the nursery. Two old truckle beds had been put up in the attic storeroom. Cook slept in the small room off the kitchen and Madame wanted the men to be quartered separate from the family. Aunt Hélène often slept on a couch in Madame's room as her pregnancy advanced.

Mending Marc's shirt gave Jenny an excuse to stay up late, by the brightest lamp in the drawing room. After the last stitches were placed and ends snipped off, she crept forward and unlocked the doors into the garden. As a last thought, she picked up the poker from beside the fire. She grabbed her shawl from the sofa, slipped on her garden shoes and locked the doors behind her. She slipped across the lawn, a half-moon silvering the long grass, an owl hooting somewhere on the island, to be answered by another. She sat huddled in the porch of the summer house and waited.

It was another half an hour, during which she got so cold she had started shivering, before she heard the subtle sound of feet crushing old leaves and brushing grass.

'Who's there?' she hissed, backing up towards the summer house. 'Tell me or I'll scream. The sound will carry to the house.'

'It's me,' a familiar voice whispered. 'Byers.'

She clamped both hands over her mouth trying not to scream or shout. '*Laurie?* But you were *arrested.*'

'I was. But I've been cleared, and they sent me back.' He walked around in front of the porch and she glimpsed his dark overalls, smelled the smoke and oil on him. 'I've taken shifts on the ferry. I'm the permanent engineer now.'

She was conflicted. 'But—'

'I'm back, and we need you to help more than ever.'

She shook her head. 'You don't understand. Things are bad here.'

'I know,' he breathed, getting closer. 'Jenny, I'm so sorry you were frightened. I was, too. They could have hanged me.'

Tears gathered on her eyelashes, making stars of the moonlight. She blinked them away. 'Why did they arrest you?'

He hesitated. 'Some bad information got through. The papers I'm given are often damaged. I must have decoded it wrong.' He took her hands, shook them. 'But they've put me back in the field, so they must be reassured that I'm trustworthy.'

'But everyone says, trust no one,' she said, pulling her hands away. 'Now Lisette may have a German beau and we are about to have more men in the house. Madame—' She took a deep breath. 'Madame is with child, she might need hospital care.'

'There's a doctor at the garrison now. You could call him out, if you need him.'

That was news to her. 'Would he come?'

'You must try to make him.'

She put the poker down. She'd been clenching it so hard that her palm stung. 'So, why are you here now?'

'We have a lot of information to pass back. I will write a simple message, and you can translate it into good Breton with maybe the odd Cornish word in case it falls into the wrong hands. I will encode it and either send it by ship or get it transmitted by radio if we can. But the Germans listen out for transmissions.'

'Augustine. Have you even seen her? She looks so ill...'

'Don't worry about anyone else, just keep yourself safe.' He took a deep breath. 'But your house is under surveillance.'

She pulled further into the shadows. 'What?'

'Everyone knows in the village. The Gestapo, Albrecht, visits the house a lot.'

'He walks his dog up the lane and onto the fields.'

He made a noise of disgust. 'That dog has already mauled a couple of sheep, and rumour says he's trained it to track and kill humans. I carry pepper just in case, for what it's worth. But I think Albrecht is interested in you.'

'Why would you say that?' she said angrily, taking the pouch of papers he held out to her. 'I don't encourage him. I try and stay out of his way. He knows my mother is British.'

'He's drawn to you, like a bee to a flower. I see what he sees,' he answered, pulling back off the porch and down the side of the building, into the deepest shadows. 'Because I'm drawn to you, too.'

His words hung in the cold, still air.

34

PRESENT DAY, 1 APRIL

The school week dragged on after Zach left the island.

Charlotte had allowed the boys a short visit with Ash each evening before settling them down to bed. Billy was thrilled to see him, climbing all over him, singing, anything to get his attention. Charlotte soon realised doing something together would be better, so they cleaned out the rabbit while she set up the classroom, or played a simple matching game while she did paperwork. Beau tended to ignore Ash, just borrowed his phone to play games. By Saturday morning Charlotte was ready to take the boys over to the big island on the ferry, to meet with the social worker who had been trying to find them a permanent home. She also planned to visit the boys' grandmother, now she was improving from her stroke.

They waited on the quay for the ferry. Merryn was there too, with an older woman. Billy was so bouncy on the short boat journey that Corinne, who was piloting the ferry, jammed the children into life jackets.

'Just in case,' she said, manoeuvring the boat away from the quay.

Charlotte sat next to her to talk. 'Where's the hospital?'

'Ask anyone for Hospital Lane,' she said, carefully guiding the boat between rocks slicing the surface of the water. 'Turn right as you leave the port. It's signposted. Clarrie's doing well, we've been taking visitors over every day.'

'Visitors?' Charlotte was surprised, but then she thought how involved the islanders were.

'We're popping in later,' the older woman with Merryn said. 'I'm Merryn's grandma, by the way, Olivia. Clarrie's been asking about the boys – it will do her good to see them.'

'Oh. Good.' For a moment Charlotte wondered if she should have taken them before. 'I was working in the school all week, or we would have gone sooner.'

'Well, it's an extra high tide, you'll have several hours.'

Billy jumped up, leaning on Charlotte. 'Will we be able to take Grandma home with us?'

Olivia caught Charlotte's eye before she could answer and shook her head very slightly.

'Not yet. She still needs to be in hospital. We'll ask her how she is.'

While Billy was occupied playing a clapping game with Merryn, Charlotte moved closer to Olivia. 'It must have been hard for Clarrie, just after losing her daughter.'

'I think it was.' Olivia glanced at Beau, who was staring out of the back of the boat and looked lost in his own world. 'I know she wanted to be a proper grandmother to the boys for so long. She used to talk about them for weeks every time Chloe made contact or shared a picture of them on social media.'

'Maybe she will be able to take them back...'

Olivia shook her head. 'She didn't want to be their mother, not at sixty. They need someone younger. Hopefully, they will find the right family.'

A familiar nausea struck Charlotte at the thought of handing them over with a couple of bags of belongings, never to see them again.

. . .

The council building in the town was open on Saturday mornings and they were directed to the small office where Traci, the social worker, operated from.

'I'm so sorry we haven't been able to help more quickly,' she said, clearing some chairs for the boys. 'Sorry, I didn't think you'd bring them both...'

Beau sat, arms crossed, staring at her. 'Of course I did,' Charlotte said, looking over at them. 'This involves Beau and Billy more than anyone.'

'How comfortable would you be having the boys for a few more weeks?'

Traci's words brought a rush of relief. 'I'd be very happy with that,' she said, her own enthusiasm ringing in her ears. Even Beau looked at her, eyebrows raised. 'I mean, if it helps.'

'Technically, we'll recruit you as a family or friends foster carer, if that's OK. You'll get all benefits due to the boys to help offset the costs. But that does mean we need to assess your suitability as a foster carer.' She handed over an envelope stuffed with paperwork. 'This is the application form, and all the information you will need for part one.'

Charlotte took it, peeked in the top. 'Part *one*?'

'Well, you'll need to be assessed, ideally in the first eight weeks, then a panel will convene to assess your appropriateness to care for them.'

Charlotte shook her head. 'I don't know how long I'll be on Morwen.'

'We'll talk about that in your interviews,' Traci said. 'One will be on the phone with me, and you'll have one with a senior social worker from the county.'

'But how long—' Charlotte was aware both boys were listening to every word. 'I did think Clarrie would be able to take the boys back, once she's better?'

'I know she wants to stay involved. She has told me how much she loves being a grandmother and she wants to stay in close contact with the boys in the future. But she feels her health isn't up to being a full-time parent.'

'I could look after her,' Beau said, his voice high and shrill. 'I can help her. We won't be naughty again, we won't give her another stroke.'

Charlotte leaned forward and Billy crept into her arms until he almost disappeared into her open coat. 'Nothing you did caused her stroke, Beau. But she needs to get better, and that means being very quiet, and letting people look after her.'

'We're looking for a permanent placement for you boys, Beau,' Traci said. 'Your Aunt Beverley has a lovely family, a nice big house and has children of her own to play with. You'd be back in London, near your old school. You could see your friends.'

Beau jumped up, his body stiff with emotion. 'I'll run away if you send me back to London!' he shouted. 'I hate it!'

Traci rode his anger, speaking over him in a calm, authoritative voice. 'It's just one option.'

'What about Daddy Ash?' Billy's voice crept out from Charlotte's hug.

'Well, he'd be able to see you too, when he's home from his job.' Traci looked up at Charlotte. 'We can arrange supervised visits.'

'Have you got any further with your investigations into Ash?' Charlotte said, lifting Billy onto her lap, feeling him tremble.

'We're looking into it. There isn't any evidence except for Chloe's boyfriend's allegations.'

'He's looking into a job on the island, to be near the boys,' Charlotte said, reaching out a hand to brush Beau's arm. 'He wants to be considered as a possible foster parent. He's really committed to them.'

'Unless he has a proper job, a home and reliable childcare, he'd struggle to compete with Beau's aunt. And she's a blood relation,' Traci said. 'I will make a note to contact him, though. Do you have his mobile number?'

While the adults exchanged information, Beau walked around the room, touching a plant, a few books, a phone.

Charlotte felt impelled to put forward Ash's case. 'It's just... he acted as a parent to them for several years. They think of him... well, as Daddy Ash.'

'I will interview him. And I do need to inspect your accommodation, check that it's suitable. You did say it was small.'

Charlotte looked at the boys. 'I hope it's not too small,' she said, starting to smile. 'But we make do.'

'We bounce on the bed,' Billy said, starting to cheer up. 'You can see the sheep from the window when you jump high.'

At the hospital, Charlotte and the boys were shown to the stroke unit day room. Most people sat out in chairs or walked up and down the ward. Clarrie looked so much better, and Charlotte was momentarily convinced she was more recovered than she was. As they got closer, Billy running over to her, she saw Clarrie's lopsided smile, and that she could only hug with one arm.

'I thought you were dead,' Billy confided to his grandma. 'But you're getting better already.'

'I am. But I'm not better yet,' she said, leaning back against the cushion in her chair. 'I hope you're being good for Miss Kingston?'

'She burned the toast this morning,' Billy said, giggling with both hands over his mouth. 'And she set off the smoke alarm.'

'I did,' Charlotte said. 'I need to buy a better toaster. But I'm glad to see you looking stronger.' She sat on the chair beside

Clarrie and beckoned for Beau to come in. 'See, Grandma's getting better.'

'But she doesn't want to have us back,' he said, biting his lip, looking at his scuffed and muddy trainers.

'Oh, I do!' Clarrie burst out. 'It's just, I really want to be a proper grandma, and have you come and stay and take you out for treats. I don't think I have enough energy to look after you every day. I think you need someone younger.'

'Then let us go with Daddy Ash,' Beau said, looking up and glaring at Clarrie. 'He's come to the island to get us. We want to live with him.'

'I thought you were cross with him, for going away,' Charlotte said.

He shrugged. 'Then he came back.'

Clarrie looked over at Charlotte. 'I only met Ash once. He seemed like a nice young man. But then social services said there was some sort of question mark?'

'I've heard that too; they're investigating. He's very good with them.' Charlotte paused. 'But his job takes him away a lot, I understand?'

'He's a sat... saturation diver.' Clarrie's voice was still weak. 'He stays under the water for weeks at a time, working in very deep water for an oil company, living in a diving bell. It's a terribly dangerous job.'

The last thing the boys needed was another dead parent. 'What about Beau's aunt, his father's sister? Have you ever met her?'

'I never did.' She looked over at the boys; they were standing at the end of the ward now, sorting through a pile of magazines. She lowered her voice. 'Edward took Chloe away from the island when she was only seventeen. We never saw eye to eye after that. I think he abandoned them when Beau was about eighteen months.'

'Oh, I see.' Charlotte smiled as the boys returned, Billy slumping onto the floor with a couple of comics.

'How are they doing?' Clarrie closed her eyes as if exhausted. 'I've been lying here worrying about them. I know they can be a handful.'

'They've been amazing,' Charlotte said. 'Beau's been out helping with Tink's sheep every morning. Billy's helping me with tidying and washing up, and he helped cook this morning.' She grinned at Billy. '*Before* I burned the toast. They've been seeing Ash regularly, and Billy is friends with Merryn.'

'I can see you're good with children,' Clarrie said, her eyes still closed. 'I suppose all teachers are.'

'They might be, to start with. It's a high burn-out profession.' Beau walked closer, leaned on the arm of her chair, just touching her arm. 'The social worker would like me to become the boys' temporary foster parent, if that's OK with you?'

Clarrie nodded, opening her eyes with difficulty. 'That's very kind of you. I don't think I can cope with social services, I'm so tired all the time. If you can be there when they meet their aunt, maybe you'll be able to persuade her to give them a permanent home. She has several children of her own, you know.'

'Of course. I'll take the boys home now. We don't want to miss the ferry and I have to pick up a few things for them. Like some proper shepherd's wellies for Beau.'

That made Clarrie smile. 'Kiss me, boys.' Billy jumped up to do so, and Beau leaned forward so she could kiss the top of his head. 'Oh, in the top drawer of my locker...'

Charlotte slid it open. Inside were a few toiletries, a purse and a key.

'Take the key,' Clarrie struggled to say, her speech more impaired. 'There are extra clothes and toys they might need.'

35

MAY 1941

Two young Polish men arrived to take up residence in the attic of the villa. Grateful for food and warm beds, they soon became helpful around the house and garden, carrying wood for fires, helping harvest vegetables and killing the odd chicken. Madame found it reassuring to have men in the house at night, even if Cook was as strong as either and slept with a two-foot rolling pin at her side. Jenny feared that there were now two more people to catch her sneaking out to the garden, but she spoke no Polish and they little French, and they kept to their room.

As Madame Boiteux's baby grew, the midwife visited more often, talking to Aunt Hélène with a serious face. Permission to travel had been denied, and now Madame was too tired and her ankles too swollen to manage the long trip to the mainland hospital. Jenny was frightened, seeing Madame burdened with her enormous belly. She wasn't able to get her own stockings on, and struggled to catch her breath just walking upstairs.

Jenny whispered to Aunt Hélène about the doctor at the garrison, but she was suspicious, preferring instead to rely on old Dr Le Tallec and the midwife.

'We shouldn't even know about a German doctor,' she said,

looking up the stairs to make sure no one was listening. 'How did you find out? Another English agent?'

'I must have overheard someone,' Jenny said. 'I might be wrong.'

Trust no one.

But as Madame became more tired, she had to stay in her room. She was too ill to play with Adela, now a sturdy toddler starting to chatter, preferring Marc to read to her until she dozed off. The midwife was frowning more and more on her visits until she caught Jenny's arm as she crossed the hallway.

'I need to speak to Hélène,' she said, quite agitated. 'Where is she?'

'She is taking food to the Aubert family. Tell me, I will pass on the message.'

'I think that Madame is having twins,' she said, in a low voice. 'I know we joked about it when she was well, but now I can hear two distinct heartbeats, feel two babies. I think her body can't cope.'

'What does it mean?' Jenny said. 'Will she be able to deliver safely?'

'I'm not sure she can manage one safely, in her condition,' the midwife said. 'But it's likely they will come very soon, weeks early. They will be small and weak, and Madame is already ill. She needs to be in hospital.'

'I will tell my aunt,' Jenny said. 'And I'll see if we can talk to the garrison commander.'

Aunt Hélène agreed she and Jenny should attempt to get an audience with the Kommandant.

'I don't know if she would survive the journey to a mainland hospital,' she said, peering out at the sea. 'A storm is coming in. No, a doctor here is her best hope. Get changed, look as well-to-do and respectable as you can. Kommandant Richter seems to be a kind man, and you met his wife. She doesn't look like she would ignore a woman in danger.'

Jenny changed into a warm skirt and jacket over a buttoned-up blouse, knitted stockings and stout shoes. Aunt Hélène wrapped herself up in a woollen cloak and they set out to the garrison.

The Germans were based in the requisitioned governor's house, south-east of the dock beyond the fishing boats and ships. Along the sea defences, a paved road ran around one third of the island, the only proper street. On one side, dozens of tiny cottages huddled together out of the winds along the shore, while opposite larger villas stood higher, looking over them to the sea. In the old orchard were new timber shacks for soldiers, a couple of what looked like temporary offices and the large house. A large Nazi flag was hung from the upper floor, as if it had just been conquered.

As they approached, Jenny felt smaller and smaller. A sign on the front door directed the locals to an office, where a bored young soldier sat with a pile of notepaper in front of him.

'Yes?' he barked, in French. 'What do you want?'

'We would like to see Frau Richter, please,' Jenny said, in careful French. She knew almost no German, although she was getting to understand some.

'I'm afraid that is impossible,' he said, looking her up and down, sneering. 'She doesn't see the peasants.'

'Nevertheless,' Hélène said, 'this is important. A matter of life and death. How will Herr Richter respond when he hears you ignored us?'

'*Kommandant* Richter,' he said, but some of the bluster was gone. 'I will ask if an appointment is possible. Wait here.'

There were no chairs for the peasants to sit on so Jenny spent the next ten minutes looking back at the beautiful seascape through the window, the turning gulls, the boats at anchor rocking in the waves.

When he returned he had an unwelcome companion.

Herr Albrecht clicked his heels and bowed to them both. 'You wish to speak to someone in authority?' He spread out his hands, smiling. His long white teeth reminded her of his dog.

Jenny answered. 'I would prefer to speak to Frau Richter. It is a problem involving our mistress.'

'Come into my office, then.' He gestured towards a door, but she stayed back. 'I can get you an audience with anyone I choose.'

'I see.'

When Hélène stepped forward, he shook his head. 'Just you,' he said to Jenny.

Hélène folded her hands together. 'I will wait for you just outside. Five minutes.'

Jenny exchanged glances with her aunt. 'Five minutes,' she said, lifting her chin up.

She followed him through the hall, darkened by the Nazi flag hanging over the upper windows, and through into what must have been the governor's own office. It was lined with books, the titles in Breton. A map of the island was spread over one wall.

'Why don't you tell me what the problem is, and I will decide who is the best person to help.' He sat behind his desk and waved her to a chair. 'I assume this is about your mistress and her... what do you call it? *Situation.*'

'She is becoming ill,' Jenny said, trying to keep her voice businesslike, not pleading. 'And the midwife believes that she is carrying twins.'

'She was certainly as fat as a cow, even a few months ago. Twin calves, huh? Can't the midwife manage?'

'Madame Boiteux is a kind and generous person.' She struggled to keep her temper from boiling over. 'Her babies are at terrible risk. Do you have a doctor at the garrison? You must have someone with medical knowledge.'

'But you have a doctor in the town, a Dr Le Tallec.'

'He's retired. He's in his seventies. And he was an anaesthetist, not an expert in pregnancy and babies.' She could hear the pleading in her own voice now. 'We're just asking for his advice, that's all. If we could get her to St Malo or another hospital...'

'Out of the question,' he said. 'But I see you want me to provide *you* with help that other local people are denied, special treatment. For no benefit to myself.'

'For the benefit of a mother and two innocent children,' she said, through clenched teeth.

'Perhaps. If she was my *friend*, perhaps. Or the friend of *my* friend. You, for example.'

Jenny heard the message, loud and clear. Indignation stiffened her spine. She sat upright. 'You mean if I was your lover, you would be more inclined to help my mistress?'

He put up his hands like a fencer warding off a blade. 'That would be explaining it at its very crudest,' he said. 'We are instructed to, at all times, be courteous to the people we have, uh, conquered. I simply invite you to act as if I was, in truth, a generous conqueror, with the fate of your dear mistress in your hands.'

Jenny stood up. 'I know what Madame Boiteux would say. I bid you good day.'

'Wait.' He had stood too, and now she could see the anger in his frown. 'You do know that if I wanted you, I could just arrest you? You think you have any rights here, in my office?'

'I think Kommandant Richter would say something about it,' she said, backing towards the wall. 'And I would hope that you were, at least, brought up to be a gentleman.'

'Don't play with me,' he said, his whisper more frightening than a shout. 'I can do what I want. I can withhold what I want. I have the power here, Cornish girl. I could arrest you as a suspected enemy citizen or a British agent, if I wanted to.'

She shrank back, hoping he would see her terror as compliance.

'But... but I'm none of those things,' she blustered. 'I have Breton nationality, I was born here. I'm Breton, through and through.' She had never longed for the soft beaches of Morwen Island and the arms of her mother more.

'I am not a monster,' he said, coming closer and reaching his arms out until his hands rested on the wall, either side of her head.

'Then... don't act like one,' she whispered.

He withdrew, stepping back slowly, and she shrank away.

'The doctor?' she said, as she slid along the wall to the door.

'Perhaps. If you ask very nicely.'

She had no doubt he would refuse her unless she acceded to his demands. She felt tears rolling down her cheeks and fled. Maybe he would think she was terrified, which she was, but they were mostly tears of rage.

36

PRESENT DAY, 2 APRIL

Charlotte was up early the next day, and was glad to feed the boys breakfast and settle them down with a children's film while she planned the following week's lessons. Even Beau seemed more relaxed, or perhaps he was just tired after going to see his grandmother. He seemed to have used masses of emotional energy, and Charlotte was feeling it herself. She really wasn't ready to face a visitor when someone knocked on the cottage door before eight.

'Who's that, so early?' she said to the boys, who were still in their pyjamas.

'It's me, Justin,' a breathless voice stammered. 'Sorry about the time. I have a favour to ask.'

Charlotte opened the door to see Merryn, clutching a backpack, standing with her dad. 'Are you OK?'

'We're fine. Can you take her, just for a few hours? We're waiting for a water taxi to take us to the big island then we have a helicopter booked to go to the mainland. Olivia will be here this afternoon to collect her.'

Merryn was looking very uncertain.

She looked down at the little girl, as she crept a cold hand into Charlotte's fingers. 'Of course. We're a bit squashed for space, I'm afraid.'

'She's always talking about you and Billy. Favourite teddies are in the bag, and her inhaler.' Justin was beaming as he dropped his voice. 'Thank you so much. Rob and I have to go to Penzance to talk to our social worker.'

'OK...' Charlotte stammered. People on the island treated everyone like extended family.

He leaned forward and whispered, 'It's Merryn's little brother. If we go straight there we could become his emergency foster placement, we'll have him from birth. But you can't tell anyone, is that OK? In case it doesn't work out.'

'I won't tell.' She could feel the excitement pouring off him. 'I can't trust the kids not to chatter, though. Go! We'll be fine. Let me know how it goes.'

'I will.' He gave Merryn one more hug and disappeared out of the door.

Charlotte shut the door and looked down at the little girl, who had put her fingers in her mouth – always a sign of distress or confusion.

'We're having toast and jam for breakfast, and Billy's watching *Magic Mountain and the Unicorns*,' she said. 'Do you want to come and see?'

Billy made room for her. 'OK,' she whispered, snuggling next to Billy. Beau seemed half asleep.

'More toast?' Charlotte asked, and Billy and Merryn had a piece each. Charlotte turned to Beau.

'You need to wake up,' she said, shaking his arm gently. 'Merryn is staying until her grandma can pick her up.'

His eyes went wide. 'Did someone...?'

Charlotte's heart skipped a beat at the shock on his face. 'No, nothing like that. But her daddies needed to go to the mainland.' The idea gave her goosebumps – a new baby. 'Get dressed. I'll let Billy and Merryn finish the film.'

Since the little ones were now absorbed in the story, she followed Beau upstairs and put some folded clothes away, turned off the nightlight and opened the tiny curtains. He sat on the bed and looked at her.

'Are you really going to foster us? Fill in all those forms?'

'I've already started filling them in.' She knelt down and looked him in the eye. 'This is all new to me. But I want to look after you until you are ready to move to your permanent home.'

'What if we never find anywhere? Would you be our new mum forever?'

She looked straight into his eyes. 'I'll still be here,' she said, her heart answering before her brain was engaged. 'I'll still be your friend. I'm not letting you go before you have somewhere lovely to go. Someone you *want* to live with.'

'It might take a long time to find that,' he said, suddenly looking more like Billy's age than his prematurely adult eight years.

'So? We'll manage as long as we need to.' Her mouth was still rambling along, but her mind was racing. Could she really take the boys permanently, if no one could be found to take them? She felt a bubble of hysteria forming, and couldn't help laughing. 'Do you know, this is the first big decision I've taken for myself in years?' The idea was growing. She really wanted to see this through and settle with them until the scared, lost look had gone in Beau's eyes, which were now filled with tired tears. 'Get dressed, clean your teeth and get ready for a walk. I thought we could go down to Seal Cove before this morning—'

She was knocked off balance when he came forward for a hug, quick and awkward, then he ran down the stairs carrying his superhero hoodie.

On the walk, Billy and Merryn were dissecting the film with speculations on mountains and unicorns as they walked ahead of Charlotte and Beau. He swung his arms, just touching her coat from time to time.

'Why are we coming down here again?' he asked.

'I don't know, really. I bought a book about the hut, and it mentions the old man's diaries. Apparently, they were donated to the museum about four years ago, but no one's read them yet. That's their next project but they put one of them online for anyone to try and decode. I thought we could try.'

'What does decode mean?'

She brought out her phone, swiped to a sample page in the e-book. 'Like this. The symbols stand in for letters in some way.'

He squinted at the page. 'All writing looks stupid to me,' he said.

'The author said the code is complicated. But he's worked some symbols out. Look, the triangle with a dot in it says E.'

'So *we* could try?'

'Exactly.' Charlotte put her phone away. 'Be careful on the steps, Billy!'

'The tide's out,' he reported back, disappearing jerkily a step at a time with Merryn following.

That made her smile; the island children were shaky on times but they always seemed to know what the tide was doing. She turned onto the top of the steps.

'After you,' she said, watching Beau scamper after the younger children, sure-footed. She took her time, especially on the steps that had weathered away. By the time she reached the little beach, the children had already run across the hard-packed, wet sand towards the hut and the tiny inlet. It looked even more desolate against the cliff, gorse and brambles reaching down over the tiny chimney, now she knew something of its history.

'I'm going to find a magic sword, like the wizards on Rainbow Island,' Billy announced, starting a search along the high tideline.

'No,' Merryn said. 'A wand. A unicorn horn!'

Beau stepped over the threshold into the hut, hands on hips, surveying the remaining walls. 'There's a lot of rubbish in here,' he said, picking up an old crisp packet.

'I suppose it washes onto the beach and the wind blows it in,' she said, finding a bottle top. The place was more sad than scary now. 'We could take it back with us.'

He stacked up the rubbish in one corner. 'Did that old man really live here?'

'He did.' Charlotte could almost smell the smoke from the chimney. 'I came here once,' she confessed. 'My Grandma Isabelle was a friend of his.'

Beau started running his hands over the fitted stones that made up the walls. 'What was he like?'

'Nice, I think. She wouldn't have taken me here if he wasn't.'

'Then he died here.' He pulled at random stones, put his fingers into crevices.

Charlotte didn't have an answer. 'What are you looking for?'

'Tink told me he used to come down here with his friends and build bonfires; he left matches. I thought we could burn the rubbish.'

Charlotte shook her head. 'That would make a lot of toxic smoke. It would be better to put it in the bin.'

'Then it goes to landfill and takes thousands of years to rot down,' Beau pointed out, quite reasonably. 'Aha!' He squeezed his fingers into one of the narrow gaps and pulled out a tin. 'Look!'

'Careful,' she said. 'It might be sharp.'

It was certainly filthy and thick with rust. She thought it might be a tobacco tin. 'Don't—' she started to say, before curiosity caught her up in the excitement too. 'Go on, can you get the lid off?'

It took both of them, but disappointingly, it was full of dried grass.

'Oh,' she said. 'Hay.'

Beau's fingers explored underneath. 'No, *tinder*! These are the matches.'

A curled, damp book of matches with 'Sunshine Bay Hotel' – barely recognisable as Merryn's home from decades before – had a few old matches still clinging to it.

'Can we light one?' he asked, excited.

'No. Well, maybe. They look horribly damp though.' She called over to the others to come and see. 'Strike away from your body.'

The first match just crumpled and the head fell off. Tutting with frustration, Beau curled himself around the match and struck the next one. It flared up and went out with a fizzle.

'That's enough, now,' she said. 'Let's put it back, with all the hay, in case someone really needs it.'

'Like a washed-up pirate!' said Billy, eyes wide.

'Or a mermaid,' Merryn contributed.

Charlotte laughed. 'Just in case, yes.' She nodded to Beau, who reluctantly replaced the box in the ledge. 'If they can find it.'

'I'd like to live in a hut like this,' Beau said. 'No school, no homework.'

Merryn showed Charlotte the three-foot stick she had found – which Billy called a magic staff – and Billy showed her several bits of old timber he called swords. They stacked them inside the hut to play with another day. Charlotte checked Billy and Merryn for splinters and caught sight of Beau, looking over the expanse of wet sand to the edge of the water.

'You'd need visitors to bring food,' she said to him. 'I think it might be lonely here, after a day or two.'

He looked over his shoulder. 'I'm always lonely,' he said, so quietly she wasn't sure she'd heard it.

37

JUNE 1940

Madame was a little eased in herself by her eighth month. The weather had improved, and occasional letters were coming from Maître Boiteux. She could waddle down the stairs, sit in a wicker chair in the garden swathed in shawls, while Jenny and Aunt Hélène read to her. The first pains caught the household by surprise, in the middle of dinner. Madame pushed her plate away, white-faced and her hands shaking.

'I shall lie down,' she said. 'I'm sure it will go off.'

'Maman?' Marc said, deemed old enough to eat with the adults now.

'Perhaps you can take a message to Midwife Kemener,' she said to Jenny. 'Take Lisette with you, come straight back. Hélène will help me.'

'Of course.' Jenny caught sight of her aunt's face, a moment of fear.

'I don't want to alarm anyone,' Madame said, holding on to the table as she rose. 'I had this with my other children. Just a little trial run. Help me up the stairs first.'

Upstairs, Adela started crying. Jenny tried to keep her voice calm. 'Perhaps Marc would like to play with Adela in her cot, for a few minutes, until we get back? Cook will keep our dinner warm.'

Lisette pulled on her warmest coat and held out Jenny's wool jacket. 'It's dark,' she said. 'We don't want to be noticed.' Jenny shuddered as she pulled on her coat, and Lisette caught her arm. 'I know,' she muttered, 'about Monsieur Albrecht.'

Jenny shook her head, tears surging into her eyes. 'Nothing happened. Not yet. But he can't be trusted.'

The two girls clattered down the steps then moderated their footfalls on the grass verge along the side of the lane. Lisette led Jenny away from the main road and along the back of a row of cottages to the one at the very end, out of sight. 'I always come this way,' she whispered. She banged on the back door of the cottage, for Monsieur Kemener to crack the door open a few inches.

'Oui?'

'Madame Boiteux, she has pains,' Lisette said.

Jenny leaned forward. 'She is only eight months gone,' she said. 'The midwife said to tell her at once.'

'I'll go for the doctor, give him some warning,' he said, pulling on a jumper. 'My wife thinks she may have a difficult time.' He shouted for her.

The two girls and the midwife half ran up the hill, the girls carrying one of her bags each. 'She labours fast,' the woman panted. 'She said the last one was two hours. And these babies are small.'

'Can you save them?' Lisette said, hugging a bag to her chest.

'That's in God's hands,' she answered, and nodded to Jenny as she tapped on the front door. 'You'll help me, with Hélène. Jenny, is it?' Turning to Lisette, she said, 'We will need clean towels and spare sheets and plenty of hot water.'

'Stoke the boiler,' Jenny added, as Cook let them in. 'Then look after the children, they're bound to be frightened. Try and reassure them. Madame has done this before, and all was well.'

'Except last time,' Lisette said, her eyes wide open.

As Jenny followed the midwife up the stairs, carrying both heavy bags, she could hear a strange moaning and panting. It sounded like a wounded animal.

'It's not coming,' Madame cried, then was lost in her pain again, twisting in the bed, as if trying to find somewhere comfortable. Aunt Hélène put a damp cloth on her sweaty brow, murmured something reassuring.

The midwife was quick to throw up the blankets and delve under them, her gloved hand coming out bloody. 'She is almost ready to bring the first one. At least he is coming headfirst, poor babe. Warm some towels by the fire, child,' and with a start, Jenny realised she was talking to her.

Madame starting grunting and heaving, and Aunt Hélène and the midwife encouraged her.

'All is well,' the midwife crooned to her.

'No!' Madame shrieked.

The swollen belly, revealed by the midwife, convulsed again and she screamed.

'Now, Marthe, push with all your strength!'

Madame seemed beyond reason, but somehow she forced her head forward and strained, her face suddenly red with effort.

Something bloody and purple and shiny unfolded into Madame Kemener's hands, and she shouted in triumph. 'Well done, my dear!'

She roughly rubbed the baby in the oldest of the worn towels, repaired by Augustine months ago. A wavering cry made all of them, Jenny included, exhale with a whoosh of relief. The midwife did things with scissors and string and held up the tiny child to show Madame.

'He is strong. Big for a twin, my dear. Rest for a minute. You will have to work hard again soon.'

She turned to Jenny without a change of expression and said, in a low voice, 'The German doctor, if you can. Madame needs help.' She had a fixed smile on her face as she said, 'Here, let his mother hold him for a minute. A little suckle wouldn't hurt, if he will take the breast.'

Jenny slipped out of the door and her aunt followed her. 'Just go up to the garrison,' she muttered. 'Scream and cry, do what you have to, to get their attention.'

'No, I can't,' Jenny started to shake. 'You don't know what you're asking, they won't listen.'

'A woman will die, very likely her baby too. We need help. She is already bleeding.' Aunt Hélène grabbed Jenny and shook her. 'I would go in your place, if I could. But perhaps the Kommandant or his wife will be there. The woman has children of her own.'

Lisette had been waiting in the shadows at the bottom of the stairs. 'I know how to get to the Kommandant,' she said, in a whisper. 'I have a friend, Hans.'

'Your lover,' Hélène said. 'If he can help in any way...'

'He's on guard duty at the north gate of the garrison until midnight,' the girl said, her face unusually pale in the shadows. 'I can ask him to help.'

'He won't be allowed to leave his post,' said Jenny, wrenching her jacket on.

'No, but they have a field telephone,' she answered. 'Let me go. I won't be long.'

Jenny was shaking inside, her hands cold. 'I'll come too. At least the Gestapo might listen to me, if no one else will.'

So the two of them crept out again. Sea mist had rolled in, making the shaded lamp Hélène had pressed upon them glow, twisting the light into ghostly dancers whirling in front of them.

'The north gate is right up over the common land,' Lisette said in a subdued voice.

'This young man of yours. It's a dangerous game to play.'

'Hans is Bavarian. He was conscripted. He's my age, he hates the German barracks, everyone bullies him.'

'But he's still a German soldier.' Jenny felt strangely young and innocent suddenly. 'Have you...?'

'No!' Lisette said, her voice suddenly infused with nervous laughter. 'We want to marry, after the war.' Her voice dropped, lost its animation. 'If we both survive.'

The north gate was attended not just by Hans, but also by two others, smoking in the fog, the ends of their cigarettes glowing.

'Halt!' The words were barked in German.

'I am sorry, officer,' Jenny said. 'We need help.'

'A girl,' some man said, and the timbre of his voice changed. 'To warm us up. Come here, let us see you.'

'I am Mademoiselle Huon,' Jenny said, letting her voice come out hard and cool. 'We need the doctor sent to the Villa de Mezareun, on the harbour lane. My mistress is in labour and may die.'

A young man Jenny half recognised stepped forward and turned to Lisette, opening a gate. 'Go through to the garrison office, I'll call ahead for the adjutant. He can authorise getting the doctor. Follow the path to the light.'

'Thank you,' Jenny said with fervour. Lisette gave him a lingering look and turned away.

'He must really love you,' Jenny said, jogging down the level part of the path.

'I pray to God that the war ends fast,' Lisette said, surprising Jenny. 'Since we have come here I've started to pray more. I even go to church, sometimes.'

'Does it help?' Jenny asked, rounding the high fence surrounding the old governor's house.

Lisette shrugged. 'Sometimes.' She tucked her arm into Jenny's. 'We'll do this together.'

The door opened at their first knock, and a man Jenny didn't recognise ushered them into the hall. Jenny dared not look towards Albrecht's closed office as they were led up broad stairs to a pleasant apartment and Kommandant Richter, who was playing a card game with his wife.

'Girls,' the woman said, looking up as they came in. 'Tell me, how is Madame Boiteux? Had she had the baby?'

'She has had a boy, Madame, but he is a twin,' Jenny said. 'The midwife thinks Madame is very unwell, and the second baby hadn't arrived when we left. She asks for a doctor. She doesn't think ours can save her.'

Jenny burst into tears at a sudden vision of Madame fighting for her babies and her own life.

'Ah, you poor child!' Frau Richter said. 'Such a lot of responsibility for young girls. Otto, can we send the garrison physician to help? I'm sure it would gain us a lot of goodwill with the villagers.' She fell into German, and the Kommandant eventually barked an order to the man who had brought them in.

'He will follow you with his medical equipment,' he said. 'But you must get back. This is not the place for you.' He nodded sternly to the man.

But as he looked at Jenny, she saw the tiniest smile.

38

PRESENT DAY, 2 APRIL

On the way back around the island from Seal Cove, Charlotte was regularly updating her phone in case Robert or Justin had sent any news.

'Why are Daddy and Pops away?' Merryn said again, gazing out to sea and shading her eyes.

'They just need to do something important,' Charlotte said. 'And Grandma Olivia will be coming to look after you, at high tide.'

'Is it something bad?' Billy chipped in, causing even Merryn's musical humming to pause.

'No, of course not. It's something good.'

Merryn stood in the middle of the slab that had once held the lighthouse tower, about ten metres across in all directions, now cracked and draped with brambles and seedling shrubs. 'Maybe it's a puppy!' she said, putting her arms out and spinning around.

'Maybe it's two puppies!' Billy chimed in. 'We can have one each.'

Billy and Merryn were swapping names for their puppies or ponies or unicorns when she felt Beau's presence just by her arm. 'Is something wrong?'

He looked so anxious. She checked the younger children were far enough away not to hear, and turned to him. 'There's a chance they are going to adopt a little baby.'

He nodded, but the anxiety was still there. 'Like Merryn's adopted?'

'That's right.'

Beau looked over at Billy. 'Someone might want to adopt Billy,' he said, his voice so resigned it tore at her heart. 'He's funny and nice and he smiles all the time.'

Charlotte bent down to his level. 'He's a baby, that's all. You, on the other hand, are kind, and brilliant with animals and good at maths. Anyone would be lucky to have you.'

He gave her a look that cut through all the sugar she was trying to pour into his life. 'No one wants a nearly nine-year-old black boy. I heard a social worker say it.'

Charlotte looked at him as if she was seeing him for the first time. His cheeks were thin, his face long and elegant, his cheekbones high. His eyes were brown but had flecks of green in them. He put his head on one side, and the slightest trace of humour flickered across his face.

It's all in there, banked down. He's a remarkable child.

Her phone beeped, a message from Tink. 'There's a ewe in labour, if you want to come and help,' she read out loud.

Beau came to life. 'Get the littlies!' he shouted and shot ahead of her down the path to the lane.

'Come on, Billy, Merryn. Shall we go and see the lambs?'

By the time they got there, Tink was looking sombre and put a hand out to stop Beau. 'Wait a minute. We're not sure the lambs are OK. Maybe you should go and help Corinne?'

'I want to see.'

Charlotte handed Merryn and Billy off to Corinne, who

invited them to see the older lambs. She looked at Tink, who shrugged his shoulders.

'Sometimes, the lambs just don't make it, Beau,' he said, as if man to man. 'It's part of farming. It doesn't look good.'

'I know,' the boy said, feet apart, unconsciously mimicking Tink. 'It's nature.'

Tink nodded, and set off for the shelter he'd erected for lambing.

Charlotte felt sick and dizzy. She was less prepared to see the birth of a dead lamb than Beau was. The ewe was grunting and straining, something poking out of the back of it. Dizzy with adrenaline, she turned away and slumped onto a hay bale.

'Miss! Miss!' Beau was looking over at her.

'I'm fine,' she said. 'Look after the sheep.'

But she couldn't tear her eyes away as Tink put on a long glove, got Beau to stand clear and did something with the bits of the lamb sticking out. After a few minutes of the ewe bellowing in distress, a dark shape slithered out. Tink told Beau to pass him a cloth. He rubbed the lamb vigorously, but even Charlotte could see it was dead. It looked horrible, its face swollen, tongue sticking out and blackened. Beau had tears rolling down his face, and Tink's shoulders were hunched in defeat, but it wasn't until the sheep turned around to nuzzle the dead baby that Charlotte started crying. Not discreet tears, proper sobbing.

'Beau, stand at this end,' Tink said sharply. 'There you go, quick. Is that one foot or two?'

The boy, without hesitation, felt with his bare hand. 'I think it's two feet and a nose.'

'Come on, Maisie, *push*!' Tink's voice was soon joined by Beau's, and when two crossed forelegs poked out, Beau grabbed them without hesitation. As Maisie heaved and bellowed, Beau pulled, and before Charlotte's eyes the boy caught another lamb, smaller than the first. He dropped to his knees and held out a hand for the cloth, still stained with its twin's blood.

'Clear his mouth first,' Tink said, crouching alongside the boy. 'Rub nice and hard.'

The little creature heaved its whole body with its first breath. Tink stood, covered the dead lamb with an armful of straw and manoeuvred the ewe around to see its baby. When the lamb bleated a high, wavery cry, Charlotte collapsed into sobbing again. Beau cheered, and he and Tink high-fived.

By the time the lamb had been introduced to Billy and Merryn, he was wobbling to his feet and the children were coming up with names. Tink discreetly removed the dead lamb and Beau organised food and water for the tired Maisie.

'I'm sorry, kids, we have to go,' Charlotte said. 'Your grandma will be on the island by now, Merryn. I'll take you home.'

'You cried,' Beau chuckled. 'You ugly cried like a baby.'

Charlotte helped Billy over the gate and Tink lifted Merryn over.

'I did,' she said, resigned to having no credibility as a teacher. On the other hand, she had never seen Beau so animated and relaxed. 'Snot and tears and everything. I even got hiccoughs.'

'We did give you the towel,' he said, giggling again.

'Yes, very kind,' she said, recalling the blood-stained rags. 'I prefer my own tissues, though. Say goodbye to Tink, kids.'

She walked around the corner of the pub to the shore path, which led to the beach in front of the hotel.

'Will the baby be all right? Merryn's brother?' Beau asked, his fingers catching a little of her sleeve.

'I hope so. I think so. They wouldn't have been told to go over unless he was.'

'What will they call him?'

Charlotte smiled and looked over at Billy and Merryn. Billy

was wearing Merryn's pink unicorn backpack and they were still talking names. 'Hopefully not Barnaby Butt Fluff,' she said, and caught Beau's gaze. 'I *hope* that's for the lamb.'

'Will his daddies get to choose his name?'

'Maybe.' She slowed down. 'The birth mother might want to name him, even though she can't look after him. She will want him to be loved.'

'Like that lamb.' She could see his long eyelashes shielding his downcast eyes,

She stopped and turned to look at him. 'If that lamb died, the sheep might have taken on an orphan lamb. If the sheep died, maybe one of the other ewes would adopt him. It happens in all sorts of animals.'

'Or Tink and Corinne could bottle feed him.'

She nodded her head, hearing Merryn squealing in excitement as they reached Olivia, waiting outside the hotel.

She squeezed his slim shoulders. 'I'm going to make sure you find the very best family. I promise.'

Even as she spoke, she was caught between two equally unanswerable ideas. How was she going to make good on her promise?

And how am I ever going to let them go?

39

JUNE 1941

When Jenny and Lisette reached the house, the local doctor was already there, and had set up the bed to help Madame. Everything was draped with white sheets, almost the same colour as Madame's face, her eyes closed, lying flat on what looked like a waterproof sheet from the nursery.

'Is she...?' Jenny asked, wondering if it was all over, until Madame sighed. 'The German doctor is coming from the garrison.'

Dr Le Tallec seemed to sag. 'Thank God,' he said. 'I can administer the anaesthetic, but someone else should operate. I've only seen the operation done, not performed it myself.'

Jenny caught sight of a basket of bloody cloths piled in the corner of the room.

'The bleeding has slowed,' the midwife said, entering behind Jenny. 'But the baby's heart is just a flicker now. He must come out, now, if he is to have a chance.'

'Can you save the mother?' Jenny addressed her question directly to the doctor.

'If I didn't think there was a chance for her, I would have

rescued the baby already,' he said. 'But she needs a transfusion, and I've never done one.'

The bang on the door heralded the appearance of a spare man in his forties, who seemed to make an immediate and wordless assessment of the patient, feeling her pulse, palpating her abdomen. The two doctors communicated with a little German, a little French and a lot of medical terms. The German turned to address Jenny and Hélène, and Lisette in the doorway.

'We will attempt a Caesarean, you understand? To get the baby out. Then we will try and save the mother.'

A mask was placed over Madame's face; a sweet, chemical smell infused the room and the women were waved aside as the doctors donned gloves and masks. Madame's poor, swollen abdomen was exposed with no dignity, and sprayed with something acrid; within seconds, the German doctor had cut a long, red line into her belly. Lisette gagged and Hélène sent her away, but Jenny was fascinated. Deeper and deeper he cut, each slice a perfect echo of the first, digging his hands into the hole, stretching and pulling and feeling his way. Then one more cut and a great gush of liquid and blood and the baby was out, held in a cloth and handed without ceremony to the midwife. She went into the dressing room and Jenny followed, grabbing a towel. This time, rubbing and cleaning didn't wake the flat, limp baby into life, and the midwife blew into his tiny chest: one, two, three.

'Keep rubbing,' she said to Jenny. 'I'll get some warm water. I think he still has a heartbeat.'

The baby twitched a little, and Jenny redoubled her efforts, remembering her Uncle Joe with his new lambs. The baby's chest moved a little, then the mouth wavered open and a little squeak escaped. In sheer relief and a wave of love, Jenny wrapped the baby up and snuggled it against her, pulling her cardigan around them both. It didn't cry, but she could see its mouth open when it breathed, and finally it opened dark blue eyes and stared up at her.

'Well done,' the German doctor said, walking in with a syringe. 'Now, I need a sample of your blood.'

'I don't even know if it's another boy or a girl,' Jenny said. 'How is Madame?'

He didn't answer, just pointed at her arm to roll up her sleeve. The needle stung like it was red hot. He made eye contact, and his face was sombre. 'She's not good,' he said as he returned to the bedroom with a syringe of Jenny's blood.

As the baby began to look around, the midwife washed it. She also discovered it was a girl, red-haired like Adela. Jenny got a clean towel and a blanket to keep the tiny baby warm, and a knitted bonnet to fit over her damp curls.

'Here, you.' The doctor came, shaking a test tube containing blood. 'You can be a donor for your mistress, you and the housekeeper.'

Jenny followed the doctor back to the room. Madame's belongings had been swept into a pile in the corner and her dressing table turned into a laboratory.

'You will have to give blood,' Dr Le Tallec said, pointing at Jenny, and told her to pull up her sleeves. He stared down at the baby in the midwife's arms, his smile widening. 'Two healthy babies. If that is all we get, by the will of God, that is already enough.' He stretched a length of the tubing around Jenny's arm.

'Will this save Madame?' Jenny looked over at Aunt Hélène, whose blood was flowing down a rubber tube into a bottle.

'We have stopped the bleeding,' Dr Le Tallec said, 'and repaired the wound. Herr Doctor is an excellent surgeon. He saved her life but now she is very weak. If she is to have a chance, we must replace the saline we are running in with good

Breton blood.' He stabbed a needle into Jenny's arm and the blood flowed quickly. 'Let me know if you feel faint.'

By the time she did start to feel dizzy, Lisette had reported that both babies were well, if under five pounds each. Finally, just when she felt quite faint, the needle was taken out and the blood taken away. When Jenny felt able to open her eyes, a bottle of blood was flowing into her mistress. Madame's face was still pale, but the fish-belly white had gone, and her lips were no longer lavender blue.

'It's too dangerous to transfuse her with more,' the German doctor said. 'I can't guarantee it's enough. Leave her to sleep. I will see her in the morning, to inspect the incision.'

Dr Le Tallec, his fingers still on Madame's wrist, nodded. 'It is in the hands of God, now,' he said.

'You did the right thing, asking me to come,' the German doctor said. 'I will talk to the Kommandant about running a clinic in the town. I have time.'

'Thank you,' Jenofeve whispered.

40

PRESENT DAY, 5 APRIL

By Wednesday, the routine of school was a relief from all the dramas of the weekend. Merryn was very excited, as her new baby brother was travelling to the island that day. It was no longer a secret, and everyone was talking about it.

Charlotte was really enjoying the challenge of teaching children aged nearly five, six, eight and almost eleven through one area of interest at a time. Although the school building was old and needed replacing, she couldn't imagine depriving the children of full-time education. Today, she had pulled the much-thumbed *Animals and Plants in British Rockpools* off the shelves. Patience Ellis, the author, had been a resident teacher at the school back in the fifties and had lived in the schoolhouse.

As the weather was good, and she had Joanna for support, they decided to take the children down to Seal Cove again, where there were some rockpools exposed at low tide. She'd found a couple of ancient nets in one of the cupboards, and a few buckets and a couple of more modern identification books and charts for seashore plants and animals.

She had made some treasure hunt sheets, laminated them

and provided whiteboard pens, for the adults as well as the children.

'One point for each species of small invertebrates,' she said to Joanna. 'Ten points for each fish or crab species. And a point for each type of seaweed.'

'What about a giant squid?' Billy said, eyes wide. 'Or a shark?'

She considered. 'One hundred points for anything bigger than me,' she announced. 'And a thousand points if it eats you.'

While the children were chattering and walking down the steps to the cove – even Beau was talking to Rhiannon – Charlotte started taking pictures of the group. Just for her own memories, she rationalised. Because this was a truly happy day. She felt a twinge as she thought about closing the school; it was like touching a bruise.

At first, the children were more interested in the little sand-swept building. Charlotte still found it oddly creepy, and evocative of something just out of her memory's reach.

'Maybe it's Stone Age,' Beau suggested. 'It's made of stones.'

'Well, so is the schoolhouse,' she reminded him. 'No, that's a good guess but this is much more recent. Do you know anything about it, Joanna?'

The teaching assistant hesitated. 'Just rumours, really. He died before I moved here.'

'Who did?' Rhiannon was as engaged as the others, which Charlotte was pleased to see.

'Well, he was a bit of a hermit. He made a little home for himself down here and lived off the seafood on the shore.' Joanna shrugged her shoulders. 'I don't remember his name, but he was supposed to be a criminal who decided to spend his last years down here.'

'I heard he was a bit of a hero,' Charlotte said. She pointed out to the rocks closer to the shoreline. 'Come on, we don't want the tide to come back in before we find some crabs.'

. . .

An hour later, Charlotte was soaking from having slipped over twice, and she was covered in wet sand, her hair drifting into her eyes and mouth as she checked the children's catches. Joanna, who had stayed dry, consulted the books.

'Tompot blenny, what a lovely name for such a strange little fish! Billy, that's a shrimp, I don't know what type, I'll take another picture... Ooh, that fish is a Cornish sucker, look at him wriggle!'

Billy had found the most species and specialised in all the shells and anemones; Rhiannon had caught the most crabs and squat lobsters, even though she couldn't bear to handle them and had to scoop them up in a net. Beau identified all the birds on the shore, some of which were flying over to see what they were doing. Even Merryn, who had dressed in purple dungarees and her unicorn wellies, was getting her fingers in the sand and finding interesting stones and seaweeds.

'I'm a mermaid,' she announced, trailing strands of emerald green plant over her shoulder.

'That's sea lettuce,' Joanna announced, showing them the book.

'The tide's creeping back and we don't want to get cut off from the steps,' Charlotte announced. 'Time to pack up. We'd better let those creatures go somewhere safe or the seagulls will eat them.'

'There's no such thing as seagulls!' the children and Joanna chorused for about the tenth time.

'What are they, then, Beau?' Charlotte said, resigned.

He had brought a laminated illustration of seabirds from the classroom. 'Herring gulls, black-headed gulls and those on the corner are waders, oystercatchers.'

It was strange how he could read the names of the birds but failed so badly on other books.

'I like their red legs,' she said, as she packed up the supplies.

With only a few minutes wasted on persuading Billy that they couldn't keep a hermit crab as a pet, and a crisis when Merryn got her boots stuck in wet sand, they retreated to the tideline to see who had won. As no one had kept score and Billy was certain he had seen a giant octopus, just in the shallows, they were all announced winners and set off up the beach to go back for lunch. Charlotte turned to the steps.

Ash was standing there. Her heart leapt as she staggered back.

'Oh, I didn't know anyone else was here!' She pressed her hand over her galloping heart and laughed.

The children all wanted to tell him what they had found, and he gave his attention equally between them, even Rhiannon joined in.

'I didn't mean to intrude. I was just going for a walk and I heard someone shouting.'

'That was Merryn, she got her boots stuck. Do you know Joanna? This is Ash.'

'I've heard all about you,' Joanna said. 'Are you working at the hotel?'

'Just about to start, tomorrow. I'm going to help out at the campsite, too.' He grinned at the children. 'This looks much more fun than being in the classroom.'

'Rhiannon's really come out of her shell since you've been teaching her,' Joanna confided as they started up the steps.

'I'm glad.' It was easy to like Rhiannon, unsubtly honest and book-smart, caring and funny. 'Maybe one day she'll be ready to tackle the secondary school.'

'I hope so,' Joanna said. 'It's a small school, it's very friendly. And I think she's intelligent enough to get past all the social stuff.'

They stood as a group at the top of the steps, the wind

rattling their clothes and tugging at their hair now they were out of the shelter of the cove.

'We're just going to have our lunch,' Billy said, grabbing Ash's hand. 'You should come.'

'Oh, we don't know if he has time...' Charlotte tried to say, but a cacophony of arguments drowned her out. 'All right! But ask him nicely, and if he's busy that's OK.'

Billy grinned up at him. 'Please?'

'That would be lovely,' Ash said, with a little bow to the children. 'Race you!' and set off in such slow motion so even Merryn passed him.

Charlotte was out of breath by the time she got back to the school. She was suddenly aware that she was sweaty, her curls were a bird's nest and her face was probably red. Ash wasn't even out of breath. She was struck by how athletic he looked, tall and slim and younger than her.

'Deep-sea diving must keep you fit,' she said, after she'd unlocked the classroom door and shouted for the kids to take off their shoes by the porch, and for everyone to wash their hands.

'It's very hard on the body,' he said. 'I'm thinking of giving it up.'

'Really?' Charlotte hung her coat up and slipped off her boots.

'Well, I'll have to if I get custody of the boys.'

She stalled. 'Have you talked to social services yet?'

'The social worker is looking into it.'

She beckoned him over to the corner of the room, by the rabbit. 'I spoke to Traci. She's looking into Beau's Aunt Beverley as well.'

'All I know about Beau's family is that they are focused on academic achievement, and very strict. Chloe didn't get on with them.'

Charlotte checked Joanna was getting the kids set up with

their lunches, wiping off odd bits of sand and quieting Billy down. Beau was watching them closely.

'Come into the schoolhouse. I'll make you a sandwich.'

Charlotte led the way into the tiny cottage. Ash looked at the foldout bed and the tiny sofa and smiled. 'It's really small.'

'We manage.' Charlotte started buttering bread. 'Is ham and cheese OK?'

'Just cheese, thanks,' he answered, looking around at the books on the shelves, the toys on the window sill. 'I can't believe how quickly they've both settled in.'

'I know. They are lovely children. You must be proud of them.'

'I really am.' He turned to face her. 'Look, Chloe was a lovely person, wild, funny, loyal to the boys. But she hated to feel hemmed in, committed.'

She managed a hollow laugh. 'Trust me, we all do.'

'That sounds painful.'

She sliced the cheese. 'Recent break-up. In fact, he's only just left the island.'

'Are you talking about the surfer dude who was staying at the pub? The local gossip – you must know you are a hot topic – says he's your ex. How long were you together?'

Her hands stalled. 'Nearly fifteen years. Since we were at university, since we were kids, really.'

'So, what happened?'

'I thought we were talking about you.'

He smiled then, a slow lift of his lips into a curve. Her heart skipped a little in her chest. It was a long time since she'd noticed another man.

She smiled back. 'We just wanted different things as we grew up.'

'Me too.' He looked down at his feet, struck quiet by some thought or memory. 'Chloe was just a child, right to the end. A lovely, fragile, enchanting child.'

'Why did you break up?'

He took a deep breath and looked back up at her. 'She couldn't cope with me going away for six weeks at a time. She said she got too lonely. She eventually met this guy, older than her. I think he was the one who hit Beau. I got the blame, but I wasn't even in the country at the time. So you see why I want to fight for them.'

'Will you have somewhere to live?'

He took the plate she handed him. 'I have savings, I could find somewhere. I would have to change my job, but I could manage.'

'What else would you like to do?' she said, as they sat down at the tiny table.

'Well, I started out as a navy diver. Did quite well, then I realised I could have more time off if I worked on oil rigs.'

'You don't look old enough to have had several careers.'

'Same career, different venues. I'm thirty-one, if you're fishing,' he said, this time smiling full on, holding her gaze until she looked away, clearing her throat.

'What's it like? Deep-sea diving?'

He chuckled. 'People find it creepy that we work in intense cold, complete darkness and we could die at any moment. I can't think why.'

She shivered at the thought. 'It sounds terrifying. You must see loads of animals down there, though.'

'We do. Some sharks, big fish, octopus. Some very odd creatures, not like the ones in your rockpools.' He took a huge bite of his sandwich.

'Look, it's highly unlikely I'm going to be able to get the kids to do any maths today. Can I interest you in talking to them for a bit? I can look up animals on the computer to show them, if you like. Nothing *too* scary.'

'I'd be happy to.' He hesitated while she finished her food. 'I just have one question, really. Why did they ask *you* to foster the boys?'

'There wasn't another appropriate adult available and I was on the island. And I didn't want them to end up being separated,' she said as they both took their empty plates to the sink.

He seemed to stare right into her, which made her feel breathless. The small room made them stand very close. 'Neither do I.'

'They are lovely children. Extraordinary little people, really.'

He nodded and stepped closer. 'Can I ask you to put in a good word for me to take them?'

'I-I don't think I would be allowed to get involved,' she stammered. 'I mean, I'm not impartial.'

'Because if they go to Beau's aunt, their lives will be completely different.' He stayed close, looking into her eyes. He was taller than she had thought, and she could feel the warmth from his body. 'I love those boys like my own. That's what they deserve, not a kind aunt bringing them up out of duty or pity. I *know* them.'

She nodded, feeling suffocated. He wasn't intimidating, but his intensity was disturbing. 'I have no doubt that you love them. You're here, away from your job, just to fight for them.'

He looked over his shoulder as he walked to the door. 'That ought to count for something, don't you think?'

41

JUNE 1941

The following day brought anxiety and relief in equal measure. Madame survived the night. The midwife managed to get the babies to suckle from their semi-conscious mother, whose experience or instincts made her attempt to cradle them. But her fever rose, making her teeth chatter in her sleep and her wits wander when she woke. Dr Le Tallec, who had only left her at dawn and returned after breakfast, redressed the wound, which seemed to bring relief, and gave her medicines to reduce her pain.

Jenny was exhausted when she went out to the summer house that evening, not to look for notes but to have a few moments to herself. She had soaked and boiled Madame's sheets. She had not known the human body could hold so much blood. A hiss made her jump and look around.

Laurie's voice came through the open window, echoing around the summer house, with its garden chairs and old tennis net and rackets. 'It's me.'

'Go away,' she said, too tired to care about whatever message he carried or which ships were in danger. 'You're mad coming here,' she said. 'The Germans are visiting the house today, and we have two Polish workers in the attic. Nowhere is safe.'

'We know what they are building at the old battery,' he said. 'They are laying a minefield around a new radar and radio post. I have to let my superiors in London know. They might want to launch a raid.'

'Didn't you hear me?' she hissed back. 'I'm too tired to talk. My mistress nearly died last night, and I am threatened by—' She couldn't say the words. Dealing with Albrecht had haunted her dreams. 'I wish I was home.' Her voice broke and her vision blurred with tears.

She heard the softest of squeaks as the door opened, and then she was caught up in his arms, her cheek against the rough wool of a fisherman's jumper and the sharpness of salt.

'Someone will see,' she whispered, tears running down her face.

'Let them. I am Yann Seznec, engineer on the ferry, known for my drunkenness and bad temper.'

She lifted her face to see him. 'We'll get caught. The Gestapo are interested in me, they could be watching the house.'

'We'll both be back in England by then,' he said. 'We're putting together as much information as you'll be able to carry, and we're going to rendezvous with a British ship in three weeks, weather permitting.'

'It will be a dark moon again,' she said.

'That will stop German fighters using us for target practice,' he said. 'They are arranging a distraction – there's an operation going on the north coast. Let's move, someone will eventually notice us. Come outside.'

Once they'd slid around the back of the building, he put his arms around her again and this time she looked up, put a finger on his lips. 'Jenny...' he sighed, and kissed her.

'Laurie, I missed you so much...' she murmured, curving her

arms around his waist, kissing him again. She could feel how thin he was. 'The Gestapo know my mother is British.'

'I know,' he whispered. 'The whole town is talking about it. Albrecht and his devil dog are dangerous. He's looking into people's personal lives, their history. He's decided to ship a Jewish family off the island, the Kellers.'

'No!' Jenny could see the children in her mind's eye, their new 'J' in their identity papers, and the haunted expression on their mother's face at the school. 'Can we get them to the mainland? They are too conspicuous on the island. They can't be sent to a labour camp.'

'Or worse,' Laurie said, hugging her close and burying his face in her hair. 'Intelligence is coming in about Germans killing Jews and gypsies.'

Jenny let herself be held for a long moment, then pulled away, looking up into his eyes. 'Can't your people take them instead of me?'

'What? No. It's all arranged, there's just room for you and me and two other agents. And a lot of intelligence.' He hesitated then, as if unable to say something.

'Laurie? What is it?'

'We'll do what we can to protect the Kellers,' he said, urgently, his hands on her shoulders, shaking them with each word. 'But we can't save everyone. We have to make sacrifices in order to achieve the greater good.'

'And one of those sacrifices might be Jewish children, who were born on the island, whose family has been here for generations?' She pulled away. 'Am I one of those sacrifices? Will I become Wolfgang Albrecht's mistress to avert suspicion?'

'Will that make him more or less mistrustful of you?' he asked, his jaw set. 'Hopefully, you can hold him off until we will get you to safety.'

'But if I can't?'

His face creased up with rage, or maybe disgust. 'This is a

reality of war,' he said, finally. 'Women are being abused all over Europe, by all sides. I can't keep you safe but the Kommandant is a decent fellow, he might intervene.'

'He's afraid of the Gestapo,' she said. 'There are more now, a whole group. No one can stand up to them.'

He pulled her back into his arms but this time his kisses didn't distract her. 'I will do something,' he mumbled into her hair. 'Just keep him at arm's length, use anything as an excuse, illness, or something...'

'I'll try,' she said, more to reassure him than herself.

Madame Boiteux was very ill for a week. Each evening she got more feverish and muddled, and she slept every morning, just rousing herself to feed the twins. A woman from the neighbouring island had given birth recently, and had been rowed over to help feed the babies. Her own child seemed twice their size, but as long as the twins were warm they were lively and hungry enough.

Jenny spent a lot of time rocking the cradle, staying out of the way of any visitors. Once Madame was well enough to sit out in a chair and have something solid to eat, Frau Richter came to visit. Her gentle conversation didn't overtire Madame. The two women seemed to find something in common and Frau Richter admired the babies when Jenny brought them in. She stared at Jenny for a long moment.

'Is it true that your mother is English?' she said, her voice neutral.

'We wouldn't say so, Madame,' Jenny said, dipping into a little curtsy to flatter the woman. 'She is Cornish, not English.'

'Ah, I see,' the woman said, her face brightening. 'Like Breton people – you do not think of yourselves as truly French.'

'Indeed, Madame. I was born here, and my father is Breton. I am a citizen of Brittany.'

It felt very strange to deny the island of her childhood, of her heart.

'You must miss your parents,' the woman said.

'I do.' The lies she had been coached in pressed to the fore of her mind. 'My father is dead, Madame. He was a fisherman.'

'Your mother, then?'

'She cares for my frail grandmother,' Jenny said. Her grandmother, the matriarch of the family and strong as an ox. Once, when her husband's trawler had started to sink a mile from shore, she had taken a couple of lads and rowed a pilot gig against the tide to fetch them. The memory of them all made Jenny's eyes fill with tears. Frau Richter's expression softened.

'You have been a good girl, and have saved your mistress,' she said. 'But, for your own safety, you should stay in the house or the garden. Our soldiers are searching the island for rebels and spies. With your Cornish mother, you are bound to be suspected.'

'Thank you, Madame,' Jenny said, managing another curtsey before carefully lifting the babies. 'I'll put them down to sleep, if you wish?'

'Thank you, Jenofeve,' Madame Boiteux said, leaning back against her pillows.

Jenny carried the babies up, smelling their hair, feeling the girl wriggle in her blanket. How could she abandon them, and throw suspicion on the whole family?

42

PRESENT DAY, 6 APRIL

After school, Charlotte braced herself for a visit from Beau's aunt, Beverley Goodwin. She had arranged to come over and chat with the boys along with Traci, to help her decide if she could offer them a home.

Charlotte was troubled by the situation. She was impressed by Ash's easy relationship with the boys and his commitment to them. Giving up a job which earned him up to a thousand pounds a day was mind-boggling. He'd made the children laugh with his stories of nosy fish and dolphins following his boat, and the time when a tiny sea spider wandered over his magnifying mask and scared him. As the story went on, the actual size of the spider got smaller and smaller until even Merryn was laughing about it.

Getting back to teaching core subjects was necessary and important, if dull even for Charlotte. Both boys were progressing with reading and playing word games, which drew on Beau's strength at recognising animal names in books. She spent some time getting their school records up to date, while Beau copied out the symbols in Byers' diary, published online by the museum.

After the girls had gone home and Beau was tidying up the classroom, Charlotte just had time to straighten Billy up before Traci arrived at the door. Mrs Goodwin was a tall, heavily built woman in a tweed suit, tights and flat shoes. She looked the epitome of sensible. Her skin was darker than Beau's, her hair in neat curls framing her face, with bright blue glasses. She looked down on the boys as they froze, Billy moving close to Charlotte.

'This is your Aunt Beverley,' Traci said, with a cheerful voice that set Charlotte's teeth on edge. 'What would you like to be called, Mrs Goodwin?'

'I think Mrs Goodwin would be fine to begin with,' the woman said. She looked around for an adult-sized chair, and Charlotte pulled out one from behind her desk. 'Do you remember me, Beaumont? I remember you. I have some pictures from your birthday when you were little, if you would like to see them.'

She stopped talking and stared over at Charlotte. Billy clutched the back of her top and she detached his fingers from her shirt.

'Why don't I go and make your favourite sandwiches for tea?' she said, crouching down to his height. 'All you have to do is chat to these nice ladies. OK?'

'Don't want to,' he whispered.

'Do it for me, sweetheart. Nothing bad is going to happen, just a talk.'

He put his finger back in his mouth, always a sign that he was unhappy. ''Kay.'

Charlotte straightened up. 'You could introduce Mrs Goodwin and Traci to the rabbit. But don't let him out, you know how hard he is to catch.'

She smiled at both women and left, shutting the door behind her with exaggerated care. Then she blew out all the air that had somehow got trapped in her chest.

She started making tea. Billy had an addiction to processed

food and fish fingers were a favourite. She found she was shaking with reaction to the threat of Mrs Goodwin's appearance. It didn't make sense; the best thing for the boys would be a loving and caring family to give them stability in their childhood. Compared to Ash, though, the older woman seemed rather cool and formal. First impressions can be misleading, she told herself. She just wanted what was best for the boys after their terrible losses. She hadn't felt this nervous since a ballet examination when she was eleven. *This is ridiculous.*

She just had time to give the kitchen a quick wipe, box up Beau's brick construction on the table and put a few loose clothes away before there was a tap at the door. The boys barrelled in without looking her in the eye, Billy heading for the bathroom and Beau bolting upstairs.

'Miss Kingston,' Mrs Goodwin said, coming in and gazing around. She looked appalled at the conditions she saw. 'May I sit down?'

Traci followed her in. 'We just have a few minutes. We don't want to miss the water taxi.'

Charlotte ignored her, locking eyes with Mrs Goodwin. 'Please have a seat.' She wasn't going to apologise about the mess. *This is what a tiny home with two small boys looks like.*

'My family is very different from Chloe's,' Mrs Goodwin said without preamble. 'When my brother Edward left Chloe, we offered to take the boy. He felt bringing Beaumont up in a good family would be the best start possible for him. I have brought up four boys and a daughter of my own, all have focused on their studies and are doing well.'

'I see.' Charlotte looked at Traci, but she was hovering by the door, obviously uncomfortable. 'Beau has had a terrible year...'

'But there is a silver lining, even in the saddest of circumstances. Beaumont can grow up in a prosperous family with structure and discipline. Opportunities.'

Silver lining to his mother's death? Charlotte processed the woman's words, feeling her shoulders tense. She folded her arms. 'You keep talking about Beau. But what about Billy?'

'William isn't part of our family,' she said with certainty. 'Of course the boys will want to keep in regular contact and we would be very open to that.'

'Beau is all the family that Billy has left,' Charlotte said, looking from one woman to the other. 'You can't split them up.'

Traci stepped in, her voice wavering. 'Of course, social services would be doing everything possible to place the boys together.'

Mrs Goodwin stood up again, looked around with the same distaste. 'That would be a confidential discussion between my family and the social workers. We won't bother the boys' *teacher* with the details.'

Charlotte found her voice. And her temper. 'I'm not just Billy and Beau's teacher. I am their de facto foster parent, and I will fight to give the boys the best life possible. And that means together.' The faintest hint of smoke reminded her of the fish fingers in the oven, whose thermostat was unreliable. 'Now, you must excuse me, I have two growing boys to feed and you don't want to miss your *tide*.'

The word came out like a pistol shot. She found her coolest smile and held out her hand. Mrs Goodwin shook it, possibly involuntarily.

'We have a claim, as his blood relations,' she snapped, dropping Charlotte's hand.

'I think the children's welfare is the most important factor here,' Charlotte said, through tight lips. 'And their wishes. Not to mention their prior and loving relationship with their stepfather.'

'The man who beat them?'

'The boys say otherwise,' Charlotte said, crisply. She took a deep breath and fixed on a smile. 'Good day.'

. . .

After Traci and Mrs Goodwin left, Charlotte found herself shaking once again, this time with adrenaline, anxiety and rage. *Separate them?* The only uncomplicated relationship the boys had was with each other. She rescued the fish fingers – only the edges had caught.

Billy slid out of the bathroom, where he'd obviously been hiding. His lip was trembling and his eyelashes sparkled with tears. The front of his trousers was soaked, the first accident he'd had for a while.

'Oh, baby, don't get upset. Let me get some wipes.' She pulled his lower garments off and he stepped out of his socks too. She shouted up the stairs. 'Beau? Can you get Billy's pyjamas, please?'

A clatter on the stairs heralded Beau. 'You told that horrible old witch!' he said with relish.

'Who's Beaumont?' Billy stepped into the clean clothes, clutching her arm for balance.

'I am,' Beau said. 'Like your proper name is William.'

'I don't like William.' Billy frowned. 'I'm always Billy.'

Charlotte buttered some bread and got the ketchup out of the fridge. 'Sorry, boys, it's just sandwiches tonight.'

Billy wriggled onto the sofa. 'Can we eat while we watch the rest of my film?'

'I suppose so,' she said, sitting between them. 'Just this once,' she qualified it, although so far this week they had eaten in front of the borrowed TV every night. The boys squashed in either side of her, and Beau put the telly on. They curled into her now like a pair of cats. She reached over to her own plate of congealing food. *Oh well, the ketchup is still good.*

The boys started to doze off, so she sent them up to bed and cleared up dinner. Then she put her papers on the table and started the report she had hardly had time to think about since she'd arrived.

Of course, it was ridiculous that a school could operate with one five-year-old and a school refuser. Wherever the boys ended up, they would be on the mainland with Ash, or worse, with Mrs Goodwin. She sat back, her laptop humming gently. She tapped out a few words, then closed her eyes.

It was wrong that a child like Merryn should be denied a proper schooling. It was shameful that Rhiannon, sharp as a bag of needles, should be held back by challenges with her social development. And it was unacceptable that Billy and Beau should be torn apart. Besides, where would Tink and Corinne's baby go to school, or Ellie and Bran's? Or Merryn's new brother, who she couldn't wait to meet?

I can't close the school.

She sighed and opened her eyes. The one job the local authority had told her to do, and she couldn't do it. She rubbed her forehead to ease the headache that was building. Some movement upstairs made her creep up to check on the boys. Beau was up, staring out into the dark beside the nightlight.

'Are you OK?' she murmured, sitting next to the starfished Billy. 'Don't let that woman upset you, she's only doing what she thought was right.'

He looked over at her, just a little smile creasing his lips. 'You called Billy "baby". You said, "Baby, don't get upset." That's what my mummy used to call me, too.'

'I'm sorry,' she whispered, mortified that she might have upset him.

'No, it's OK. I don't like calling you Miss, that's all.'

'How about...' She thought fast. 'In class you call me Miss Kingston. Then the rest of the time you can call me Charlotte.'

He chuckled. '*Charlotte?* Don't you have a nickname or something?'

Char. Zach had always called her Char.

'My granddad used to call me Lottie, but I think I outgrew it when I was about six.'

'I'll think of something,' he said, lying back down. 'Then we'll all have nicknames.'

'OK. You do that, but while you're asleep. We've got a big day tomorrow. We're going to meet the baby.'

'And see my lamb.' His voice was definitely softer now. She walked to the door, feeling the need to kiss them goodnight even more keenly.

'Goodnight,' she said.

The word 'baby' hung silently between them.

43

A second week crawled past since the babies were born, and Jenny had heard nothing from Albrecht. Perhaps he had just enjoyed scaring her; maybe he had no intention of following up his threat. He had certainly succeeded; she was afraid to leave the house, letting Aunt Hélène and Lisette collect Marc from school. The little boy seemed to have grown up since the twins were born. He seemed older and harder, and had tackled one of his bullies at school and made the larger child back down. He had a hint of his father's authority creeping in, which made him argumentative and sometimes disobedient in the nursery. Jenny found a pleasure in helping him with schoolwork, bonding over mathematical principles. He was affectionate, too, leaning against her arm as they tackled algebraic problems, even if he would argue about bedtime an hour later. She lay awake worrying about what would happen to the Boiteux family when she escaped.

Sharing her fears with Hélène, they came up with a plan. Jenny would act fearful and upset, not too distant from the truth, and would then disappear. Her aunt could suggest she had stowed away on a ship to escape the Gestapo officer's advances.

A letter arrived one evening, just as Madame had gone back up to bed after her first afternoon downstairs, eating with the family and servants. Jenny waited until the dishes had been washed up before taking the letter into Maître Boiteux's study to read it.

Mademoiselle Jenofeve Huon.

You will present yourself for questioning tomorrow morning, eleven o'clock, at the office of Geheime Staatspolizei Kriminaldirektor Wolfgang Albrecht.

Jenny's hands shook, making the spiky, black words tremble on the page. Questioning? The idea made her feel like laughing, with an edge of terror. *Hysteria.* She shook off the feelings and examined the letter again. As he increased the pressure, she would be expected to dress up, do her hair and submit to his desires. Although she was repelled by Albrecht, her life – and others' – might depend on her compliance. She felt sick as she looked in the mirror. Her face was almost as white as Madame's had been, making her hair look mousy. It was time to accelerate the plans to get off the island.

She tucked the letter in her pocket and went down to the drawing room, where Aunt Hélène was reading a book by the only lamp. Even with her glasses on, she was holding the book close to the dim light.

Hélène spoke first. 'Was that a letter from the German?'

'The Gestapo, yes.'

'I thought he would contact you sooner,' Hélène said, not looking up from the book. 'I hoped he had thought better of his disgusting threat.'

'So did I. Lisette has fallen asleep in the nursery. She's worn out running about with Adela.'

'Shut the door, child. We need a private word.'

Jenny did so, and walked over to sit on the footstool in front of the dying fire. 'I'm supposed to be getting away in a week,' she said in a whisper, tears welling up, dropping through her fingers as she covered her face. 'I'm so scared. I just want to go home.'

'We're all scared. If anything you or I, or Augustine or Laurie, might do would help end this filthy war, I would ask you to stay, and fight. But not like this.' She paused. 'We must get you away.'

'What will happen to the Jewish family, the Kellers?' The idea felt like a grenade dropped into the room, hissing. 'I asked Laurie to take them too, but the British won't. They can't stay, not with Albrecht here. He'll put them in a labour camp.'

'Or worse. Death may be a certainty for the Jews. The stories people are bringing out of Poland... The German government passed a law in March to intern people just for being Jewish.'

'If I escape, won't you and the whole family be in trouble?'

Hélène shrugged. 'We will be questioned. But what do we know, really? A few rumours, a frightened girl so homesick she ran away. We'll try to get the Kellers away to the mainland. Jews are pouring out of France.'

'Albrecht won't believe that,' Jenny said. 'He'll think I was part of it.'

'Well, what if he does?' Hélène leaned over and put a hand on her shoulder for a second. 'Augustine has been in Paris, did you know?'

Jenny was glad. 'What about Laurie?'

'He's off with one of the cargo ships. I saw him embark. He looks ten years older. I think he's been gathering information in St Malo – he has a web of contacts with the Resistance. Some of them are nationalists, unhappy that the Germans haven't supported independence for Brittany despite their early promises.'

'But how will the British get us home?' It seemed like an impossible task.

'Don't worry about that. There are three or four crossings a month just from the north-west corner of Brittany. Laurie's crossed several times this year, taking dissidents away from the Germans, rescuing a couple of airmen and several agents.' She shot a glance at Jenny. 'You seem very interested in Laurie.'

'I like him.'

Jenny couldn't explain the attraction, except that life seemed very precious and dangerous when he was nearby. It was as if an instinct to connect and hold on built inside her when she saw him, knowing he and Augustine dealt with the Germans every day. Suppose one of the crewmen on the ship realised he wasn't French? He had never pretended to be Breton; he didn't have the language and the local seamen didn't like the reclusive French character he played.

'I think he's very brave,' she added.

Hélène pursed her lips. 'Brave, maybe. But I am suspicious about his return. I was certain his own government thought he was a traitor. Don't trust him.'

But I have to entrust my life to him.

Jenofeve Huon was ready for Kriminaldirektor Wolfgang Albrecht in his office at five minutes to eleven. She had borrowed some of her aunt's clothes, a severe black work dress that fell unflatteringly to her shins. Her hair was braided into plaits and coiled tight to her head. She knew she was pale and made no effort to look otherwise.

He walked into his office and indicated the small, upright wooden chair in the middle of the room.

'Sit,' he said, tapping his cane against his ankle before sitting in the leather chair behind his desk. His dog slunk around his heels, looking up at him as if for orders.

'I see you are looking well, after your ordeal. How is your mistress?'

'Hers was the ordeal, Herr Albrecht,' she answered, in a flat voice. 'She is recovering slowly.'

'And the children were saved,' he said. He picked up a silver inkwell, put it down. 'Because our *German* doctor was superior to the old Breton one.'

'Yes.'

The dog walked over to her, pushed his cold nose into her hand at her side. She allowed herself to caress the animal's face for a moment before she remembered what people said about Bruno. She glanced down at the German shepherd. His eyes seemed filled with intelligence rather than malice, and when she put her hand on the top of his head, his tail swished.

'You have enchanted my dog,' Albrecht said, pausing in his examination of his desk to stare at her. 'As you have me.'

Jenny couldn't think of anything dignified to say. There was something about his dark eyes that reminded her of his dog's. Curious, questioning. Predatory.

'He doesn't like the French,' his master said, moving to sit on the corner of his desk, very close to her. The dog was sandwiched between them. When Albrecht smiled, he showed a lot of teeth. 'Perhaps he prefers the Cornish. *Tsk*, Bruno, disloyal.'

'I am neither French nor Cornish,' she said, the words sounding very repetitive. 'I am Breton and a native of this island.'

'Of course, of course.' He put one finger under her chin and lifted it a little. 'You don't *look* like a spy.'

'I am not,' she said, trembling inside. She lifted her chin away from his touch.

'And yet, you have an unfortunate taste in friends.'

'If you mean Augustine Berthou, she is a harmless seamstress.'

'Who travels more frequently off this godforsaken rock than I do.' His voice was sharp. He walked around her chair, making her shudder as he passed behind her. 'I think you know more about this *Augustine's* activities than you are telling me.'

His dog let out a tiny whine, and the man immediately hissed. Bruno shrank down to his belly.

'I know nothing but my duties, to help Madame Boiteux and her children.'

He ran a finger down the side of her face, brushed her lips. 'I thought you would be grateful for the lives of your mistress and her brats.'

'I am grateful,' she said, lifting her chin. Her knees were beginning to wobble and she pressed them together. 'Thank you.'

'But not grateful enough. I thought we had a deal, you and I?'

'Monsieur—' she said, her voice shaky.

'Call me Wolfgang.' He sat in front of her on the desk again, his knees either side of her. 'I do not want you to fear me, hate me. But I do need you to tell me everything you know about Augustine Berthou.'

'I don't know much,' she said, meeting his dark eyes. He had a ring of lashes so long and dark they looked like a woman's. 'She is a stepsister of my late father, but I had never met her until she came to the island.'

A twisted smile crossed his face for a second. 'So the local peasants say. Why do you believe her story?'

'She told me details about my father, from when he was a boy. But she was sent away to a convent school, so she didn't know him as an adult. Nor me.'

'But she is known to your aunt, Hélène Huon. I wouldn't

want to have to interrogate your old aunt because you weren't completely candid with me.'

She blinked back tears, clenched her teeth. 'My aunt doesn't know anything, nor do I.'

'Yet messages have been leaving this island, with its few hundred sheep and surly Breton fishermen. At least one boat has landed.'

'I don't know anything about that,' she said, sitting bolt upright, staring at him. 'And I think you called me here for another reason.'

He stepped away. 'If that's all I wanted, I could take it,' he said. 'But you are right. I want more. I would regret brutality.'

She nodded, almost afraid to speak. She selected her words carefully.

'I am not a spy. No one at the Villa is.'

'Then there is no reason we can't be... friends.'

She couldn't answer, just nod slowly. He bowed, clicked his fingers to his canine shadow, and opened the door for her.

44

The meeting with Mrs Goodwin had left a sour taste for Charlotte and upset the boys. Billy looked tired in the morning, and Beau was tense. So she got them dressed early and set out to walk along to the hotel to pick up Merryn to play with Billy. It was Good Friday and the children had the day off school.

'Morning, Charlotte!'

She waved to Birdie, standing on the quay beside his boat. 'Hi, Birdie. How's Jayne?'

'Good. Off to see the baby?' He grinned at her. 'Half the island's queueing up to see him. I, of course, brought him back on the ferry so *I've* already met him.'

She laughed and waved, spoke to Maggi, the white-haired post lady, and greeted a woman walking her terrier, while the boys ran over to stroke the cat sitting outside the pub. This community had taken her to its heart but there was something hesitant and watchful about them, too. They knew she was there to close their school. She walked faster up the path, and she remembered that Ash was working at the hotel.

'Beau, Billy, keep up!' she called. They powered along the gravel path beside the beach, towards the hotel.

Justin opened the restaurant door for her, holding a tiny bundle that could only be the baby. The boys immediately quietened down.

'Look!' Beau breathed, as enchanted as he had been by the lamb.

'Come in, come in.' Justin waved them all inside. 'If you sit still you can hold him. Would you like that?'

Beau rushed to a chair and held out his arms for the bundle of blanket, fuzzy pale hair and rosebud lips. Billy leaned over just as the baby sneezed, and the laughter woke him up, making him grizzle. Beau rocked him a few times and he stopped crying, screwed up one eye and stared at Billy.

'He likes me,' breathed the little boy.

Merryn came over, the new big sister, Robert trailing behind her with a hairbrush.

'I bet you're swamped with visitors,' Charlotte said.

'Mum has a sort of appointment system going,' he said. 'We just thought you would like to come by early, since you were so helpful with Merryn.'

'She was lovely. So confident. I thought she might be a bit fazed, but she was great.'

Robert looked over at the children. 'It's not great news that she isn't clingier, to be honest. These kids, they've lost their faith in people. Merryn never developed strong early attachments.'

'But she talks about you all the time,' Charlotte was able to say. 'And just because she didn't act upset doesn't mean she wasn't. And she adores Billy.'

Robert smiled at that. 'You should prepare yourself. Apparently, they are getting married and you will be invited to be a bridesmaid. Along with a random lamb she and Billy are adopting. They just can't agree on the name.'

'Are they still at Barnaby Butt Fluff?' she asked. 'If so, you might like them to name the baby.'

Robert walked over and retrieved the baby from Beau, laying him in Charlotte's arms. She caught her breath at the lightness of him, and his enormous, vital presence in the middle of the blanket.

'Wow,' she said softly. She'd held babies before – friends' children, colleagues' babies. But this was different, as if something had changed within her, some emotion forced open by the island.

'His mother had already named him Luca when we saw her,' he said softly. 'We might keep it as a middle name. We were able to talk to her about Merryn, too. She was devastated to be losing him but very happy he was going to be with his sister.' He paused. 'She has eight children, all in care of some sort or another. It's awful for her, but she can't care for them.'

'It must be.' She was dropped into the agony of giving a child away, making tears rise into her eyes. 'He looks like you,' she said, looking at his elegant long face. Justin had ginger colouring and there was a hint of that in the baby's delicate eyebrows. 'He looks like both of you. How is that possible?'

'Mum said that, too. I don't know, it's weird.'

She handed the baby over gently. 'I have to get back. I can take Merryn all day if you like. Save your energy for holding court with the baby.' She hesitated, looked around. 'Uh, is Ash around?'

'Who do you think got Merryn's breakfast, helped her dress, listened to her reading and got her backpack ready?' He rolled his eyes. 'All we've done is carry the baby around going *Wow*.'

Now neatly plaited and dressed in denim dungarees and a sparkly jumper, Merryn came to kiss the top of the baby's head, followed by both boys.

As she took Billy's hand, Charlotte caught sight of Ash, standing in the shade by the kitchen door holding a hairbrush. Her heart skipped a beat, then another, and he raised a hand in greeting. She gave a little wave, unable to stop herself smiling, for a moment locking eyes with him.

45

JULY 1941

Jenny checked behind the summer house as soon as she got back from her interview with the Gestapo officer, careless of whether or not the house was being watched. There were no notes, so she sat on the step and let thoughts of escape and rescue chase around her mind like cats. The urge to steal a rowing boat and row for home consumed her with longing, even though she knew she'd founder on the rocks before she got away from the island's brutal currents. But sixty miles north lay the sandy shore of Morwen island, the bells ringing from the church, boats humming in and out of the quay, children running along the cobbled streets and up to the school.

The Gestapo officer had mesmerised her like a snake, and now she was filled with the poison of fear. If she was on the mainland, she could have run. Hidden away on a train or walked across the fields, caught a lift, anything. Here, she was so visible. The Breton locals, even the ones who remembered her father from when she was a baby, thought of her as different. The Germans certainly thought of her as half-English, probably working against them. This man could do what he liked just by arresting her and holding her for interrogation. The kindness of the Kommandant and his wife came back to her. Could she ask them for protection, refuge? They were decent people, she was sure, like Lisette's young Bavarian. Perhaps they felt powerless against the Gestapo, too?

It seemed, from the limited information they had, the Gestapo had gained in power as they created an initiative to imprison all the Jews of occupied Europe. Everyone knew, but no one dared say, that there weren't enough prison cells nor camps to hold all the Jews. The rumours that they were being randomly executed ran among the islanders as they whispered about the Keller family.

She dried her eyes and walked back to the kitchen. Maybe Cook was making something small to tempt Madame, who had lost a great deal of weight since her ordeal. The babies would need their changes and bottles. Although Madame had fed them small amounts, and the wet nurse more, the doctor still advised giving them extra bottles as they were so small. Boiling and sterilising the bottles, as well as worrying about where to get tinned milk, took up a lot of the household's time. Someone had to go down to the shop every time the boat came in, to queue to make sure they got enough. Everyone in the house was severely rationed for milk, and even Madame was drinking black tea.

Jenny had fed and cleaned all the children by half past one, her mind still distracted by thoughts of escape, when Lisette put the baby boy in his crib with his sister.

'He's much more of a fusspot than she is,' she said. 'I'll make sure Madame has everything she needs, then I'll be out in the garden. I promised to help Cook pull up a few vegetables and do some weeding.' She rolled her eyes. She used to be a little lazy, but now worked as hard as anyone.

'Will Hans be by at some point?' Jenny asked.

'He might be.' Lisette grinned and flicked her ponytail over her shoulder. 'I couldn't say...'

'Can you ask him if he's heard anything about the Keller family, the Jews? I'm worried about them.'

'He might not be allowed to say.'

'Don't press him. I just wondered.'

Lisette leaned forward. 'There's something big going on, I do know that. They're building something on the north coast, and we're going to get more German ships soon. Maybe they're planning to invade England?'

'Oh. Goodness.' The thought made Jenny sick. She watched Lisette leave the room, and sat back in the nursing chair, rocking the crib. Here, among the babies she had nurtured, she felt guilty at even thinking of leaving them. Especially when their mother hadn't yet turned the corner into full health, but was beset by odd fevers and faints. There wasn't a ship that could take them all, and Madame couldn't travel. Tears came easily in these tense days, but she fought them back.

Think, Jenny, think.

That evening, Lisette caught Jenny in a quiet corner of her bedroom as she rocked the baby boy. Madame refused to name the twins until she had heard from her husband, and letters to and from the island still took weeks.

'I spoke to Hans,' Lisette said, in a whisper so she didn't wake the baby. 'The Keller family are going to be deported to stay with Jewish relatives in St Malo. Hans said many families managed to get across to England before the Germans arrived, but some boats were sunk and many people have drowned.' She shuddered. 'He said the body of a little girl washed up on the north coast of Ushant and two more people on Kadoran.' The uninhabited neighbouring island often caught debris from shipwrecks.

'That's awful...' Jenny murmured.

'One of the bodies was a spy, they think. He had some British papers on him.'

Laurie.

The world spun around Jenny for a moment, and she sagged against the chair as the baby started to cry. She pulled herself up, shushing and rocking.

'How terrible,' she choked out. Lisette's face looked so curious she felt she had to say something. 'It could be a fisherman from Cornwall, even from the islands where my family live.'

'You have fishermen in your family, don't you? It must be strange, knowing they are just across the sea.'

'Many, many kilometres away,' Jenny answered, walking back to the nursery with Lisette. 'A hundred *stormy* kilometres.'

But she was right, it did feel like she could reach out and touch the same air that had flowed over Morwen. While Jenny put the baby in the cot next to his sister, Lisette started tidying baby clothes.

'Tell me about your island,' she said, folding nappies ready to use.

'It's a lot like Ushant,' Jenny said, rocking the cradle as images of Morwen flooded her mind. 'It's very rocky on the western coast, the side that looks out over the ocean. But it slopes down to the quay on the eastern coast, which is where our fishing fleet is, and we can look over the other islands.' She smiled at the thought. 'And at night, the lighthouses shine, but nothing like here.'

Ushant had nine lighthouses, some of them the most powerful in Europe, maybe the world. The Germans had ordered some of them turned down or off to confuse the British. She just hoped the information she had decoded helped the Allies navigate close to Ushant and the rest of the coast.

'What happened with that Gestapo man? Albrecht? Hans

said everyone is scared of him. He seems to make up the rules to suit himself.'

'He wants us to be lovers,' Jenny said, her voice hollow.

'No.' Lisette looked up, her eyes now wide. 'If you can get away, you would take the chance, wouldn't you?'

Jenny froze. 'Why do you say that? How could I get away?'

'I don't know. Maybe hide away on the ferry and head for the north coast. People have.'

'Yes, and many of them ended up arrested or dead on the shore,' Jenny said, feeling a pressure in her chest at the thought of a drowned doll on the sand, swept in on the tide.

Lisette looked back down at her hands. 'You know the whole island would help. There are people that think you're English and should go home.'

'You might all be questioned, even be punished if I went away,' Jenny said softly. 'Life is hard enough as it is for the family.'

'We'd just blame you and bad-mouth you once you'd gone. You were untidy, neglected the children, hogged the sugar—'

Jenny lobbed a cushion in her direction and Lisette laughed. Jenny rocked the cradle again to stop the babies waking.

Swamped in the baby clothes of their bigger siblings, the twins curved together like puppies, maybe as they had in the womb. They were getting bigger, and it hurt her heart to think she wouldn't see them grow up.

After the war, I will come back.

46

PRESENT DAY, 11 APRIL

The village had a full social calendar. Monday evenings was pottery, down in Bran's studio, with half a dozen people walking past the school each week. Alternate Tuesdays was a dance class with Emily who also worked at the café. Since Billy was feeling so much more relaxed, Charlotte suggested that rather than just retrieving the rabbit and clearing the floor, ready for the class, she and Billy might give dance a go. Beau refused blankly.

'You and Percival can watch a film,' Charlotte said. 'As long as you clear it with me first.' Beau seemed accustomed to watching any film he fancied, whether suitable or not, and Charlotte had had to put parental controls on everything from the computer to the streaming services on her laptop. They compromised on a science fiction he had seen before.

She walked over to the classroom just as Emily arrived, trailing scarves from a box of props and smiling widely.

'Do I have to dress up?' Billy asked, starting to back away.

'No! Of course not,' Emily said. 'Do you want to help move tables? You look super strong.'

'I am,' he said, puffing out his chest.

Convinced Emily had Billy's measure, Charlotte scooped up the rabbit and put him in his carrier. Beau was waiting in the porch for him. 'You know where I am, if you need something,' she said.

'I won't.' He'd closed down again; his shutters had a hair trigger.

Several women had walked up to the school and Corinne met them at the door with Merryn. 'Hi, Billy! I hope you're going to help me, I'm terrible at dancing.'

Charlotte could see Billy was nervous now – he kept swallowing – and she was worried about his bladder. 'Come on, let's go to the bathroom while Emily sets up.'

'I don't think I want to dance,' he whispered as she shepherded him into the cubicle. She stood in the door to obstruct anyone else's view.

'It's just for fun, like exercise. You're very good at exercises. I think I'll be worn out in two minutes.'

'You can shut the door a bit,' he said. 'And you won't go anywhere, will you?'

'Certainly not. I'll guard you like a lion.' She tried a small roar, which made him laugh.

She had wondered whether the group of five women of all ages, one middle-aged man and two small children might find it difficult to work together, but once she'd got the warm-up exercises out of the way, she started copying what the teacher was doing. Emily was as graceful and elongated as a willow tree and Charlotte felt like a rooted shrub. There was a lot of laughter, but by the end Billy and Merryn were leading the group, having easily taken on the movements. Charlotte didn't have the coordination to follow the music, but Billy really seemed to embody the Moroccan CD playing in the background. As people fell out or got to talking, Emily gradually brought them back to the movement until, by the end, Charlotte was tired but brought to life by her own body's response to the melodies and drum beats. Even Billy had grabbed two scarves to form shapes in the air.

'That's it for tonight,' Emily said at the end, packing up.

'Don't forget, Liz is doing a drumming class here next week,' someone said. 'Or outside if the weather's good.'

An older woman, smiling broadly, introduced herself as Sorcha. 'I was wondering… We were going to have a meeting in the church hall at the end of the week, but we were wondering if we could have it here? We've got more people interested than we expected.'

'Of course. Yoga is on Thursday so it would have to be Friday. Is it another class?' Charlotte started setting chairs around the tables Emily had put back.

Sorcha hesitated. 'Actually, no. It's a meeting of the village committee.'

'Oh, great. Yes, of course. I'll open the doors. Any particular time?'

'Seven. Thank you so much. We'll bring a few extra chairs but put it all back at the end.'

She smiled and walked away, clearly unwilling to discuss what the meeting was about with Charlotte.

Charlotte returned the rabbit to his sleeping quarters, locked the schoolroom and escorted Billy home for bed. The light outside was silvery, the moon almost full, and she took a moment to stand outside looking over the field. An owl hooted far away, possibly on the nearby island, and one replied close by. A lamb called, his mother answered, a gentle, reassuring sound. Someone's footsteps crunched on the gravel of the lane, and she shrank back into the porch for a moment, then wondered why she would be scared. She already knew almost everyone on the island.

'Hello?' he called out nervously anyway.

'Charlotte?' A young man's voice.

Ash.

'I was just going for a walk before bed,' he said. 'Can I have a quick word?'

She succumbed to an impulse before she'd thought about it or the implications. 'I was about to make a cup of something. Do you want one?'

His face came into view, made darker by the night, the moonlight picking up his cheekbones, so like Beau's. Maybe you do end up looking like your children, she wondered, a bit like people taking on traits of their dogs.

'Something low in caffeine,' he suggested. 'Are the boys in bed?'

'Just going,' she said. 'Although Beau was asleep on the sofa when we came in. Billy's a bit wired, he's been dancing. Come and say goodnight.'

'He was always singing and dancing as a toddler.'

Billy let out a squeal of delight that made Beau groan and, although he didn't hug Ash, he managed a creditable high five. By the time Charlotte had wrangled both boys to bed and come back downstairs, Ash had found the decaffeinated coffee and had made a decent pot.

They sat on the sofa talking, Charlotte feeling her tension flowing away. He was funny, intelligent and well educated. They talked about his years in the navy, his wish that he had studied oceanography and his time with Chloe. They compared funny childhood stories and, somehow, he drew out of her a little of the difficulties with Zach.

'It sounds like you really loved him,' he said, looking at her thoughtfully over his cup.

'Oh, I did. I fell in love with who I thought he was going to be. The romance of his sport, his energy and enthusiasm for everything.' That felt as if it pulled loose one of the strands of love that bound them. She looked down into her coffee. 'I got it wrong. It turned out the things he was enthusiastic about were more important than me.'

He was silent for a minute, and she glanced up at him. 'I think we all do that when we're young,' he said, staring at the floor, enunciating each word. 'I know I did with Chloe.'

She didn't know how to respond to this, and she certainly didn't want to talk about Chloe while the kids were upstairs.

'When I first met Beau he was a cute four-year-old. A lot more like Billy back then, like his mother. I enjoyed taking them all to the zoo, out for a burger. Then Chloe invited me to an eco festival, all camping and earth toilets, nudity and music. I literally fell for her. Like falling into a pool of emotion; I nearly drowned. And in the pool were the boys. I didn't see them as separate from Chloe.' He smiled at the memory. 'I learned tai chi, did laughter yoga, sang in a choir even though I can't carry a tune. I was the happiest I'd ever been, I think, at least for that week.'

'That's lovely,' Charlotte said, suddenly sad. 'That must have been hard to lose.'

'It worked for more than two years.' He shrugged, stood up and replaced the cup in the sink. 'Chloe was skittish around commitment and I always knew I loved her more than she loved me. I had to let go of her when she found someone else, but I couldn't detach from the boys. I thought about them, missed them. In saturation diving you have a ridiculous amount of time to think. Some people literally go a bit mad with the isolation in the pressure tank, just three divers locked away for weeks at a time at nine atmospheres.'

She couldn't imagine. His brief description of deep diving had enthralled the children but painted a picture of dark, lonely hazards to her. 'So, you missed them even more?'

'I started writing to Chloe. Just gentle, funny letters, trying not to put pressure on her. She allowed me to see the kids when

I was off duty, but the guy she was with hated it. He wanted her to cut off all communication with me.'

'So she came up with the story of you being harsh with the boys?'

'I never touched them.' He sighed and the expression on his face was heartbreaking. 'But step-parents don't have the same rights as parents, or any blood relatives, really. Apart from her dubious taste in men she was a good mother. In the end I had to back down.'

Charlotte put her cup down slowly, deliberately, choosing her words carefully.

'But you want them back now?'

She already knew the answer. She stood up, and he put a hand on her waist, bent down a little and moved closer. Without thinking, she lifted her face and met his lips. It was as if her body and his were having a conversation that her mind wasn't invited to, the kiss deepening, ending, him pulling away a few inches, frowning slightly, his breathing ragged and fast. Or was that hers?

'I'm sorry. I'd better go.'

'No!' Charlotte said breathlessly. 'I mean, don't be sorry.'

He pulled his coat off the hook by the door. 'You're working your way through letting go of Zach. You explained how you still care for him. And I have enough on my plate trying to get the boys back.'

'Of course.' Prim, sensible Charlotte, teacher, was back. 'You're right. Thank you for the chat. It was nice to talk to another grown-up.'

He looked back at the door, a small smile growing. 'Maybe we can do this again, over a drink, sometime?'

Common sense flooded in like the cold, black water of his work. 'I'll be leaving the school at the end of term,' she said. 'And you're right, we shouldn't get... involved.'

He frowned at that. 'What will happen to the school? It seems like such a lovely place for the kids.'

'The local authority can't run it for just one child,' she said, because she knew the patter off by heart.

'So they'll close it down?' His expression hardened. *'You're* here to close it down, aren't you? You're just tying up the loose ends.'

'Every closure is hard. But the funding just isn't there and they can't recruit a new teacher.' She tried to keep her tone light. 'You won't have to worry about it. You'll have your own life to go back to, especially if you get the boys.'

As he shut the door behind him, the hollow feeling returned in her chest. She curled up on the sofa, trying to hold on to the feeling that the impulsive kiss had given her, the feeling of not being alone in the world.

47

JULY 1941

On one of his house calls, the German doctor changed Madame's dressing and released a lot of infection, which soaked into her nightdress. It eased the dragging pain that had beset her, and she was able to feed her twins more comfortably. While the whole family was distracted by the babies, who in the absence of proper names had been temporarily named Pierrick and Brigitte, after Madame's two siblings, Jenny did find a note in the rat hole. It was stark.

> Be at Kerzoncou beach at 8 p.m. Friday, with all the documents. Don't pack a bag, it will cause suspicion. Don't tell your aunt nor anyone in your household. Carry on as usual, don't deviate from your normal pattern.

As it was in code, and in unfamiliar handwriting, she couldn't tell who had sent it.

Under the softened floorboards of the summer house was the leather bag Laurie always carried, filled with schedules, maps, notebooks with tiny writing in them, some of it encoded, some in other languages, and canisters that were sealed tight against water or light. Inside, she saw letters inked on the leather. L.B. *Laurie?*

She felt sick. She couldn't work out how to avoid Albrecht's attentions, and she couldn't bear the idea that she was running away and leaving the children, the Keller family, Hélène and Madame and Lisette behind. If she could, she would take them all.

On the back of the note were more, very explicit, instructions. What she was to wear, what she was to do if she was challenged. She needed men's trousers; she could take those from Maître Boiteux's wardrobe – he had a few pairs of casual trousers he used for fishing or sailing. His shoes would all be too big, she would have to wear her own.

She would be carrying enough information to get them all shot. It was a horrible dilemma. She left the bag jammed under the summer house until she could get it away. She got the children ready to walk with Marc to school.

Adela, in her perambulator, was now so mobile she had to be securely strapped in, and it grieved Jenny that she wouldn't be taking her to the sandy beach south of the fishing port. But no one was playing on the beach any more, and the Germans planned to mine it.

Jenny slipped down the lane, meeting up with two mothers progressing towards the school. With barely forty pupils of all ages from six to fourteen, the building was only half used, with two teachers. One was a veteran of the first war; he trembled whenever he heard gunshots from the range or warship engines cruising past the island. The other was a spinster in her forties, a long-necked turkey of a woman. Jenny secretly thought they would be perfect together.

Jenny pushed the perambulator alongside Madame Keller, who was walking with her six-year-old Artur and toddler Pierre, and carrying baby Cécile.

'Madame, may I speak for a moment?'

'You'd better not be seen talking to me,' Madame Keller said, tossing her head back. 'People are afraid of becoming Jewish by association.'

'I was wondering if you had given any thought to leaving the island?'

The woman looked around quickly, to make sure they weren't overheard. 'I heard that people have been executed for trying to get away. But...' She swallowed hard and shrank closer to Adela's pram. 'We have been informed we will be given a date, by which time our property is to be disposed of and the money raised used to pay for our transport.' Her eyes were filled with tears. 'We dream of stealing a fishing boat and sailing away. But we know we would be caught, or drowned. We are not sailors.'

Jenny dropped her voice even further as they walked along the road towards the lane. 'The British have boats moving across the Channel all the time. They drop agents, equipment, guns for the Resistance.'

'But we know nothing about that!' Madame Keller said, looking around wildly.

'If I heard of a ship leaving Ushant, taking people straight to England, would you come?'

She couldn't believe she was saying this. Laurie and his fellow agents would be horrified. But she couldn't leave them behind, to go to their certain death.

'Why would you do that?' Madame Keller said, flushed with emotion, maybe even anger.

'I'm half-English,' Jenny said. 'I come from an Atlantic Island called Morwen. If I stay, the Gestapo will arrest me. I have to get away, and I have heard a whisper of a possible ship, just a fishing boat, that might take that chance.'

'Are there such kind people?' Madame Keller said, eyes open wide, clinging to her baby until Cécile began to cry, then rocking her gently.

'Talk with your husband,' Jenny said. Her own eyes were stinging with tears too. 'I couldn't escape and leave you, the most vulnerable, behind.'

'I know he would say yes,' Madame Keller said, staunchly. 'And maybe we will sink and drown, or get arrested and shot, but I can't just wait for what's coming. Have you heard what the Gestapo are doing across Poland?'

'I have,' said Jenny softly. 'Shush. Someone is coming.'

'Uh, so, a little ice is excellent for teething,' said Madame Keller, her hands shaking as she lifted one in farewell. 'Good day, Mademoiselle Huon.' She managed a watery smile, before Jenny saw who was approaching.

'Ah, of course. The little English girl is friends with the *Jews*.' Albrecht's dog trotted forward, sniffed at Jenny's shoes.

'Her son is in Marc's class,' she explained.

'Jews are already barred from schools in some places,' he said, idly tapping the side of his boot with his cane. 'It won't be long before we stop them wasting our time and resources in schooling they are ill-suited to.'

'Some of the world's greatest scientists and philosophers are Jewish,' Jenny burst out.

He shrugged, and when Bruno nudged her hand with his head, she stroked him.

'Myself, I don't care,' he said. 'But they suck up money, gold and property. We can't afford these invaders, the immigrants. We need to build a successful and healthy race.' He winced at the words. 'I don't believe in the Aryan ideal,' he said. 'I hardly fit it myself.' Thin, tall, dark, saturnine. No, he didn't look like the powerful, blond Hitler Youth that the posters promoted.

'I must go. We have the babies to look after and Madame is still unwell.'

'But I so enjoy our talks,' he said, smiling with his teeth bared, like his dog. 'Perhaps I should arrest you, interrogate you some more.' His eyes roamed over her body then, his smile widening.

She kept her lips tightly shut, mutely refusing to engage with the idea. 'I must go.' She ground the words out.

'Very well. But we will meet soon, when there is no one to interrupt our little chat.'

48

After the impulsive kiss with Ash, Charlotte's sleep was broken by disturbing dreams of him underwater, lost and alone. She woke feeling tired and achy, and as it was early she ran a bath. She had got the antiquated shower working but it was full of limescale and was little more than a trickle.

She dried herself on one of the towels she had bought, a bit of luxury she would use in her new home. When she found one. The idea seemed strange: a quiet space, coming home to a dark house. *I'll get a pet.* Life would seem very empty without the children, and without Zach, although in the last few years he had hardly ever been there in person.

She towel-dried her hair. It was getting a bit wild now; she should have booked a trim at a hairdresser on the big island, and maybe got some advice on the boys' hair. Billy's fell in wild ringlets around his face and Beau's grew straight out of his head like a soft halo. She opened the door just in time to meet Billy coming the other way.

'I need to pee!' he shouted.

She smiled, pleased to see him bouncing again. He was also

managing to stay dry at night, which seemed related to his stress levels.

'What did you think of the dancing?' she called through the door.

'I want to go to ballet with Merryn!' he shouted back, loud enough to make her wince.

She walked into the kitchen and pulled some clean clothes out of the stationery cupboard she was using as a wardrobe. By the time she was dressed, Billy was out, and she sent him back to clean his teeth while she sorted out the fresh laundry. Being able to use Clarrie's washing machine and drier had been a life-saver, especially with the volume of clothes two active boys got through running about outside.

Billy bounded upstairs, waking Beau. He wasn't a morning person; she could have drawn his morning scowl on with a marker pen.

'I hate Billy,' he growled, as he walked past her to the bathroom.

'No, you don't,' she said, mostly to herself. She had researched some history of the island for this morning. A local history website was full of references and old photographs of the hut in the cove.

Laurence Byers had lived in the tiny home he had made by hand, stacking the rocks he found at low tide. He'd died there, his body discovered by someone who delivered food to him every day, possibly Charlotte's Grandma Isabelle. There would probably have been a group of people that kept an eye on him, like the support web that was forming around Robert and Justin as they tackled looking after a new baby, and the circle that had formed around her with Billy and Beau.

Laurence Byers. She had to do a wider search to find a mention of his past on the mainland. She knew the name, but where from? She checked the time: ten past eight. She had some time before the girls arrived. She called her mother, who was always an early riser.

'Hi, darling.' Her mother always sounded different on the phone, a hint of her West Country childhood in her voice.

'I was wondering if you have any ideas on something the children and I are working on. A project on a little hut down in Seal Cove. It's a stone—'

'I know what it is.' Her mother's voice was suddenly alert, sharp. 'I don't think it's all that suitable for young children.'

'Why not?' She got the milk out of the fridge for Billy, and watched Beau pour him some.

'My mother used to visit him regularly, and she even took you a few times. I think he died around 1994, you must have been about six or seven.'

'That doesn't make him sound unsuitable,' Charlotte said, trying to get the top on the bottle with one hand. She gave up and pulled hot toast out onto a plate for Beau. 'I mean, if Grandma Isabelle took me to visit.'

'Well, the rumour was that he had been convicted of a crime – something during the war. He worked as a secret agent, and he went to prison afterwards.'

Charlotte crunched a bite from an apple. 'I knew I'd been there before.'

'He refused to go into a care home. Grandma was terribly upset, although he was just an old recluse by then. I suppose you get attached when you look after someone.'

'You do.' For a moment, Charlotte almost spoke about her growing feelings for the boys.

Her mother stayed silent for so long Charlotte wondered if she'd lost the connection. 'I do have some photos in one of your grandmother's albums,' she said, finally.

'Could you scan some and send them over for me, for the project?'

'I'll try.' Charlotte's mum ran a busy medical practice in Bath. 'Did Zach come over to see you?'

Zach. She put the apple down. 'We just signed off the last bits of our relationship.'

'You know he's given up competitions? I think he's ready to settle down. And he's teaching.'

Zach always had her mother charmed, her father less so.

'But when I saw him, I was just sad.' Charlotte turned away from the boys. 'I've been getting less emotional over him. It's been over for years, really, I was just his support system between big competitions.'

'At least you still have *some* feelings for him,' her mother suggested. 'Just keep that door open. Oh, there they are. Grandma kept several pictures of the hut. I'll take them out of the album and scan them at work.'

Over the rustling, Charlotte could hear something, as if her mother had caught her breath. 'What is it?'

'I'll scan the backs of the pictures for you, too. Maybe you can decipher the writing on there, it's just in pencil. Looks like – yes, it's "Uncle Laurie, 1956". I didn't think he was a relative. The National Archives might have something on Laurence Byers.'

'I'll look him up. Thanks, Mum.'

Was Byers a *relative*?

'Are you upset?' Billy asked her. His fingers were in his mouth already and he hadn't eaten his cereal.

'No, not really. My mum is sending me a picture of the man who lived in the hut. Come on, eat up.'

'I dreamed about your nickname, too,' Billy said.

'I had a friend, once, who was a bit of a hippy. She used to call me Charlie and I called her Stevie because her name was Stephanie.'

'Charlie!' shouted the apparently restored Billy. He blew hot and cold so easily.

'But Miss Kingston in class,' she said, rescuing the last of the milk in the bowl before it went flying.

'Charlie,' Beau said, putting his head on one side. 'I like it, it suits you. You don't sound like a teacher, though.'

'No, Charlie falls over in rockpools and burns fishfingers,' she replied, laughing back at his expression. His smile slowly widened.

He grabbed the last piece of buttered toast and walked towards the stairs with it.

'And kisses Daddy Ash,' he added from the bottom step.

49

Jenny almost jogged home with the pram. She made an excuse when she got in, saying she felt unwell and would use the outside privy, the one normally used by the gardeners. Instead, she slipped along the other side of the summer house and felt inside the usual hiding places.

There. A note for her, simple: confirming where on the beach she would meet the boat. She memorised the few words easily, written as they were in clumsy Breton. She took out the stub of a pencil she carried for the purpose and wrote a simple message on the back: 'Must see you.'

She also found an extra parcel wrapped in oilcloth. She unrolled it into her lap and found a tiny gun, the type she'd heard referred to in books as a derringer, an American weapon. She cautiously picked it up; it was heavy, and when she examined it further, she found it was loaded.

She felt the cold bulk of it in her palm. This would give her confidence facing Herr Albrecht. A moment's reflection told her it would only help if she was prepared to point it and maybe shoot it. But if she was caught with a gun...

She slipped it back into the fabric, wondering where on earth she could hide it. The idea came to her in a rush.

Every month she put her soiled sanitary napkins in a little bin she kept for the purpose, up high on the wardrobe. If she put the gun under there, surely no one would touch it? When she got to her room, she put the derringer at the bottom of the bin, and covered it with underwear.

The next three days, after dinner, she went to the summer house. Under cover of the noise of the bent-over trees, the wind rapping their branches on the roof, she waited for someone she could talk to about the rescue.

She huddled under a picnic blanket at the back of the shack, hidden behind a couple of folding chairs. Maybe they wouldn't come, as they hadn't managed to the previous days. She squinted at her watch, but it was too dark to see, and she didn't dare use her torch.

The squeak of the door – reduced to a faint whisper after she had pressed candle wax into it weeks ago – alerted her in a moment.

'Jenofeve?'

His voice, his accent, were so familiar.

'Laurie,' she breathed and pushed the chairs back, her heart bounding with relief. 'Thank God. I thought... I'm back here,' she whispered.

'We lost an agent,' he said. 'Two sailors, too.' He crept into her little cave and sat against the wall, his legs under the chairs. She leaned against him, so glad he was here, relieved that he hadn't been killed, and he put his arm around her.

'Did you get my message? Did you understand it?'

'I did.' His voice was strange in the dark – soft, more like a boy. 'There's a boat coming over, the *Talisman*. It's a Breton fishing boat, like many of the ones in the western fishing fleet.

We'll pick you up at dusk tomorrow at the beach beyond the sheep shelters at Kerzoncou farm. Do you know it?'

'I do,' she whispered, shivering.

The words hung in the air. When he leaned over, it felt natural to reach up. His first kiss fumbled on her cheek in the dark, but then his fingers framed her face and he found her lips.

'I'm afraid for you,' he whispered, before she could say the words. 'Suppose you're challenged? The Germans will certainly treat you like a spy.'

'They'll decide I'm a spy anyway,' she said. 'Albrecht has only left me free because he wants me. Willingly, if he can seduce me, but otherwise...'

'God, I can't bear to think—'

'But you don't have to. I'm ready to go.'

'Your Breton coxswain was a pilot for more than twenty years. He'll get you through the currents to the *Talisman*. The boat is an old sardine pinasse, you have several in the port, it's called *An Durzunel*. It has a green hull, brown sail. I doubt there will be anything else like it moored offshore. They will come inshore with a dinghy, take us over in twos and threes.'

'You're coming with me?'

'I hope so, with another agent. We have ordered two people from the nationalists to create a diversion over at the old fort, where the Germans are building. They're going to loosen some of the scaffolding, to organise an "accidental" collapse.'

She caught him by the shoulders, pulling him closer, shaking him. 'What about the Kellers?'

'When I come back I will be overhauling the bilge pump on the cargo ship, as grumpy a Frenchman as you can imagine. I'll try and smuggle them onboard then, but it's hard with the children.'

'Why would you risk that?'

'I have to,' he said, a tiny light from the house gleaming in his eye. 'I am chasing my redemption.'

'Why?'

He looked away. 'Years ago, I was a sympathiser of Oswald Mosley, from the British Union of Fascists. I was in his inner circle at one point. I was won over by his nationalist principles. When the secret service told me to betray an old friend and colleague from those days, I just couldn't. I sabotaged the mission. What I didn't realise was that I left eighteen people in danger, and two died. I was convicted of treason, with an automatic death sentence.'

Jenny shrank back a little. 'Why did they let you come back?'

'I'm now a double agent, sending misleading information to the enemy. People like you and Augustine are the engines that pass on the information, which saves ships and lives. I am expendable.'

'Expendable.' The idea struck her in the chest and she found herself trembling again. 'Laurie...'

He kissed her again with more urgency. 'If things were different,' he groaned, 'I would—'

She kissed him back, and let her feelings overcome her. Here, they were just Laurie and Jenny, and maybe he would be shot, or Jenny would drown in the vicious shallows, but right now...

50

PRESENT DAY, 13 APRIL

The local authority education officer called on Thursday evening, when the school was full of people doing yoga. Charlotte took her mobile outside to speak.

'We haven't had your report yet,' the woman at the end of the phone said. 'I thought you would have finished your pupil profiles, at least.' There was humour but also firmness there.

'Well, as you know, we have two extra children at the moment, and they all have additional needs.'

'But they are only temporarily resident.'

Charlotte took a deep breath. 'I can't say whether they will be permanent or not. Their grandmother lives on the island and is recovering from a stroke, and their stepfather is presently living and working on the island. Also, there are two babies and one expected soon, all likely to grow up on Morwen.'

'The decision has been made. You are to find ways to soften the blow, and manage our responsibility to the present permanent students.'

Charlotte turned her face away from the wind. 'That wasn't how the project was pitched to me. I was told to examine the viability of Morwen School for the children of the island.'

'Of which there is just *one*, a rising five-year-old. The older student must be encouraged and supported to go to the high school.'

'The school isn't just a provider of education to the *four* children presently attending,' she said. 'It's one of the few community buildings, and the only council-owned one. It's used for adult education as well.' She looked over at the yoga students, all in warrior poses. 'It's as much a community centre as a school. The villagers are even holding a committee meeting here tomorrow night.'

'Yes,' the dry voice echoed in her ear. 'The Save Our School group. I heard.'

Save Our School? She had seen posters for SOS but assumed they were something to do with the lifeboat.

'Well, I can see why they want to save the school,' she said, her voice sharp in her own ears. 'If there was no school here, younger people would have even fewer reasons to stay. Morwen would become a holiday park, closed in the winter.'

'Our responsibility is to look after the education of island children as cost effectively as we can. One child just isn't enough. The boys, as far as I am aware, are likely to end up in foster care or on the mainland.' Her voice softened. 'All I'm asking you to do is to think how lonely school would be for Merryn if she's the only child. We're looking at alternatives at this end, we just need *you* to write your report.'

As she said goodbye and hung up, Charlotte sat on the steps of the school. It was old, shabby; it had been a temporary replacement when the original school burned down forty years ago.

She rubbed her forehead. It was time to get Billy ready for bed. The yoga group would lock up and put the key through the letter box.

She didn't feel up to talking to anyone right now.

. . .

Beau was looking at something but shoved it into the cushions when he saw her. She knew he would rather struggle with natural history books than let her teach him, and his writing was abysmal. He wasn't reliable at his own name and mixed lower-case and upper-case letters all the time. She was failing him as a teacher, as well.

'I've got something for you,' she said, reaching over to the printer next to her laptop. 'Where's Billy?'

'I put him to bed.'

Great. Now she wasn't even parenting. She walked upstairs to check on Billy. He was snuggled under the duvet; all she could do was tuck him in and, more for herself, bend over and kiss his warm forehead.

'I'm sorry,' she breathed.

Downstairs, Beau was watching her. 'Why are you sad?'

'I don't know,' she said. Which was true, because nothing new had really happened. 'Just work stuff.'

She spread out two pages on a lap tray. 'Do you remember that man who wrote the diaries?'

'Yes.' He looked curious.

'I got these from the museum website.' One page was an entry from the diaries, just a long string of symbols, and the other was a partly filled-in code sheet. 'The author of the book, Mr Thurston, shows how to work out the messages.' She started transcribing the first three letters. 'Look, he was really clever. He used this character for the first E, then this one for the next two, then back to the first one.'

'So you can work out the words,' he said, leaning forward and peering at the letters. 'I worked out that triangle thing must be an O,' he said, triumphantly. 'And look, that mushroom shape is an S.' He held the page closer. She wondered again if he might need glasses and wondered where to get him an eye test.

'We should be able to decode it now,' she said. 'You could work on it.'

'I like it here.' He spread his fingers over a page. 'I don't want to go.'

'Are you worried?'

'Well, that lady wanted me, and Daddy Ash wants us both. We're going to end up with one of them, aren't we?'

'I won't let Billy be on his own,' she said, finding a fierceness she hadn't expected. 'I'll fight to keep you together, and Ash will too.'

He shrugged, making himself smaller, and curled up on the sofa. 'I don't know if I want just a dad,' he said. 'I'm used to a mum. I liked being with Grandma, but she was strict.'

She sat next to him. 'Sometimes children need strictness.' She looked away. 'Sometimes grown-ups need strictness, too.'

He allowed the top of his shoulder to brush hers. He traced a few more letters. 'This is a funny word, look.'

'*The child*,' she read. 'That's weird, is he writing about Isabelle?'

Beau traced the name further in his scruffy, but legible translation. 'Is that your grandma's name?'

She studied the words. 'I think it must be, but why does he call her "the child"? Anyway, time for bed.'

As if without thinking, he threw his arms around her for a lightning hug, and had gone before she realised he was on the stairs.

'Night, Charlie,' his voice came down the stairs.

'Night, Beau.' She smiled as the tears spilled over her eyelashes onto her cheeks.

51

JULY 1941

Jenny slipped into the house via the window she had left ajar in the pantry. Aunt Hélène must have locked up, not aware that anyone was out. A nightjar called across the island, answered by a distant call, maybe from the small neighbouring islets.

She was exhilarated at the feelings between her and Laurie, and the freedom that was within her grasp. But now she needed to pack up her small collection of belongings and decide which, if any, she could take. One thing she would not leave was a slender signet ring of Laurie's which he had pushed onto her finger before she left. For this night, they had been man and wife, lovers.

She slipped her clothes off and pulled her nightdress over her head, although she knew that the babies would be awake soon. Lisette must have kept an eye on the nursery while she was out. Her cheeks burned at what Lisette thought she was doing. She pressed cold hands to her face and tried to sleep. It was pointless; her mind was filled with so many memories – a touch, a word, the feeling as he sought her face in the dark. Her words, his words, love, happiness... *yes*.

. . .

The next evening, Aunt Hélène came into her room.

'Augustine is at the back door. You need to get ready soon.'

Augustine was sat outside looking thin and old. 'Are you prepared? You can take almost nothing, just what will go in your pockets.'

'I'm afraid to leave them all,' Jenny said, filled with doubts about leaving the family. 'They will all be suspected. And I could be caught by Herr Albrecht. I think he has people watching the house.'

'That's the excuse your aunt will circulate.' Augustine took a deep breath. 'People will think a girl ran away from the advances of the Gestapo.'

Jenny shut her eyes, remembering the wild waters just off the cliffs. 'When?'

'You will rendezvous with Laurie at the beach at Kerzoncou farm. The sardine boat is waiting off the coast. Then you'll transfer to the malamok *Talisman* in the fishing grounds.'

Jenny knew the traditional Breton motor fishing boats well, deep hulled, resilient in the stormy waters around the island.

'I'll bring the bag. And the gun Laurie gave me,' Jenny said. She had practised unloading and loading the single-shot gun.

'Fire only in an absolute emergency,' Augustine said. 'It has a very limited range. Here, I altered these for you.' A bundle of men's clothes had been hastily adapted for Jenny's slim frame. They smelled, and when Jenny wrinkled her nose, Augustine smiled. 'We didn't want you to be the cleanest fisherman in the fleet. We won't cut your hair – there are several women fishing now.'

'Not too different from the past,' Jenny said, remembering fishing with her father. 'Won't the malamok be too slow?' The engines were designed to drag long nets very slowly; the engines might overheat if they were pushed to the maximum.

'I imagine it's been adapted,' Aunt Hélène said, stepping

forward to hug her and kiss her cheeks. 'I'm astonished how often they do come across.'

'Thank you,' Jenny said, her heart pounding. 'Will I see you again, Aunt Hélène?'

'Maybe, maybe not. Tell your father, *this* is my love for him,' she said. 'Now, go. I will attend to the babies.'

Jenny crept out of the side door with the bag over her shoulder, heavy with papers and film canisters. She slipped to the edge of the family garden and into the large vegetable plot, well-used now food was short. One corner was used by a few hens and ducks scavenging under fruit trees; she could get onto the huge compost area there. Climbing on hot, smelly lawn clippings and vegetable scraps, she straddled the top of the wall, and after checking no one was below, let herself drop to the lane below. Crouched down, she waited to see if anyone had heard her. Far off, she heard a small dog bark, then answering it, a deep baying. Stories of Gestapo attack dogs came back to her.

She started to run, scrambling up the lane and then cutting through their neighbour's grounds, past their wash house, squeezing through the leggy shrubs onto the back field. She raced through puzzled sheep, their dark faces turned to her then scattering. Maybe, she thought, the dogs would be distracted by the animals, but the thought of the lambs at their mothers' heels made her stop. No, she would turn left, clamber over the stone water tank and drop down onto common lands, marked by a few fallen stones that were believed to be prehistoric. She kept low, afraid her silhouette would show in the dusk.

She ran across a new field, this one waist high with long grasses and probably ticks; she brushed her arms and legs off as she reached the cove. The last inlet before the beach was bisected by a rocky outcrop, maybe thirty or forty metres into the water. As the tide was dropping already, she saw where she could wade out, maybe cling, walk or swim around to the beach.

No, it is still too deep.

She turned to see if she could clamber over the top when she saw the dog. Its hackles were raised, bristling into a shadow monster in the shadow of the cliff. Its teeth gleamed, lips were drawn back and its growl vibrated through the ground under her feet. She knew it could kill her, and for a moment, she looked back at the sea, heart pounding.

She turned to face the dog, the strap of the bag wrapped around her arm. Maybe if she could wedge the bag in its throat – but then the Germans would find all the intelligence that agents had spent weeks collecting. But the dog hadn't moved. Its mouth was now more relaxed and she could hear him panting.

'Bruno?' Her voice came in a squeak. 'Bruno! Here, boy.'

All those times Albrecht had allowed the dog to befriend her. Maybe he preferred her to his cold, manipulative master. The dog bounded up, nudged his snout under her waiting hand. She gave his head a stroke, rubbed behind his ears.

Then he lifted his head, as if he could hear something Jenny couldn't.

His master's call.

52

Charlotte had struggled to sleep. Was the SOS group conspiring against her behind her back? Should she back off? But the local authority was right – Merryn already suffered from insufficient contact with other children her age.

She got up, looked over the empty field. Tink was supposed to mow it today. She felt like the world was shifting around her and she couldn't rely on anything. Losing Zach had left her unsure of what she wanted any more. That must be how Beau and Billy felt, uncertain about their future.

The boys were the warm centre of her world. And the thought of Ash was a glow of excitement too. She watched out for glimpses of him walking down the lane now he was camping out in the lorry. He still came to take the boys to the village green to kick a ball, or go for a walk. She had given up supervising him; Traci the social worker said they were satisfied that he wasn't a danger to the boys, but she missed being part of their little gang.

She hesitated over whether to call him. Their kiss still lingered in her mind. He hadn't said anything, and neither had she. The gap of awkwardness was growing out of control now, let alone her uneasiness that the boys knew. She texted him, and immediately wished she could retrieve the message.

Can we talk? I need someone to speak to.

Before she could add an even more awkward message of explanation, he replied.

Make some coffee and I'll come up.

She watched him walk up the lane, his head bobbing above the hedge, and all she could think about was the kiss. He smiled at her as he walked through the school gate.

'Can we get something out of the way?' he said. 'The kiss. I'm sorry if it embarrassed you.'

'I'm not embarrassed,' she lied. 'I'm confused. I haven't kissed anyone apart from Zach for years.'

'I just wanted to, that's all. You looked so lovely, and you did look like you were leaning in. And you did kiss me back...'

She smiled. So, this was what it was like to be an adult and single. Then the situation folded in on her. 'You're going to have a battle with social services over who gets the boys.'

'As long as you are honest with them – and me – about who you think they will be better off with, I don't mind.'

'Beau did say he wanted to live with a woman rather than a single man. He misses having a mum. Maybe Mrs Goodwin would work, if she would take Billy as well. And you could still visit them.'

And I could still visit them.

'I bet he does,' he said, slumping onto the classroom steps. 'I grew up with a single mum. I can't imagine how it feels to lose your mother. The boys and Chloe were a lovely unit. A bit chaotic and bonkers, but totally loving.'

'I'm sorry.' She sat next to him. 'Do you still miss Chloe?'

'I did for a long time.' He stared over the field. 'But I always knew she didn't feel the same about me.'

She bowed her head, hearing some pain in his voice that, if she was honest, she didn't feel about Zach.

He turned to her. 'So, what's going on? Is it the boys?'

'Not really. I've just found out the whole island is scheming to save the school behind my back. They think I am the enemy.'

'Aren't you? Everyone knows you're here to close it down.'

'Except me.' Charlotte winced. 'I thought I was doing a feasibility study to help the local authority decide *whether* to save the school or not.'

He laughed at that. 'Did you believe that?'

'Honestly, I'm struggling to make a case for saving it.'

He put his hands on his knees. He had long, slim fingers, to go with his lean physique. 'I think they need their school. Three babies will have been born within one year. They will all need somewhere to go.'

'So you're on their side.'

'Absolutely.' He patted her arm. 'And so are you. If Billy and Beau were going to stay here with me, say, they would need a good school.'

'But the permanent teacher has retired,' she blurted. 'I've only been keeping it running as a temp. I don't have the resources or the time to put together a really effective programme for the kids. And if you get custody, won't you go back to the mainland? Where the work is?'

'I don't know.' He sighed. 'I'm loving it here.'

She glanced at the side of his face. He always looked like he was thinking fast – he wasn't a restful person. When Zach wasn't talking about or actually surfing, he used to fall asleep. 'Although...' An idea began to grow. 'Let me think about it.'

He looked at her then, and smiled. 'If they had you on their side, they might have a chance.'

'I need to hear their plans, but I haven't been invited.'

'It's an open meeting, anyone can come. I'll be there.'

She stared at him, feeling a pressure building in her chest, realising she was holding her breath. At first she thought she was drawn to him because she was connecting with the boys, but it was more than that. It was *him*. She could smell his soap, his skin. His smile faded and he looked intense, like he was concentrating on something. Finally he leaned closer.

'You have to make the first move, this time,' he said.

She did, and his lips were as welcoming as before, his arm sliding around her waist to draw her to him. Dizziness swept in, and she had to remember to breathe.

She drew back and looked at him. His eyes were still closed, so she kissed him again, putting her arms around him, pulling him closer.

'It's not just me, is it?' He looked into her eyes. 'This feeling.'

'No. But I'm scared we will end up on different sides when it comes to the boys. *I'm* their foster parent.'

'But I am the best parent for them,' he said, taking a step back. 'I was their dad for more than two years, I knew them as small boys. I can keep their memories of their mother alive.' He reached forward and tucked a stray curl behind her ear. The touch made her jump, her heart skip a beat. 'Now, I'd better get back. See you tonight?'

'I'll be there,' she answered, looking up at him as he stood. 'Even though I'm the designated bad guy. But I do have a couple of ideas.'

She couldn't wait to start exploring alternatives.

Mid-morning, she sent the children out into the field before Tink mowed it. She set up her laptop overlooking the green so she could keep an eye on them. It would be unthinkable on any mainland campus, but where were they going to disappear to? She fired off email after email, to every contact and teacher in the islands she could think of, or discover online.

One of her previous internet queries had paid off. The diaries of Laurie Byers had been donated to the museum on the big island, St Brannock's, after it was found in the belongings of Jenofeve Macintosh, her great-grandmother. Tink walked up to the field gate, saw the children and looked around for her. He vanished around the side of the building to come in.

'I was thinking of cutting the grass while the weather's dry. I should get a decent amount of hay off. Is that OK?'

'Could you give them five more minutes? They're full of fidgets today and could do with shaking them out. Oh, Tink, do you know anything about Laurie Byers? The old man who lived in Seal Cove?'

'A bit before my time but...' He looked over at the children. 'I would have thought you would know more about that than I would, anyway.'

'Oh?'

'Well, wasn't he your great-grandmother's friend? I think she persuaded people to let him come back to the island after his prison sentence was over.'

She made a note. 'So, he *was* in prison?'

'I believe he served about eleven years. The museum would know more, but you should ask your mum. I'm sure she knew him, so did Isabelle.' He was holding something back.

'Go on. Tell me.'

'He was awarded a medal of valour, it was all in the papers. Laurence Byers, the only man to have been in prison *and* win a medal for bravery, all for the same war.'

She made a mental note to look up the details online. 'Thanks. Oh, before you go, do you know what Mr Byers was in prison for?'

She just hoped it wasn't murder – the sentence seemed long enough.

'Sure,' Tink said, frowning as he looked away. He cleared his throat. 'He was convicted of treason.'

53

In the distance, Jenny could hear voices shouting, maybe even calling Bruno's name. 'Go, boy,' she said, climbing up the rocks along the cliff. 'Find your master! It's all right...'

The dog whined, followed her a few yards, then looked back. Far away, a whistle sounded. 'Go!' she hissed. 'Good dog.'

He looked torn, trotted away a little, then looked back as she scrambled over rocks and through gorse bushes that tore at her clothes and her hands.

He barked then; maybe he was confused between his master and his friend. She hoped he wouldn't want to run through the thorns.

'Jenofeve?' The low Breton accent penetrated her racing brain. 'Is that you?'

'Here,' she panted, stumbling down onto the shaded beach, the pale sand wet at the top.

'The boat, it hasn't come,' Madame Keller sobbed, cradling her baby.

'It will be here,' she promised, turning back to hear if the dog was coming. 'Be quiet, I have been followed by one of the dogs.'

'That dog, he bit Joël Vourc'h, ripped his arm right open.' Her voice was trembling.

'Maybe we'll get away before he gets here,' Jenny said. 'Now, listen.' An oystercatcher sounded to the left of their position. Then it called again. 'Follow the sound of the bird,' she hissed, taking the hand of one of the children.

They stumbled on the soft sand, the light was going, the glitter on the dark water showing the falling tide.

'Here,' called a man's voice, in English. 'Here,' in Breton.

The dog howled, once, twice, louder now.

Two men were pulling on the oars of a small boat, their dark outlines against the glittering sea. It didn't slow, just crunched up the sand.

'Who are all these people?' The man repeated himself in French.

Jenny stepped forward. 'These are the Kellers. I want them to be given my place.'

The man's teeth flashed in a grin. 'Byers said you were going to be a challenge.'

'I have the information for you,' she said, holding up the leather bag. 'Just get them away.' Her voice was choked with tears. She felt cold at the thought of being captured by Albrecht.

'We'll fit you in.' The man beckoned to the family. 'Quick, come. We'll come back for you, Monsieur, just help your wife.'

The father lifted his wife in, the baby in her arms, then reached back for his oldest boy, Artur. 'Here, you take Pierre,' he panted, and Jenny passed the younger son to the sailor.

'Get in,' said the quiet English voice, almost in her ear. 'We'll come back for the father, if we can.'

'No,' Jenny said, 'leave us both. The dog will attack him if I go, but he knows me. Just come back quickly.'

'As quick as we can, then. Brave girl,' the man said, and she sensed rather than saw his smile.

The dog bounded onto the beach in a spray of sand, just as the sailors pushed the boat into the water. Jenny could hear the first strokes of the oars as she turned to face the dog.

'Good boy,' she called, but the dog was sniffing the air audibly, snarling as if he was about to attack. Monsieur Keller waded further out into the water.

'Bruno! *Halt!*' she shouted. The snarling stopped. She clicked her fingers as she'd seen Herr Albrecht do and he came to her, sniffing her hand. She could hear the shouts of many Germans now, see pools of light from lanterns or torches shining across the fields.

She stroked the dog, praising him, but she could feel that he was torn between her and something else, maybe his master.

'We must swim for it,' Monsieur Keller said. He was further into the water now. 'Come!'

'They will be back,' she said, sinking her hand into the dog's thick coat.

'Before or after that hellhound tears us to bits?' he said, up to his waist in water.

'He won't hurt me,' she said, feeling him nuzzle against her side. 'I'd take him with me if I could.'

The sound of oars approaching again gave her hope.

'Jenofeve.' The clipped, cold voice of Albrecht. Boots crunched through the shells and stones at the top of the beach.

She whirled around, just able to see the tall shape of the Gestapo officer. She fumbled in her pocket, even as the dog started whining.

'Don't come near,' she snapped. 'I'm armed.'

'Of course you are,' he scoffed. 'All you little English spies are armed.'

He didn't stop walking, though, and she dragged the little gun out, held it straight. 'I mean it.'

The torchlight dazzled her when he turned it towards her face. 'So I see. But are you ready to fire it? Are you ready to kill a man?' But his footsteps had stopped; he was barely a dozen metres away. The little gun was shaking in her hand.

'Are you ready to bet your life on it?' she snapped, as she put one hand over the other to steady it.

The oars had stopped a little off shore. 'Miss Huon!' came a voice over the water. 'You must come now!'

'Jenofeve!' shouted Monsieur Keller from the water.

'Bruno will attack if I command him to.' The smooth voice came over the beach. 'He has been trained to kill *spies*.'

'Try him,' Jenny said, hearing the dog's whining, almost feeling his confusion.

For a long moment she didn't hear him reply, then he started laughing. 'You are such a child. I should have taken you as a plaything months ago.'

'Go, Monsieur Keller!' she shouted, and Bruno barked.

'Fass! *Fass*,' Albrecht shouted, but the dog just howled.

Jenny fired over the man's head, making him fall to his knees, cursing her. She threw the gun, turned and raced for the waterline and splashed forward, hearing shouts and barks behind her. She waded out to her waist, the cold shocking, and ducked as a bullet flew past her.

'Halt!' he was shouting, but she half-swam towards the boat. Another bullet whined over her.

She was up to her neck in water before fingers reached down and heaved her up. It took several hands, roughly hooking into the back of her trousers and grabbing her feet to haul her in. They immediately laid her next to the soaked Monsieur Keller and they rowed in earnest for their fishing boat. They flinched from bullets, but it was getting dark – perhaps the Germans couldn't see them.

Eventually, they came alongside a bigger, open sardine boat, a pinasse.

'Up, now,' the man said. It was lovely to hear an English voice. The man boosted her and Monsieur Keller up a short ladder before leaping up himself. They abandoned the dinghy and started heaving up sails as more bullets splashed around them, but falling just short of their position. Jenny was grabbed by someone in a thick woollen sweater, the common uniform of both British and Breton fisherman along the Celtic Sea.

'Steady, girl.' English, which sounded strange after two years of Breton and French. Her next thought was a shock of recognition.

'Tad?' Her father hugged her, heedless of her soaked clothes, her shoes squelching on the deck. For a moment she forgot the danger of the German bullets and the patrol ships that were probably already looking for them,

'There, my girl,' he said, rocking her against him for a moment. 'We're not safe yet. Down below with you all, we've got the currents to run yet and then we're joining the fishing fleet.'

As the sails rustled and snapped in the wind and the boat pulled and leaned, Jenny heard the voice she feared. Albrecht, screaming at Bruno. Then, a single shot, a yelp from the dog, and silence.

54

Charlotte changed after dinner with the kids, and put on a bit of make-up. It was the first time she'd cared about her appearance since she had come to the island, mostly just putting on her 'teacher' clothes to help her act the role. *It doesn't really feel like a role now, though.* Tonight, she would have to put on her senior inspector gravitas.

When she walked into the schoolroom a few minutes before the meeting started, the chatter in the room fell quiet. Someone had lifted the rabbit cage onto the cupboards as there were several dogs in the room. People of all ages were there; she didn't recognise all of them. She worked her way to the back of the room and sat beside the rabbit cage. The talk in the room slowly dialled back up, and eventually several women, including Jayne, stepped up to the front.

'Welcome,' said Sorcha, who had booked the room. She caught Charlotte's eye. 'And thank you, Miss Kingston, for letting us hold the meeting here.'

All eyes swivelled to Charlotte. She cleared her throat. 'My pleasure.'

'Perhaps, as you're here, I could address a question directly to you?'

'Certainly.' She stood up so everyone could see her, just as Corinne and Ash slid through the doorway.

'Is it true that the council is trying to close down the school?' She spread her hands. 'As a former headteacher, I know how these decisions are made.'

'Actually, while the local authority *are* exploring that option, I am personally not decided about what will best serve the community.'

A babble of protest rose, people talking over each other until Sorcha waved her arms around and shushed.

'You understand that the island committee is very anxious to retain the school?'

'I do, and I know why. But you need to come up with a better reason than "the community benefits from having the school here". There has to be an educational benefit to each and every child.'

She looked around the room, picking out the faces that were turned towards her. Jayne, smiling encouragingly. Justin, with the baby strapped to his chest. Corinne, arms folded.

'Hi. I'm Lizzie Cameron from the school on St Piran's.' A woman stood and waved at the room. 'Charlotte and I have been in email communication,' she said. 'We had the same problems on West Island twelve years ago but we kept going, and now we have seven children attending. Charlotte specialises in art, history and English literature, I qualified in science and mathematics education. We need to be more effective at sharing our skills over the whole group of schools.'

A man in his forties stood up. 'Hi, Lizzie, Charlotte. Most of you know me. I'm Jim Barclay, teacher on St Petroc's. I'm normally up at the high school, but got seconded because we couldn't recruit a teacher to replace Ellen Jamieson when she left St Petroc's. As you know, we tried to recruit a replacement for Jayne for more than two years. No one wants to move to an island where the property is prohibitively expensive and the job is difficult. My school is vulnerable to closure, too. I don't want Morwen School to set a precedent.' He nodded to Charlotte, who continued.

'What we propose is to still have a teacher living on each island, but share the teaching over all the schools. Morwen children will be based at Morwen, but have a curriculum delivered over the islands, via the internet. When the tides and weather are good, we will take children over to another island for a weekly session of four hours of focused teaching, enrichment and socialisation.'

Before the ripple of conversation could drown her out, she stood tall and increased her volume. 'Which will start, with the parents' permission, next Wednesday when West Island School will be welcoming primary children from all over the islands for a maths day, preceded and followed up with planned work set by Lizzie.'

This created a tumult of people talking over each other, asking questions, putting their hands up. Sorcha pointed to one.

'Corinne. What do you want to ask?'

'The main concern about travelling between the islands has always been the transport. How do children travel back and forth in bad weather?'

Jim Barclay stood up to answer that. 'This would be weather-dependent. And we'd need to have contingency if our students got stuck in one school or another because of the tides or storms.'

Joanna put her hand up. 'Patience Ellis used to keep camping equipment in her school to accommodate visitors who couldn't get home. It hardly ever happened but we all got to have a sleepover with our Westy friends or St Petroc's kids. It's just part of island living.'

Jim nodded approvingly. 'And I remember going home on

the lifeboat a couple of times,' he said, eyes twinkling. 'But who hasn't been stuck in Penzance or on St Brannock's once or twice? Part of an island education, I would say.'

Sorcha fielded another few observations from people. Ash threaded his way through the chairs and the standing crowd to Charlotte.

'Are you OK?'

'I am.'

A woman she recognised – Lucy, who owned the café on the quay – moved closer. 'I was hoping to have a chat with you soon. About the school.'

'Oh? Good or bad news?' Charlotte laughed, a release of tension. She had been worried she might be in real trouble with the whole island.

The crowd quietened down, and Lucy went red as people listened. 'Sort of private.' She looked around, her ponytail swishing. 'Oh, well, nothing's ever really private on the island. My partner Marcus is moving permanently to Morwen, and he's bringing his daughter to live with us.' There were cheers and shouted congratulations. Lucy, now very red but smiling widely, put her head on one side. 'So, I was hoping you'd have room at the school for a nine-year-old who loves animals and horses?'

Charlotte laughed at that. 'I think we can squeeze her in.'

Sorcha called out for people to be quiet. 'But that does still leave a question over how to recruit a new teacher? Unless you want to stay?'

All eyes seemed to swivel to Charlotte.

'That's another problem. I'm not actually a working teacher,' she said. 'I've realised how horribly out of practice I am. I'm a school inspector, and I'll have to go back to my real job at some point. And the boys will be going to their forever family, eventually, and they will probably move to the mainland.'

Out of the corner of her eye she saw Billy standing in the

porch, just beyond the open door to the classroom. He was in his pyjamas already, and looking vulnerable. Before she could say anything he walked around the edge of room towards her. 'Need a kiss goodnight,' he said.

He leaned against her while she kissed his head. 'And say goodnight to Daddy Ash,' she said, and he hugged him. She realised the quiet room was watching her closely.

'Night, baby. Go and see Beau. I'll be in in a moment.'

She stood tall, meeting as many people's eyes as she could.

'I had no idea how important the school was until I came here. And I think the school is still underused, and investment has been inadequate for many years. Look at this old building! It was a temporary classroom back in the *eighties*. And how long has it been since someone thought about the accommodation for teachers? Most teachers are couples, or have children themselves. Who can afford to live here?'

'But you manage,' someone said from the front of the room.

'Because I don't have most of my stuff, or most of the boys' belongings, either. Keeping this school will need commitment and major investment.'

There was a round of applause and she realised she really needed to take a few deep breaths. She made her way through the crowd. She nodded to Sorcha. 'Thank you for letting me speak. Drop the key through the letter box when you've finished.'

Sorcha smiled as she took the key. 'So, you're working on a plan?'

'I'd like to be part of the solution,' she said. 'But we'll have to make a much better case than we have so far to sway the local authority.'

Outside, the cold air caught her as if she'd had too much wine. She staggered, and an arm went around her waist to balance her for a second, then dropped.

'I had no idea you had all that passion in you,' Ash said. He pushed the front door open. 'Do you mind if I come in?'

'No. I mean, I'd like that.'

She slumped onto the sofa and shut her eyes. 'I'm going to get fired,' she said, resigned. She could hear Ash filling the kettle.

'After earning this large slice of cake,' he said and she opened one eye. Slightly squashed but still wedge-shaped on a paper plate were two large slices of caramel-coloured cake. 'Coffee and walnut, from the hotel.'

She looked around. 'Where's Beau?' He must have dropped off. She'd tuck him in later if he didn't come down.

'He looked a bit upset earlier, outside the school.' He handed her a mug of her favourite night-time tea blend and the cake. 'Is that OK?'

'Heaven,' she said through the crumbs on her lips as he sat down beside her. 'Do we have to talk about' – she waved her hand between them – 'this?'

'I thought if we quantified it, it might be harder to find out what this' – he smiled, waved between them – 'is.'

'I'm not really a very spontaneous person,' she admitted.

'You don't know what kind of person you are if you've been in the same relationship since you were a teenager.' He leaned back. 'You're enjoying spontaneous cake, you've just winged a declaration of intent at the meeting. You're full of surprises.'

'I surprised myself,' she said, licking a bit of coffee butter-cream off one finger. 'This cake is delightful.'

He sipped his tea and looked over at the kitchen as she admired his profile. He had a long, thin nose, it made him look rather like an Egyptian pharaoh. She savoured every bite of the cake, and when she'd finished she clambered out of the embrace of the sagging sofa to check on Beau.

She pushed the door open a few inches; the room was very

quiet, and the curtains had been drawn around the nightlight so she couldn't see the boys. She let her eyes adjust to the dark then realised only one of them was in the narrow bed. Billy was asleep on his back, a pillow hugged tightly in his arms, as if holding his brother. But Beau was nowhere. She checked behind the door, looked under the bed, then ran downstairs to look in the bathroom.

'Beau's gone,' she said, her breath coming harshly in her throat. 'Where is he? Did he sneak into the classroom?'

'I don't think so. I'll go and check.' Ash put the remains of his cake and the cup down in the kitchen. 'He probably wanted to listen to the new plans.'

'No, I'll go,' she said, slipping out into the cold, dark yard. The meeting was winding up, people walking down the lane with torches, the schoolroom being put back to order by half a dozen people. She checked the lobby and even the store cupboard. By the time she slid to a halt in the classroom, Ash was already beside her.

'Have you seen Beau?' she called out, generally. She could hear the shrill note of panic in her voice.

Sorcha, just putting the rabbit cage back on the floor with Tink, looked confused. 'No. Why?'

'I can't find him.' Charlotte looked over at Tink. 'What do I do?'

'I'll call out the emergency services if we can't find him. Are you quite sure he hasn't fallen asleep in the house?'

'I looked everywhere, there aren't many places to hide,' Ash said, his mouth tight and narrow with tension. 'He'd be with Billy. He's very protective.'

'Where could he even go?' she said, swinging around as if Beau was somehow in the cupboards or hiding behind something.

Sorcha took her arm. 'He can't go far. He's probably just out in the field.'

'Or with the sheep,' Tink said. 'We've still got a few lambs due. I'll run down and search the field and the lorry before we panic anyone. Is there anywhere else he likes to go?'

She couldn't think straight. 'I don't know, maybe his grandmother's house?' She hadn't thought to check whether the key was still hanging up with the others. 'I don't know what to do.'

Sorcha's voice was kind but firm. 'I'll check at Clarrie's. Billy might know where his brother has gone, you should talk to him.'

Charlotte ran back to the house, just beaten to the door by Ash. Clarrie's key was still there, hanging by the door.

'Don't scare Billy,' he said, panting with the effort. 'We'll go and look for Beau, but let's hear what he knows.'

Tink spoke out of the darkness. 'He isn't in the field or with the sheep. I've asked for the ferry to be searched before it sails. But the cargo ship stopped here at eight thirty and it's just gone. The police are going to have to handle that search, it's a big vessel.'

Charlotte froze, her hands clenched on the door knob. 'He can't swim. What if he tried to get on one of the ships to run away? What if he fell off the quay or the tide cut him off?'

Ash put his hand over hers. 'He's so serious and he's grown-up for his age. He'll be careful.'

'But he's unhappy.' Charlotte dragged her sleeve across her face, which was wet with tears, and spoke fiercely. 'We've got to find him.'

She pushed Ash aside and headed upstairs. Billy was a huddle in the bed, the sound outside must have woken him up.

She sat on the side and he immediately came into her arms the way she had seen children curl into their mothers when they were terrified or upset.

'What's happening?' he asked.

'We can't find Beau,' she said, surprised at how the words

came out quite calmly. 'Where would he go if he was going off to frighten us?'

Billy shook his head. She cupped his heart-shaped face in her hands, lifting it to hers. 'I'm not cross, sweetheart, I'm just trying to find your brother.'

His bottom lip trembled, tears beading his eyelashes. He really was beautiful; she had known it since she first met him. But now she never wanted to let him go, and was hit by the knowledge that she loved him intensely. She recognised the emotions that were flitting across his features, but she needed to know what he was thinking.

'I don't know,' he wailed, and she let him burrow into her again.

Charlotte glanced up at Ash.

'Stay with Billy, I'll take the first shift,' he said. 'You man the phones. Sorcha is organising the islanders to search the town, and Tink has alerted the fire brigade, police and the coastguard.'

'OK.' It came out as a whisper. She hugged Billy, kissed his head. 'We'll find him,' she promised. 'Was he upset about something?'

She could feel Billy's nod against her collarbone. 'He said you were going away,' he said, snuggling closer and relaxing. He pulled away to stare up at her. 'You aren't, are you? Because we need you here.'

'I'm not going anywhere, right now,' she promised. 'Let's just think how to find Beau, and bring him back safely. Then we can explain it to him.'

She looked up to find Ash staring at her, seeing something stiff about his blank expression as he watched her with Billy.

'I'll call you if we find anything,' he said, holding up his phone.

'Thank you. Good luck.'

And then the tears came.

55

JULY 1941

Jenny woke when the rocking of the ship changed. She was lying on a narrow bunk with the eldest of the Keller children, and crawled over him, only bumping her head once, before squeezing into the tiny foredeck. The stink of wet clothes and fish was horrible. She pulled on her discarded and still-damp jacket to crawl out of the low door for some fresh air.

She found two trawlermen and three British naval officers, all dressed like fishermen. They had already made it through the Rail d'Ouessant current, only safe for smaller ships, and out into the Celtic Sea. Their boat was in a mixed fleet of perhaps two hundred fishing vessels from the north of Brittany and the islands. Many were out of Lorient, and there were two distinct types. Larger trawlers had trammel nets with cork floats out, and smaller boats were after herrings and sardines on long lines or short nets. Their boat was one of the smaller ones, and the fishermen had already started filling baskets with the silvery fish. The simple rig of jib, foresail and mainsail were just employed in the breeze, and the boat created a foaming wake.

Jenny shaded her eyes, her hair salty and tangled, to pick

her father out from the men on board. All were in old and torn clothes, glistening with spray and salt.

'Are you picking up the other agents?' she asked her father. 'I'm sorry I brought the Kellers, but I just couldn't leave them to be deported.'

'No, maid, they've moved to one of the uninhabited islands. I don't know if they will be picked up before the Germans find them.'

His expression was sombre.

'What have I done?' she said, putting a hand to her mouth. 'Oh, Tad...'

Have I condemned Laurie or one of the other agents to death? Maybe I'll never love anyone like that again. The thought of Albrecht's revenge made her feel sick.

'They'll look after themselves. They are all well trained.' Her father gestured to her to join him sorting through the small catch, throwing the smaller fish overboard. 'Look like you're fishing. There are quite a few wives and daughters out here.'

'The Breton way.' Jenny looked at him, tears filling her eyes. 'Oh, Tad, it's good to see you. How is Mam? And the boys?'

'Your mam's good, working at the cannery, earning more than me lately. Theo has joined up, he's in the North Atlantic, escorting convoys. Ben's away on St Brannock's, working at the airbase.' He looked across the sea, against the glare of the sun. He pulled his cap further down. 'German patrol, south-east, about a mile. Torpedo boat.'

He hadn't raised his voice. Jenny froze.

'What do we do?'

'Look like we're chasing a shoal,' her father said. 'Let them have a good look at us and they won't board. Jenofeve, start gutting those herring. The slimier and smellier the deck, the less likely they are to bother us.'

A young man with fair hair stepped down and sat by the

door to the tiny cubby, opening it a few inches. A few words of French and the door clicked shut again. He nodded to Jenny.

'You might not recognise me in daylight, but we met last night. Miles Macintosh, at your service. You can call me Mac. We'll just act surly and unhelpful if they pull us over. We all know a bit of Breton, most of it swearing, I'm afraid. I've told Madame to take the children into the crew quarters, right in the bows.'

That meant in front of the huge fish-well, now starting to fill with the herring. The stink of fish would be suffocating, and she hoped the parents could keep the children quiet. Jenny took the folding knife she was offered and started cutting and gutting on the top of the foredeck, her legs right up against the little door. It just looked like she was preparing some fish for lunch, and Mac pulled out a small but smelly petrol cooker and put it within reach.

For a couple of minutes the boat veered towards them. The crew glanced over at them at slow speed but then passed, their wake just rocking the boat.

'He's not bothering with us, he's going straight by,' her father said in French.

Mac smiled at her. 'All right, girl?'

'Jenny to you,' she said, sick with relief.

Mac went down into the fish locker to let the family out, at least into the roomier space beside the fish-well, where they could sit up in comfort. Jenny offered them some fried herring, but the whole family seemed to be struggling with sickness, so she rinsed out their bucket and left them to their suffering.

'It won't be long now,' her father said, sitting beside her. 'We'll try and get to the edge of the licensed fishing area, as the light goes. Then we'll transfer to the malamok and race for home.'

As the evening drew on, Jenny saw the local fleet turn,

dividing up to different ports. 'They aren't all from Ushant,' she said.

'No, they're from all over northern Brittany. We just have to hope no one reports us. We'll appear to be struggling to get the sails down – that would be a good reason to be stuck out here past dark.'

While two of the men pretended to wrestle with the sails, eventually getting them right down, Tad set a sea anchor to control their drift and attitude. Stars came out as the last of the light went, and by their light, the Keller family could finally emerge. One of the sailors offered a tin of milk to Madame Keller but she shook her head, patting her chest.

'I think they have all been really sick,' Jenny said, in English, to be instantly shushed. 'She can feed the baby herself,' she whispered.

'Voices carry over a calm sea, especially now the wind has dropped,' her father said. 'Very quiet, and just in French or Breton.'

Chastened, she hugged his arm and listened. It was quiet, until a splash beside the boat made her look overboard.

Mackerel, their swimming trails highlighted by phosphorescent ribbons, were being chased by playful dolphins. Even the Keller children, who had been too ill to sit up earlier, now sat on their father's lap and pointed and whispered.

One of the other sailors came around with hot tea, brewed on the petrol stove, and a tot of rum for the adults. A motor boat could be heard, first in snatches between waves, then constant and getting nearer.

'Quiet,' Mac said. 'It could be a patrol.'

But the *Talisman* emerged from the darkness, barely lit with a couple of deck lights, a rusty, deep-hulled boat. Tad helped Jenny clamber aboard, handing her the children one by one as Mac helped the adults.

'Get them below. The exhaust builds up in there, so only

shut it if we're challenged,' he said to Jenny. 'You go with them, we need to run hard for British waters until dawn.'

The engine coughed into life, sounding like a brass band, and Jenny was convinced the German ships would hear and investigate. One of the sailors, Rick, showed her the route he was plotting on the chart. She recognised the Celtic Sea, was able to see how far they had drifted and the route they needed to take.

'We'll be in home waters in about four hours,' he said, poring over the chart with a tiny red bulb almost touching his hair. 'Then we should get an air escort.' He smiled at her. 'Sleep. We'll wake you if we need to. The other two will take the pinasse back, hopefully pick up the agents.'

With a lurch she remembered Laurie. She closed her eyes, said an intense little prayer that her insistence on taking the Kellers hadn't got him killed.

She lay down in the bunk, short even for her, and rested her head on a folded-up jumper, thinking she would never sleep. But then she was gone.

56

PRESENT DAY, 14 APRIL

The search dragged on. Billy had cried himself to sleep and was now entangled in a quilt next to Charlotte on the sofa. She jumped at every sound, and the house was cold because people kept putting their heads around the door to tell her more bad news or offer support. It was such a small island, yet Beau seemed to have completely vanished.

The cargo ship had arrived at St Brannock's and the police were helping the crew search every box, container and cubby. Search parties were being coordinated by the fire brigade, and the coastguards were checking boats at anchor off the quay. Messages of support kept coming in from the islanders.

'I can take over, if you like.' Corinne's voice came from the doorway. 'I can't go and search with the baby, so I may as well sit on your sofa and worry as sit at home on my own. Maybe you could get a couple of hours' sleep.'

Charlotte slid out from under Billy. 'I don't need to sleep,' she said, her voice strained. 'I need to find Beau.' She lifted Billy easily, fuelled by adrenaline. 'I'll put him to bed. But yes, I'd be really grateful if you could take over.'

When she came down, Corinne was feeding baby Kitto.

Charlotte couldn't identify the raging river of emotions inside her. She was angry at Beau, at herself, at the world that had left the child so vulnerable. But under that was an ocean of terror.

'I'm going to retrace his steps from this morning,' she said, thinking over where he played in the field, the walk to the shop to get sweets. And over again, the trips to see the lambs. She had to see the pens and the fields for herself.

She rummaged under the sink for the large torch. She tried it, the batteries were OK. 'Look, I'm just going to check the lambs again.'

'He's not there, Tink already looked.' The baby started crying, and Corinne crooned gently to settle him.

'But he might have hidden from Tink,' Charlotte said, pulling on her jacket. 'If he thought he was cross with him. He'll come to me.'

'Will he?'

But Charlotte didn't have time to answer. She bolted out of the door, pulled it shut behind her, and walked out onto the gravel path to the school gate. She had been thinking back to what she had said in the meeting, one or two moments that, if taken in isolation, might suggest she was giving up on the boys.

Beau would come out to talk to her because he was enraged and felt betrayed – that, she was sure of.

By the time Charlotte arrived at the field, she had convinced herself he would be there. But he wasn't, not even with Barnaby, the lamb he had saved. When she shouted his name the silence was profound. Ewes and lambs called to each other, the sound mournful. She stopped, her legs shaking with the tension, and tried to catch her breath.

The cove. He was fascinated by the story of the man in the hut. She raced back to the lane, shutting the gates against the half-asleep flock, and checked her watch. Two fifteen, less than an hour to high tide.

What had they been talking about? Seal Cove. He was fascinated by the story of the man in the hut, the mysterious coded notebooks he was learning to decipher. She raced, stumbling on the uneven path, the bobbing torchlight almost useless. She could feel the breath catching in her throat, her chest burning.

She rounded the viewpoint at the south of the island, the stars making a million sparks of light on the sea.

'Beau,' she gasped, hoping he would answer. She had to stop to really yell. 'Beau!'

There was a whisper of a reply, unless it was in her head. She ran along the path, this time keeping the glow of the torch on the ground until she reached the top of the steps.

'Beau!'

The sound could have been an animal moving or a stone falling, but in her head it was Beau, lost in the water or fallen down the cliff. Even as common sense told her to alert someone else, instinct led her onto the uneven steps.

'I'm coming, Beau!' The sand behind the wooden risers got into her shoes. She grabbed the handrail where it hadn't fallen away, and half fell onto the triangle of sand at the bottom. The incoming tide almost reached the steps, and had created recesses either side along the beach.

She would have to wade through the water to get to the sand in front of Laurie Byers' hut. Her shoes filled with the icy water, and the sand underneath was unexpectedly soft and deep. She sank up to her knees quickly, gasping at the cold, struggling to get her feet out for each step.

'Beau!' *God, please let him be there. Please let him be all right.*

'Go away.' She could barely hear him at first, then his voice came sharp and hard. 'Go away! I hate you!'

'Beau, it's OK...' She slipped again, falling to one knee, soaking herself almost to the waist before she staggered upright again. 'I'm coming,' she said, managing to lurch ashore by the side of the hut. She slipped in the dry sand and shells, and grabbed the doorway to get her balance. 'I was so scared.' The torch lit him up with its last yellow glow, before going out.

Beau was curled up in a ball by the fireplace opening. He unfolded himself and stood up as her eyes adjusted to the darkness. He was moving slowly; she was afraid he was injured.

'What do you care? You're leaving us.'

'I don't want to,' she said, putting a hand to her chest while she caught her breath.

'You're going to close the school!' His voice was shaky, and she could see he was trembling. 'And then you'll let someone take us away. You want to get *rid* of us.'

'I do not,' she said, stepping into the shelter of the hut and pulling out her phone. No signal, not on the cliff side of the island. 'I would keep you if I could, but I'm just not the best person. Ash knows you, he could make you all into a family. Or your aunt – wouldn't it be nice to live with your cousins?'

'*Billy* is my family!' His legs gave way and he slumped against the wall, his head falling forward onto his knees.

She knelt down and felt his face, his neck. His skin was freezing.

'Beau, you have to warm up,' she said urgently.

'I'm tired,' he sighed, as if his outburst had used up the last of his energy. She looked down at her wet clothes. Her jacket was wet along the bottom but the rest was warm, and he was only in jeans and T-shirt. She pulled off her coat and, after a moment's thought, her long-sleeved top as well.

'Put this on,' she said, feeling the breeze on her bare skin. She had a lacy vest over her bra, but she was going to cool down fast. He seemed to be semi-conscious, she could barely rouse him.

She pulled the top over his head, forced his unresisting arms into it, then wrapped him with the driest bit of the coat. The best she could do now was get help. She might be able to wade back but it looked deeper now, and more dangerous. If anything happened to her, they might not find him in time. She looked up at the sandy, brambly cliff above the hut. She might be able to climb up a few metres, but again, what if she fell?

She pulled Beau onto her lap, wrapping her arms around him, and leaned up against the back wall.

Think.

When they were here before, Beau had found the tobacco tin. A box of matches, a wisp of dry grass. She turned to look behind them, Beau grunting in protest at the movement. She felt around for the dried sticks they had collected before – Merryn's magic staff, Billy's swords. She needed to make smoke to attract attention. And if she could create some warmth for Beau, that would help. She put a few bits of dry twig together in the fireplace, feeling her way with one arm while supporting Beau with the other.

'What?' he slurred, as she propped him against the wall to the side of the chimney. His eyes gleamed in the starlight, half open.

'I'm going to try and make a fire,' she said, fumbling around the wall for the alcove. She hadn't seen exactly where Beau had put the tin back while she was busy with the other children.

'There,' he said, one arm creeping out of the bundle of clothes to point, his arm wavering and drooping.

She felt around where he had pointed, a gap a finger's width between two stones. Her own hands were stiff with cold and she pulled the rusted tobacco tin out with difficulty. She fought to open it, laid the grass in the tiny fireplace, and added a few more twigs. It was harder to break the children's bigger sticks. Eventually, she managed to crack them into pieces and pile them in the hole.

When she opened the matchbox, panic rose in Charlotte's chest. She could only feel three matches.

The first one blew out almost as soon as she lifted it towards the tiny fire. The draught running up the chimney had too much pull. She fumbled in her jacket pockets as Beau watched. Two receipts, a tissue and a shopping list.

She twisted the papers and, shielding the flame with her body, managed to get the papers to light, then carefully dropped them on the dried grass. They caught, and almost immediately she realised it would burn out before the sticks caught. She reached up through the open roof, grabbing at the black bramble sticks, the thorns dragging into her skin, and snapped some off. With them came handfuls of dry grass.

Carefully feeding the fire, she could already feel a little warmth, even as each gust of wind blew smoke down and around them both.

'Seaweed,' Beau said.

'What?' She followed his gaze. Along the highest tideline was a load of dried, blackened weed. Bladderwrack, she remembered.

She crawled out of the hut, hitting the cold air, and scooped up a load of the crispy stuff. Putting some on the fire almost extinguished it, but then a foul, fishy smoke erupted, curling up towards the cliff.

She fed it more, and made frequent excursions along the edge of the sand for dried wood and weed, grass, anything that would burn. A discarded water bottle stank so badly she and Beau retreated from the warmth of the fire. Every couple of moments, she stood outside the hut and screamed up the cliff.

'Help! Help! We're here!'

After what seemed like hours but was probably only ten minutes, someone shouted back.

'Charlotte!' She could hear the tremor in Ash's voice. 'I'm coming down!'

'I've got him,' she called back, but between the smoke and the cold her voice was raspy. She turned back to Beau, now lying curled in the corner like a cat, eyes closed, face shadowed in the glow from the fire. 'He's here.' She started to cry.

She held his frozen hand and tried to warm him through her sheer need for him to be OK.

Ash had to wade through the water, now at the top of the high tide, to get to them. He reached indiscriminately for both of them, gathering them in his long arms. He crushed Charlotte against his wet clothes and squashed Beau in the middle.

'He's cold,' she managed to say. 'He's freezing. I don't know —' She couldn't finish the thought.

Ash pulled back, put his fingers against Beau's throat. 'He's cold, pulse is slow. He's probably hypothermic.' He looked over at the fire. 'I smelled the smoke. I should have thought of here, I knew he was fascinated. I was so certain he'd gone on the ship.'

'Me too,' she said. 'But he was so interested in Byers.'

'Beau?' Ash said, as the boy stirred a little. He shone his phone torch on his face. 'You're going to be OK.'

'I want Mum,' Beau breathed. His eyes filled with tears, and he closed his eyes again.

Charlotte hugged him again. 'How do we get him out?'

Ash was already pulling off his jacket and scarf. 'We'll keep him warm. I told Tink about the smoke, he's going to round up the fire brigade.'

'The fire brigade is pretty useful,' she said, a humourless smile tightening her face.

'I'd think of joining,' he said, looking at Beau with concern, feeling inside his clothes. 'If I was staying.' He glanced up at her, and turned the light on her. 'His core isn't too bad. I'm a bit worried about you, though. I don't think I've seen that shade of blue on someone's arms before.'

'Oh.' Charlotte pulled Beau a bit closer, to cover her semi-nakedness a bit. 'Well, I had to do something...'

'You did great,' he said, reaching a hand out and touching her shoulder. She could barely feel his warmth. 'But you are freezing too. Share the coats with Beau.' He went outside and called up the cliff. Charlotte relaxed a bit. She hadn't realised how tense she was, clinging to Beau as if to breathe life into him.

'Stay with me, sweetheart,' she murmured to him. 'I won't let you go.'

They swathed Beau in blankets and strapped him to a rescue cradle, to be hauled up the cliff as the stars faded and the sky lightened. The fire brigade's leader, Ed, had decided speed was more important than the high tide. Ash wrapped Charlotte in the blankets and waterproof they had left for her.

'The tide's started to turn now. They'll take Beau over to the big island to get him checked out.'

'I want to go with him. It's not so deep now.' She staggered to her feet, her legs stiff. The tideline had retreated a few metres, and the water was glassy. It wasn't quite as freezing or deep as she remembered, barely over her calves, and Ash steadied her in the soft sand.

'He thinks I'm abandoning him,' she said, struggling up the first few steps. 'He thinks I don't want him, that it's just a competition between you and Mrs Goodwin.'

'Do you love him?'

'Of course I do.' She caught her breath halfway up. 'What did you think?' she answered sharply. 'That doesn't mean I should *adopt* him. If he and Billy didn't have anyone else, I would, in a heartbeat. But they have family.'

'I do want to adopt them. I always have.'

'I know.' She looked over his shoulder at the sea, achingly

beautiful in many shades of deep blue-green. 'Which is why I'm going to support your application to have the boys,' she said, the words sounding flat. 'It's the right thing to do. You'll keep them together, you'll make a home for them.' Her voice broke. 'And if I could come and visit...'

'Of course you can,' he said, his hand cupping her elbow, firm, warm. 'All the time. Thank you, Charlotte, that's a huge sacrifice, I know.'

'I'm just a stopgap emergency foster carer,' she said, starting up the steps again. 'I'm going to try and save the school, then maybe do something completely different for a change. Go on my own adventure.'

He was quiet as they got to the top, and she watched the quad bike-turned-ambulance slowly bounce Beau along the path, the rest of the rescuers following behind. 'I mean it. Your support could give me a real chance. Although I've come to wonder if Traci isn't too keen on Mrs Goodwin's determination to split the boys up.'

Charlotte was already feeling more alert. She had started shivering again, painfully. 'I'm going to let Billy know Beau is OK, then put all my winter jumpers on,' she said. 'Then I'm going to have a *massive* hot chocolate.'

57

JULY 1941

Jenny woke in terror to the sound of planes overhead. She jumped up and scrambled to poke her head out of the locker door. Two Spitfires, with their British colours, wheeled and spun overhead, like playful birds.

'We're about two hours from St Piran's harbour,' her father said, looking exhausted. 'Do you want to get our guests?'

The family looked pale and sickly and struggled to climb the few steps onto deck. Mac insisted they all drank something, even a few mouthfuls of tea. The baby just latched on to his mother, who probably wouldn't have chosen to feed him in front of five strange men, but looked beyond caring.

'Madame,' Jenny said, passing her some sweetened tea. 'For your milk.'

'Thank you, Jenofeve. We will never forget your kindness, your bravery.'

Jenny felt herself flush. 'No, Madame. These men, who came all this way to fetch us, they are brave.'

Madame sipped, grimaced, sipped again. 'You stood up to that dog, you got us on that boat before it attacked.' Her eyes filled with tears. 'I thought... my children...'

'Are well. And will be safe until the war ends.'

The oldest boy, Pierre, shouted, pointing at the horizon.

Within a few minutes the adults could see what the young eyes had picked out, the low silhouette that almost looked like a cloud bank.

'Îles de l'Atlantique?' he asked Jenny.

'Yes.' Jenny started to smile. 'Sí,' she affirmed in Breton. It had been almost two years since she was home. She could almost smell Morwen, the fresh wind off the sea, the valerian sprouting out of the walls. Ushant was so Breton, with its homes and pubs smelling of coffee and garlic. She couldn't stop smiling, while at the same time tears trickled down her face.

58

Beau needed a few hours in hospital to thaw out and be monitored, just as a precaution. Ash stayed with him, all questions over his suitability as a parent gone. Charlotte got back to the schoolhouse before dawn and curled up on the bed next to Billy. He was too wound up to sleep for a while, and kept calling out questions from his half-sleep. Eventually, he dozed off holding her hand, and once she read the message from Ash that he and Beau were coming home on the afternoon tide, she was able to catch a couple of hours' sleep herself.

She woke around lunchtime to find that people had left croissants downstairs, with orange juice and her favourite brownies from the café. They had also left notes and cards for her. The common thread was how relieved her new friends and neighbours were that they were all right. These people who had been strangers just a few weeks ago.

She dressed, leaving the restless Billy to sleep, and put some coffee on. She felt hollow, because something had resolved in her head while she was fighting for Beau.

She hadn't been grieving for her lost relationship with Zach, after all. She hadn't even been falling for Ash, although that possibility was zinging through her. Somehow, without her permission or knowledge, she had become a mother. Maybe only a temporary foster mother – her eyes filled with tears at the thought – but the boys had made it easy to love them.

She sighed into her coffee, wiped away the tears, closed her eyes and let the uncertainty in. She couldn't predict or control what was going to happen – fifteen years with Zach had cured her of that illusion. The idea of being a mother was even more of a pull, and her life would be empty without a child in it. Ash, Billy and Beau would soon be building their new life, and seeing pictures on social media or making the odd visit wasn't going to be enough. But she would rather take crumbs than no cake at all.

She picked up the phone to call Traci on her out-of-hours number.

When Beau walked into the house, she saw instantly that he was mortified with embarrassment. She reached out, hugged him, kissing the top of his head.

'You need a haircut,' she said, running her fingers through his hair. 'We need to find a hairdresser who knows something about black hair.'

He shrugged and pulled away, but there was a tiny smile. 'Just buzz it off,' he said.

'No! I like it longer.' She smiled over his head at Ash, who put a couple of plastic bags down. 'Thank you, for everything.'

He looked into her eyes and she got that breathless feeling again. She didn't fight it, or try to hide it.

She hugged Beau again until he started to fight her off. 'I'm glad you're both home and OK. Billy's watching TV upstairs, can you go and get him?'

Ash put his coat on the back of one of the kitchen chairs. 'I'm guessing you've spoken to Traci?'

'I have. Have *you*?'

'Mrs Goodwin is formally applying for Beau's custody. She is going to consider taking Billy too, to strengthen her claim. She has made an accusation that you can't control him or keep him safe.'

Ouch. She winced. 'There's some truth in that.'

'No, there isn't. Beau didn't really run away because he thought that you or I were giving up on him, no matter what he says. He couldn't cope with his feelings any more because his mother died. That's what's driving him to act out.' He sat at the table, looking down at his hands. 'How is Beverley Goodwin going to help him with that? She hasn't committed to taking Billy or hidden her opinion of Chloe—' He stopped as he heard footsteps in the bedroom overhead. 'I need to fight for them.' His face was set, determined. 'I'm sorry, I know you care for them, but I have history with them, they love me—'

'Stop.' She waved his argument away. 'You're right. Anything I can do to help, I will.'

Billy scampered down the stairs and shot into Ash's arms, then climbed onto his lap.

'You're back!'

'I am. Did Beau tell you?' He looked up at Charlotte. 'Are you going to tell Charlotte our news, or would you like me to?'

'Me.' He bounced onto the floor. 'Me and Ash and Beau are going to live in Grandma's Clarrie's house! She says we can have the house because she's going to live... somewhere else, I can't remember the name...'

'Clarrie is going into a stroke rehabilitation centre in Penzance,' he said. 'Hopefully we'll be able to help her build a relationship with the boys. Long term, there's a co-housing place for older women there; she's looking into that.'

'She can be a proper grandmother,' Charlotte said with delight, remembering Clarrie's words.

'She might sell the cottage for the buy-in money, but not for a while. So she's letting us stay there.'

Charlotte let Billy hug her around the waist, and hugged him back. 'That's good for the island, and the school.'

'Absolutely. As she says, it keeps it in the family.'

'And,' said Billy, looking up at her, 'you can carry on being our teacher.'

She crouched down to hold him closer. 'I will as long as I can,' she said, her voice husky. 'Until the summer. But they will have to replace me in September.'

Beau stood at the bottom of the stairs. 'I went to the museum,' he said, holding up an envelope. 'I picked this up for us. It's from Mr Thurston, the man who wrote the book.'

She reached for the package before she recalled what it was. 'Oh. Laurie Byers' records?'

Billy jumped up. 'Can I see them, too?'

She sat on a chair, lifted him onto her lap to keep him still, and pushed the envelope back to Beau. 'You open it.'

Ash leaned forward. 'What's this?'

'This is the diary Laurie Byers left in the hut in Seal Cove. No one's read it because it's in code, but we – Beau and I – are learning a way to decode it.'

Beau lifted out the photocopied sheets. He squinted at the very top of one. 'See?' He read the first line, glancing at the decoding sheet. 'M-A-Y-1-9-5-8.'

Ash turned his head to read along with Beau. 'How are you doing that?'

Beau lifted a smaller sheet. 'This is it, Charlie, isn't it? It's the translation.'

She smiled. 'Carry on.' She pushed it over.

'It's really small,' he said, but leaned closer. 'May 12. That's what it says at the top, doesn't it?'

'Exactly! Can you carry on?'

'Gr... grey seals, with – is that pups? Are baby seals called pups or cubs?'

Charlotte looked at Ash, who was grinning. 'Oh, yeah, he reads now, but mostly natural history and secret codes. It turns out he's a great decoder.'

She could see Beau's lips moving as he picked out some words. 'Jenny came, something Isabelle, gave her two – some-thing – crabs.'

'Isabelle is my grandmother's name, Jenny's daughter. Born in 1942.'

Ash read over his shoulder. 'Spider? Spider crabs – they are amazing creatures with long legs. I've seen them deep down, crawling about. They look like aliens but they taste good.'

Charlotte remembered Patience Ellis's rockpool book. She lifted Billy down and took the book off the shelf, leafing through until she found a sketch of crab shells washed up on the beach. 'Really spiky things,' she said. 'Big, too. I didn't know people ate them.'

Ash lifted the stack of papers. 'There are dozens of pages here.'

'And that's just one diary,' Charlotte said. 'The museum has nine of them from the hut. Laurie worked in intelligence on St Brannock's during the war. He worked out a special cipher with Jenofeve, my great-grandmother. They ran messages in and out of Ushant off Brittany. They were part of the preparations for D-Day.'

He looked from Charlotte to Beau. 'What cipher?'

Beau leaned against Charlotte's arm, his warmth reassuring after their time in the hut. 'Laurie and Jenny would code German messages – what did they call them?'

Charlotte smiled. 'Intel.'

'They turned them into Breton, it's a special language of Brittany.' Beau spoke with confidence. 'They muddled that up into code. Jenofeve was on Ushant Island, sending messages to her dad. He would translate it back into English, then the army people knew what the Germans were doing.'

'Wow.' Ash looked genuinely impressed. 'So you've been looking at the same code? Good for you.'

'Just in English. But it's teaching me to read. That and the bird books.' Beau shrugged as if he wasn't thrilled with the praise but the raised shoulder and half-smile said otherwise.

Ash rummaged through his shopping. 'Which reminds me... The bird book we bought on the big island, you might like to show Billy.'

Charlotte looked through the transcript which the historian had provided, finding more and more information – and puzzles.

'*She brought the child to see me...*' She looked at another entry. '*Child is going away to school. Desolate.* Who was this child he keeps talking about? Grandma Isabelle?' That triggered something. 'Grandma left me a bag, hang on...' She rummaged on the table for the old messenger bag. Inside, written in loopy letters, was 'Iz Macintosh'. Beside it was a faded inscription, dug into the leather. *L.B.*

'*She* must be your great-grandmother – Jenny.' Ash started reading aloud from another page. '*The Americans landed by the radar station.* Is he writing about his exploits as a spy?'

Charlotte showed him the bag. 'This must have been his even before the war. I didn't make the connection. He could even have carried this back and forth to France. My Grandma Isabelle left it to me.'

She looked at another document, a scanned photo album. Inside, the pictures were tiny squares in black and white, many images of the seals, the cove, the waves.

'These were his photographs.'

A child running around the cove. A woman in her thirties in the doorway of the hut, the door open, a bag of things at her feet. Then a middle-aged man, sitting on a picnic rug on the sand, the child standing behind him. They looked as comfortable together as family members.

'That looks like Isabelle.' Charlotte bent over the grainy picture. 'I see a family resemblance with my mother. My great-grandmother – I suppose that's Jenofeve – married Miles Macintosh during the war.'

'You need to see the original,' Ash said. 'Scan it, blow it up. Similar eyebrows and eye shape, too, don't you think?'

'That could be my grandmother Isabelle Macintosh,' Charlotte breathed. 'What's the relationship with Byers?'

A search on the laptop led to a copy of a birth certificate, viewed online by Ash. 'Here, Laurence Gillespie Byers, born 11 January, 1914.'

There was a death certificate too. 'He died in Seal Cove,' she said, glancing over at the boys who were sat under the enormous glossy bird book. 'He died of old age, in the hut.'

A wave of fear that she would end up old and alone swept through her. She shrugged it off.

'If Clarrie is lending you the house, you'll be staying for a while,' she said. 'Will you carry on working at the hotel?'

'Actually, I'm going to see if I can get a diving job here. It's a great maritime location, and there's work for me.'

'Deep-sea diving?'

He laughed. 'Not much deep sea around here. I had a chat to a diving school on the big island. They have plenty of instructors for beginners but find it hard to recruit instructors from intermediate qualifications onwards. They usually have to fly one in, hardly worth it if it's just a couple of students. The rest of the time I could be a diver for hire for salvage projects.'

'So, you could stay here. The boys would go to the school.'

'Well, they would if you stayed to teach them,' he said softly.

She looked up at the familiar high cheekbones, the seashell whorl of his ear, the hazel eyes. 'I can't,' she murmured. 'My heart is breaking right now. I'm going to concentrate on the island schools set-up. Jayne will be filling in.' Tears filled her eyes, and he fetched her some tissue as she leaned away from the copied documents. One tear had splashed onto them, making a ring of ink blots. 'I'll help you keep the boys, if I can, of course I will.'

'But you love them.'

She smiled, despite the tightness in her chest. 'I do. So I want what's best for them over everything.'

He nodded, looked over at the boys. 'Would it be OK to take them to Clarrie's house tomorrow? I think they need to remind themselves of the cottage and I've never actually been there.'

That was it – she could feel the tearing, of her heart actually breaking. She summoned the last of her composure into a watery smile. 'Of course.'

'I'd ask you to come too but...'

'No. They need to see how it would work with the three of you. There are three bedrooms, you know, although one is tiny. Beau said he liked it, he can hear the sea at night. I used to love that sound at night, too.' Her common sense kicked in. 'You'll need Billy's pull-ups. He still wets the bed occasionally and any change makes him more vulnerable.'

'You know them so well, already.' He raised his voice. 'Boys. I thought we would go and see Clarrie's house tomorrow, see if we need to buy anything because Grandma will be taking some of her stuff with her.'

Billy bounced over like a kangaroo. 'Can we have a dog? Please?'

Ash smiled. 'No. But you could walk other people's dogs, if you like.'

Beau gave Charlotte one of his sharp stares. 'What if that other lady wants to keep us?'

Charlotte shook her head. 'We're going to fight for you. I

mean, we're going to argue that Ash will make a brilliant father for you both.'

'Are you staying on the island?'

Charlotte closed her eyes for a moment to block him out. 'For a little while. I've got a big fight on my hands too, to save the school. Then we have to find a proper, experienced teacher for you all.'

'You're already a teacher.' Billy started jumping around. 'And then we could see you every day and Beau will learn to read.'

Charlotte swept her fingers over the photographs in the document bundle. 'He is learning to read already. Who knows, I might come back one day. Some people really can't get away from the island, can they? Look at Laurie Byers. He still came back after everyone knew he was a convicted criminal.'

'Here's a wild idea,' Ash said. 'Did he stay for the child? I mean, was she really *his*?'

She stood up, feeling heavy and aching after the stress of the last few days, and lifted down the folder she had been keeping. 'She could have been. Jenofeve married in 1941. My grandmother was born fairly soon after.'

'So she could have already been pregnant.' Ash looked excited, and even Beau was listening.

Charlotte could almost feel her grandmother's disapproving frown. 'More likely by the man she married.'

'Where was Laurie back then?' Beau said.

She looked back through her notes. 'It just said he was on duty.'

'He could have been in Brittany, with Jenny,' Ash said. 'She could have married to give her child a father.'

Charlotte looked at the scribbled family tree they had cobbled from their notes. 'She could have been twenty-one, pregnant and looking for a home.'

'Well, Byers couldn't have married her, could he? He was already convicted of treason and going to prison.'

'She was on Ushant nine months before she had the baby.' Charlotte looked through the pictures, found one of mother and daughter. 'She was pretty. This was her and Miles, on their wedding day. They look happy, don't they? And maybe he let her visit Byers, bring Isabelle to the beach.'

'She was a kind person, to overlook his crime,' Ash said, letting Billy clamber into his lap. 'Like her great-granddaughter. Picking up waifs and strays.'

He smiled at her, and somehow it made her feel even more lonely. This cottage would go back to being an empty, cold, temporary home when they left.

'When do you want the boys to move into Clarrie's? The weekend?'

Billy looked from one to the other. 'And you're coming too?'

'Well, I have to be here for the school,' she said, improvising. 'And you need to get used to Ash looking after you. I expect you'll want to change the rooms around, too, if Grandma Clarrie won't be able to be there.'

'She can't walk upstairs any more,' Billy said, his mouth turning down.

'But we'll go and see her in her new place, all the time,' Ash said. 'And I expect Charlotte will help us pack up Clarrie's things and get my stuff from the truck.' He looked over his shoulder at Beau, who was hiding behind the book but clearly listening. 'We can go to the mainland and pick up my games console and big TV.' The book twitched and Billy jumped off, shouting in celebration. Ash rolled his eyes at her. 'Boys' toys, huh?'

'It's going to be a boys' house,' she said. 'Let's make sure the court chooses you over Beverley.'

59

Despite, or perhaps as a consequence of, all the stress and exhaustion, Jenny slipped back into home life feeling like a child. While her parents and siblings worked, she slept late, often waking in her tiny bed under the eaves in broad sunshine. The house would be empty, food left out for her.

The food. Despite rationing, the English had more food than the French could dream of. The island's fields had been dug up and were producing potatoes, onions and cabbages, topped with lazy white butterflies, diligent children picking off the eggs to prevent caterpillars.

There was enough bread, and there was fresh meat from the big island even if it was supplemented by a lot of offal. Her mother's pastry made her mouth water at the very thought.

So when Jenny woke one day to nausea and faintness, she knew the consequence she had both dreaded and longed for. A memento of one night, while life and death flirted with them, in the summer house, on a heap of beach towels behind the lawn chairs. She shut her eyes against the sickness, took a few deep breaths, and turned the signet ring Laurie had given her around her finger.

Since that terrible night on the sea, waiting for a torpedo or machine-gun fire, she had spent a lot of time with Miles Macintosh. When he got leave from his post on St Piran's, he came over, talked about his home in Northumberland. He made her laugh, telling her his exploits and adventures, where he always came out the fool having to be rescued by his friends or his brothers. She thought about Laurie every day, but she knew that he was never going to be with her. Her debriefing had made it clear. After his duty, if he survived, he was going to prison, perhaps for a very long time.

Sometimes she thought she had fallen for him because he was the connection to home, because what he was doing was so dangerous and brave. But sometimes she just woke up in tears, feeling the pressure of his arms fade into the daylight.

She dressed, walked up onto the cliff path, and sat at the top of Seal Cove. The tide was right up to the steps, leaving a patch of cut-off sand either side; pink sea thrift grew in great clumps all down the rock face. She waited. This was where Mac often found her, looking out to sea. He said she was waiting for the rest of the mermaids to join her.

Today it was an hour before he came, and she was ready to stretch her cramped knees and walk back by the time she heard his footfall.

He reached out a tanned hand to pull her up. 'I have news,' he said. His voice was sombre, and he didn't look at her and grin as he normally did.

'Oh?' Her heart started to race. 'About Mr Byers?'

He turned away, his profile sterner than normal. 'He's back on the island, to do some training with new equipment.' He shrugged a shoulder. 'He wants to see you.'

'I can't.' She could feel the panic fluttering in her throat.

Mac turned back to her, took her cold hands in his warm ones. 'I won't ask why you won't see him,' he said softly. 'Things happen in war.'

'Yes,' she said, her eyes filling up.

'You like me, don't you?' He smiled, his mouth lopsided. 'As a friend.'

'Yes, of course. Mac, what is this?'

'In military terms, this is an ambush.' He tried to joke, but he looked down, his smile slipping. 'You love him, don't you? Byers.'

'I thought I did,' she said. 'But then I thought one or both of us would die.'

'Well, I love you *now*.'

She caught her breath. He was staring at her quite seriously, not his normal playing around. 'You hardly know me,' she answered. 'And now—'

'I fell in love with a scruffy mermaid I heaved into the boat at Kerzoncou beach.'

'It was dark,' she said, without thinking. 'You couldn't even see me.'

'Enough to see how hard you tried to save a family you hardly knew, in defiance of your orders, even your own safety. And with all your wet clothes I wasn't sure we'd get you in, so I imagined you as a beautiful sea creature as I almost dislocated my shoulders.'

'Then you saw me.'

'And you were even more beautiful. I helped you down the steps, I took off that awful jacket and inside was this pearl, this brave, generous girl. I lost my heart right then.'

Jenofeve looked out to sea, frightened by his intensity. 'I have nothing to offer you. I love – if I love anyone – someone else. Laurie.'

Mac shook his head. 'I wish you could understand. He was convicted of *treason*.'

'No, *you* need to understand,' she said, not wanting to see the warm look in his eyes fade. 'I'm pregnant. The secret service say they can give me some medicine to make me miscarry, but I can't do it.'

He shook his head and smiled again, even more warmly. 'I love you, Jenofeve Huon. I can wait for you to fall in love with me. In the meantime, shall we give that baby a family?'

Looking up at him, Jenny thought maybe she could. 'I have nightmares of those weeks before we escaped. The things that happened, the boat, the Gestapo...'

He nodded, closed his mouth as if to stop himself saying anything else, and hugged her. She let him hold her close, breathed in his smell of laundry starch and hair cream. She shut her eyes. Mac was a safe harbour. Laurie was a winter storm.

'I need to talk to my mother,' she said. 'Then I can answer you. Then you've got time to change your mind. You would be bringing up someone else's baby.'

'I'll be bringing up *your* baby. I don't doubt Byers' courage, and I know he's going back to Brittany. I'm not going to feel any different about you in a few weeks' time.'

He put his hand slowly onto her belly which unexpectedly moved her; she fleetingly wondered what it would be like to be married to Mac, to lie in his arms on the island, listening to the sea.

60

PRESENT DAY, 1 SEPTEMBER

By the end of summer, Charlotte had been through a madly busy time. She'd successfully argued that Morwen School should stay open as part of the shared primary initiative on all six islands, and undergone an intensive return-to-teaching course in Bristol. She'd let go of Zach, and grieved moving away from the boys. They contacted her regularly and she'd visited them a couple of times, not wanting to distract them as they attached to Ash.

Now, after a bit of a battle with Beverley Goodwin – who finally admitted she felt taking Billy would be a duty rather than a joy – the adoption panel had done the many checks and reports they needed. Billy and Beau's biological fathers had given up their parental rights, and the adoption was going through.

Charlotte turned up at the court in the county town of Cornwall, Truro. She was a little shaky at seeing them all again.

Seeing Ash again.

'It's Charlie!' Billy charged along the pavement outside the court, dragging Beau behind him. 'We're getting adopted!'

'I know, I know!' She bent a little to catch him as he

cannoned into her, taller and heavier than when she had last seen him. 'Oh, my goodness. Look at you two!'

Beau smoothed down his jacket. 'We got new clothes.'

She put her hands on his shoulders and looked into his relaxed face. 'You look great.'

'Your hair grew long,' Billy said, catching her hand.

She ran her hand over his close-cropped head. 'And you got haircuts. Very smooth.' Then Ash was there, and she had to take a deep breath to stop the dizziness.

'Hi, Charlie. Is it OK if I call you Charlie, too?'

'Of course. Congratulations.' They'd had a few phone calls, always about the boys, after she left the school to Jayne's capable management.

'Thank you. Beverley's here somewhere, too, and Traci. They both want to make sure I go through with it, I think. Tie these rascals down.'

'Great. Should we go in?'

Ash reached for her hand, his skin warm. She looked down at it, uncertainly.

'I... we... need to talk afterwards. Don't run off, OK?'

By the time Charlotte had greeted friends from the island, Clarrie with a walker but looking so much better, Justin and Rob from the hotel with Merryn and baby Max, Corinne and Tink, Ellie with her newborn baby, Zillah, in a sling, the ceremony was beginning. The judge confirmed the adoption, solemnly asked the boys and Ash if they agreed with the adoption, and declared them all a family. Ash had booked a function room and caterers to celebrate, and people had started to disperse to the venue when he caught her hand again.

'We want to ask you something,' he said, sounding a little out of breath.

She'd been overcome by seeing the boys' shining eyes, their happiness with Ash, his emotion when the judgement was recorded.

'I'm not sure—' *I can cope, right now.*

'Beau. You're up.' Ash's hand was so warm and strong, and she felt Billy grab the other one, pulling her around.

'Charlie,' Beau said, an awkward grin on his face. 'You love us, don't you?'

'I do,' she said, choked with tears. 'Of course I do.'

'We love you too. So we would like to adopt you,' Beau said, his grin widening.

Ash squeezed her fingers. 'We mean, on whatever terms you want us. Friends, family, anything you want.'

She stared into his dark eyes. She had longed for him, as much as the boys. 'Any terms?'

His kiss cut off any more words, and she was vaguely aware of Billy shrieking with delight and someone clapping. Ash pulled away a little. 'We'll come to you, whenever you want. Maybe we could go on holiday together, and you could visit us on the island. We could get to know each other.'

'That will be easier than you think. I applied to be the new teacher of Morwen Island,' she said, and he kissed her again, this time hungrily. 'I start on the sixteenth.'

'Well, I'm going to buy Clarrie's cottage,' he murmured when he hugged her. 'We're going to extend it.'

'Will there be room for me, one day?' The idea of living on the island, surrounded by friends and her new family, was intoxicating. Grandma Isabelle and Great-Grandma Jenny would understand the need to return to the nest, like a homing seabird to Seal Cove.

He smiled and leaned back. 'If you wanted to, we'd all squeeze in the schoolhouse but it wouldn't be very private.'

'I think it needs to be private,' she whispered, more of a promise. Charlotte looked at the boys, hugging each other and holding on to Ash's jacket. She threw her head back and laughed. 'You can adopt me too, then.'

EPILOGUE

SEPTEMBER 1953

'Isabelle! Let me...' Jenny's deft fingers worked a plait out of the trailing curls falling from her ribbon.

'Oh, Mam,' sighed Isabelle, impatient at eleven. 'Daddy, look at the soldiers in their funny hats!'

Mac smiled and pointed something else out as the two of them looked down the grand street in front of Buckingham Palace. Jenny tugged at her smart dress, the most expensive thing she had ever bought, and straightened the matching hat and its wisp of net. She was much more comfortable in her normal clothes, her normal life. Caring for three boys and Iz, that was enough. Mac beckoned her over.

'We're off to our seats,' he said, grinning. 'You go with that gentleman.'

The gentleman was an equerry, who kindly explained where and how she was to act and where to go. She threw a last anxious look over her shoulder at Mac before being led into a massive hallway milling with beautifully dressed people. A stocky woman wearing a massive fur stepped towards her in elegant heels, pearls draped to her waist over a silk dress.

'Jenofeve?'

Jenny took a long moment to stare at the woman, and she felt her mouth fall open into an inelegant gape.

'*Augustine?*'

'My dear child.' Jenny was crushed in a cloud of silk, fur and perfume. When she stood back, she saw that Augustine, although her hair was now striped with shades of silver, seemed younger than the part she'd played in France. She even had a full set of teeth.

'I didn't know... they never told me what happened to anyone,' Jenny said, in a rush.

'Laurie got me to the mainland of Brittany. I spent most of the war mending things: petticoats, cameras, radios...' Her eyes gleamed with the humour Jenny recognised. 'I escaped to Switzerland – that's where I was brought up – in 1944. Then back to my husband and family in London.'

Jenny was shaking with surprise. 'Is Augustine even your real name?'

'It is. I was born Augustine-Marie de Montmollin. But I married an Englishman so I'm just Mrs Hamilton-White now. I'm here to get an award, like you.'

Jenny couldn't stop shaking her head. 'I'm so glad you got out. I wasn't sure.' Tears were running down her cheeks. 'What happened to Madame Boiteux?'

'They all survived the war, except Hélène, as your family will have told you, had tuberculosis. Madame went back to Rennes with the children. Oh, my dear.' Augustine brought out a lace handkerchief from her handbag and dabbed Jenny's face. 'You mustn't meet Her Majesty in that state.' She smiled as she looked critically at her. 'Perfect. Of course, you're still very young. Do you ever hear from Mr Byers?'

Jenny's cheeks grew warm. 'I write to him, twice a year. I think more would be disloyal to my husband. He's due to be released soon.'

'I know.' Augustine shrugged. 'My husband is a diplomat; I

get all the news. Ah, here we are. Stand tall, my child, you can be proud.'

An hour later, they stood outside, photographers snapping shots of them, Augustine's husband talking to Mac, and Isabelle hanging on Jenny's arm. A tall gentleman she hadn't seen before stepped forward and asked for a private word. Thinking it was something to do with the palace, she told Iz to stay with Daddy and walked a few paces apart from the families.

'Mrs Macintosh. A medal was presented in private today, before the ceremony. The recipient asked to speak with you.'

Her heart thudded in her ears. 'Here?'

'In one of the private offices. Follow me, Madam.'

Jenny didn't have time to react, think, she just threw a look over her shoulder at Mac, who stopped talking and frowned. She walked back inside the palace and into a small office.

The man looking out of the window was tall, gaunt and dressed in an ill-fitting suit. Before he turned, she recognised the angle of his shoulder, the shape of his chin.

'Laurie?'

His smile made him look a decade younger. 'Jenny.'

She almost ran into his arms like a child, but something stopped her, something different in her. The part of her that had yearned for him for so long, the part that agonised over every polite letter for eleven years, was overwhelmed by her love for Isabelle and the boys. And Mac – kind, lovely Mac, whose very voice made her heart race. Laurie's face changed, as if he could read her thoughts.

'I'm so proud of you,' he said, looking away. 'An MBE, a wonderful thing for you, for the bravery you showed in helping the war effort.'

'It's for my charitable work on the islands,' she said, staring up at him, at the grey in his dark hair, the creases around his eyes.

His smile returned. 'It's for all the work you did that we can't talk about.' He staggered a little, and sat on a chair by the desk. 'Do you mind? I picked up a bullet in Normandy, it still aches.'

'You were there for the D-Day landings?' She allowed herself to drink in his smile, the shape of his face. 'You should write a book.'

'Or you should,' he laughed. 'But we both signed the Official Secrets Act, remember? Maybe I will write one, but all in code.'

She laughed at that. Then she remembered. 'Are you out of prison now?'

He winced as he shifted in the chair. 'Just. They couldn't have a serving felon, a traitor, receive a medal.'

'What happens now?'

He reached out his hand. 'My first thought is to go away, and disappear. Live in the wilderness somewhere. Read books, own a dog. Breathe the fresh air, maybe by the sea or on the moors.'

She nodded, and let him take her hand for a moment.

'Are you happy?' he asked urgently.

'I am, truly. What you and I had was... wartime madness.' She looked over at the door. 'I have to go. Mac will be wondering where I am.'

'Will you keep in touch? I love to hear what the child is doing.'

She nodded, then pulled her fingers from his light touch and walked back to the door. 'Of course. Maybe you can visit the island? I'll check with my family, but I think you would be welcome. You can meet Isabelle in person.'

'I would like that,' he said, smiling again.

A LETTER FROM REBECCA

Dear Reader,

I'm so glad you found *Memories of the Cottage by the Sea*. I hope you enjoyed meeting Charlotte and following her journey towards finding love on the island, and Jenny's journey to safe harbour in terrible times. If you did, you can keep in touch with future island stories by following the link below. Your email will never be shared and you can unsubscribe at any time.

www.bookouture.com/rebecca-alexander

I have spent many years living on islands. I love the feeling that we have to find everything we need within our community, and even now, a trip on a ferry seems like a new story is being written. My imaginary island of Morwen is based on the village where I live, and wonderful islands all around the south-west of England, like Lundy, St George's and St Agnes. The cobbled alleys, narrow streets and tiny cottages all seemed to have their own stories – and histories.

I'm looking forward to writing more stories based on the islands. Living in a community where everyone knows everyone means history has to be buried very deep indeed.

If you want to support me and the books, it's always helpful to write a review. This also helps me develop and polish future stories!

You can contact me directly via my website, Facebook or Twitter.

Thank you and happy reading,

Rebecca

www.rebecca-alexander.co.uk

 twitter.com/RebAlexander1

ACKNOWLEDGEMENTS

This book wouldn't be in your hands without the hard work and patience of my editor, Jess Whitlum-Cooper. I'm astonished at how I deliver a rambling pile of nonsense chapters into her hands to get an orderly book back. Somehow, she divines what I *meant* to say – no mean skill!

Thank you also to the wonderful team at Bookouture, for continuing the process of shaping the novel and making the story shipshape and my characters consistent. They also design the lovely covers and organise all the business end, which is a mystery to me. I am truly grateful.

Much gratitude goes to my son Carey Bave, my first reader and editor, who knows all my books. He keeps me writing and asks unexpected questions, and advocates for the characters all the way.

As always, much love goes to my patient family, especially my five-year-old granddaughter Lily. She knows just when to be quiet and let me concentrate! And the support and tolerance of my husband Russell, who knows when to drive me to a field by the sea, and leave me to work off-grid in my vintage caravan.

Printed in Great Britain
by Amazon

17259770R00189